Also by Sara Cate

Keep Me

Keep Me

SARA CATE

sourcebooks
casablanca

Copyright © 2025 by Sara Cate
Cover and internal design © 2025 by Sourcebooks
Cover design by Stephanie Gafron/Sourcebooks
Cover image © Stock Story/Shutterstock
Internal design by Tara Jaggers/Sourcebooks
Internal art © Chloe Friedlein

Published by Sourcebooks Casablanca, an imprint of Sourcebooks
P.O. Box 4410, Naperville, Illinois 60567–4410
(630) 961-3900
sourcebooks.com

Cataloging-in-Publication Data is on file with the Library of Congress.

Printed and bound in the United States of America.
LSC 10 9 8 7 6 5 4 3 2 1

For my mom—if you read this, let's never, ever talk about it.

Content Warning

Keep Me is a sexually explicit romance with elements of kink and BDSM—to include exhibitionism, partner swapping, impact play, and bondage. There is no use of a condom in this story. As always, my books are works of fiction meant to serve as entertainment and should not be used for instruction, but rather, inspiration. Should you and your partner(s) choose to explore the practices in any work of fiction, please do your research first. Be safe. Have fun.

Please be aware there are also elements of parental neglect, cheating (not between main characters), alcohol abuse, death, PTSD, and agoraphobia in this story. Read with caution.

PART ONE

Sylvie

Chapter One

"You've arrived at your destination," the GPS announces.

"That's the one, on the left," Aaron says, looking up from the map on his phone to the large brick mansion on the hill.

"That?" I reply in shock.

"Barclay Manor. That's it," he says, staring out the window. Rain pelts against the windows of the car.

"Aaron, you said your family had a *house* in Scotland. *That* is a castle."

"Technically, it's a manor."

"Semantics," I reply, gaping through the windshield at the massive gray stone building. It looms over us like a bad omen. Aaron pulls off on the side of the road, and I turn toward him in confusion. "What are you doing? Drive up there."

"I can't," he argues. "That sign says *Private Property.*"

My jaw drops. "So what? It's not like people *actually* live here."

"That's exactly what *private residence* means, Sylvie."

"We came all this way."

"So? What would I tell them? They're not going to let me in just because my great-great-grandfather once visited here in the summer and wrote his book on the typewriter."

"That is *exactly* what you tell them. Based on these photos, we have proof that the typewriter is in there. We came all the way to fucking Scotland to see it. Now you're telling me you're going to just drive away because of a tiny little sign?"

He turns toward me and gives me a condescending glare. "Don't talk to me like that, Sylvie. I'm not afraid."

I roll my eyes. "So at least drive up there."

He lets out a huff. "Fine. You want to go to jail in a foreign country, let's drive up there."

He's so dramatic. I don't say a word as he pulls the car up the long gravel drive, through an open gate framed by two tall brick structures on either side. The one on the right displays the words BARCLAY MANOR 1837, and the one on the left has the PRIVATE PROPERTY sign.

The driveway is long but secluded. There are dense trees on either side, and judging by the map on Aaron's phone, there's a body of water not far on the other side of the manor. As we travel up the hill toward the manor, the rain continues to pour. It's rained every damn day since we got here last week. New York isn't sunny, but at least it's better than this.

"See, there is no one up here," I say when we get closer to the house. Aaron slows the car, clearly nervous. "Go around back."

His head snaps in my direction. "What? Why?"

"Because it's probably easier to get in back there."

"Get in? No, no, no," he barks, quickly turning the car around like he's about to flip a bitch on this narrow drive.

"Aaron, will you just relax? No one lives here. There's not a car in sight. My friends and I used to sneak into our school all the time as kids, and that had much better security than this place has."

"You're going to just walk into this nearly two-hundred-year-old manor like you own the place? Are you out of your fucking mind, Sylvie?"

"If someone sees us, we pretend we don't speak English and act like tourists."

When it's clear he can't turn his car around on this road, he pulls up farther to where the road winds around the building. He goes to the back first, his knuckles white around the steering wheel.

"Look!" I say, pointing from the passenger side. "There's a door on the side."

"Yeah, and it's probably locked," he replies, coasting the car to a stop.

Just then, the door pops open. Aaron and I both gasp and duck at the same time as we watch a woman emerge. She's wearing a black miniskirt and a white shimmery blouse missing a few buttons in the front.

One step out the door, she suddenly realizes it's raining. Instead of pulling an umbrella out, she covers her head with a black jacket and gazes around the yard as if looking for something.

Then, she's jogging in the mud and rain with her shoes hanging from her fingers instead of on her feet. And she's running straight toward *us*.

"What the…?" Aaron murmurs.

She stops by his driver's window and waits as he slowly rolls it down a few inches.

"Are you my lift?" she asks with her thick Scottish accent. There is black makeup streaking down her face and her lipstick is smeared around her mouth.

If I didn't know any better, I'd assume this woman is doing the quote-unquote *walk of shame*.

"Uh…no," Aaron stammers.

Her head pops up as she stares down the drive we just came from. "Och!" she chirps, then takes off in a jog through the mud toward another car slowly crawling up toward the house.

Aaron rolls the window back up and turns toward me in astonishment.

"Can we get out of here now?"

"What?" I reply. "No. The door is totally unlocked!"

His eyes widen further. "It's someone's house, Sylvie! Did you not just see the woman walk out of there?"

"Even better," I reply as I unclip my seat belt. "I can claim I'm her friend if someone sees me. I came all this way, Aaron. I'm getting in that fucking house."

"You're unhinged," he mutters as he faces forward and stares in shock. "People tried to warn me that you're a loose cannon, but I figured that would mean you're fun and unpredictable. I didn't think they meant it in a criminal way."

"Wait, who said I was a loose cannon? Never mind. It doesn't matter."

It really doesn't matter. I can think of a handful of people off the bat who I know would say that to my boyfriend. People in our social circle define *fun and entertainment* as tearing down other people and talking shit as if they're so much better than anyone.

The only way I've figured out how to avoid that is to beat them at their own game.

They want to call me irrational, then I'll show them irrational. With that, I smile at Aaron and snatch my phone off the center console, shoving it into my pocket before throwing the hood of my rain jacket over my head.

"Be right back," I say as I open the car door and jump into the downpour.

"Sylvie!" Aaron calls from the car, but I cut him off by slamming the door shut and sprinting toward the place we just watched the girl emerge from.

There's a moment somewhere between the car and the door when I realize that this is, in fact, a bad idea. I'm walking into someone else's home uninvited. I could just knock and ask nicely to see the library, but where's the fun in that?

This is the moment when the adrenaline kicks in. It's invigorating. Fear, anticipation, and excitement all blend into one as I reach for the door handle without a clue as to what's on the other side.

It's an antique brass doorknob on an old wooden door. The

forest-green paint is chipping away at the edges, and the knob squeaks as I turn it. As expected, it opens without an issue.

Once inside, I pull the door to just an inch from latching closed. It's my idea of a quick escape plan just in case these particular Scottish homeowners are the kind that like to pull an axe on their intruders or have large wolfhounds to protect the residence.

Shit, dogs. I didn't think about that.

The house is seemingly quiet from here. I'm standing in a large entryway, although, to be technical, this is the back of the house. So maybe it's called an exit way?

The floor is all hardwood, and the walls are painted. It looks as if it was recently renovated instead of featuring the stale, dated decor I was expecting. It smells nice, as if there's incense burning somewhere or men's cologne sprayed nearby.

In front of me is a long hallway, and I take each step slowly, listening for people or voices in the house. I pull my phone out of my back pocket and pull up the camera app to have it ready. When I get a picture of that typewriter, Aaron is going to eat his words. This will be nothing more than a funny story someday.

There are closed doors on either side of the long hallway, but none of them look like the kinds of doors that would lead to a large library like the one we saw in that photo of the typewriter. So, I keep walking slowly while listening.

At the end of the hall, I step into a giant entranceway with a grand staircase that leads to the second and third floors. The height of the ceiling in this part is massive, and I'm struck silent as I stare upward at it. This place is like nothing I've ever seen.

And if it wasn't for the warm smell of spice and musk, I wouldn't believe this is a residence.

My phone buzzes in my hand, drawing my attention from the ceiling and grand staircase.

I glance down to see a text from Aaron.

Get the fuck out of there. Now, Sylvie.

I roll my eyes and swipe the message closed. He's always so paranoid. Such a rule follower. He used to be fun, but the last year with him has been painfully boring. Every day is so predictable it makes me sick. I'm going to prove to him right now how fun and spontaneous I can be. I'll snap a picture of that old typewriter that his great-great-whatever wrote some dumb old classic novel on, and that'll show him.

When I glance up again, I spot an open door on the second floor. In the room, I spot a shelf of old books. *A library.*

Pocketing my phone, I carefully tiptoe up the stairs. I don't hear a single sound in the rest of the house. If anyone is here, they're probably sleeping or in the shower or something. They'll never know I was even here.

There is a single stair that creaks as I settle my weight on it. With a wince, I freeze and wait for the sound of footsteps, but there's nothing. Quickly, I finish my climb, reaching the top and slowly creeping into the large room. The ceilings in this room are far taller than I expected. Each wall has a tall ladder attached to a slider. For a moment, I can do nothing but stare at the massive space.

As my gaze casts downward, it catches on something on the other side of the room. Resting on a large ornate wooden table is a huge vase full of flowers next to a dusty old typewriter.

"Gotcha," I whisper as I quickly tiptoe through the room. The floor in here has a thick rug that muffles my footsteps.

I slip my phone from my back pocket and open the camera app. Aiming at the typewriter, I take a multitude of shots from various angles.

"Eat your words, Aaron," I whisper.

Then, while I'm at it, I take a few shots of the library too. It's so old-fashioned looking, like something out of a fairy tale. I don't know anyone who owns this many books, and if I did, they wouldn't store them in a room like this.

There's a creak in the house, and I quickly spin around, watching the door.

Fuck.

Time to go.

With my phone clutched in my hand, I make my way toward the door I came in through. There's no sign of anyone on the second floor, so I book it for the stairs. My heart is pounding, and adrenaline is coursing through my veins. The long hallway ahead leads to the exit. Just a few more feet and I'll be outside, sprinting toward Aaron's car in the rain, laughing about how wild this was.

Reaching the bottom step, I leap to the right.

An enormous hand wraps around my arm, hauling me to a stop before I can make my escape. I let out a scream, turning around to gape at the impossibly large man scowling down at me with my arm still gripped in his fist.

"Who the fuck are you?" the man bellows in a deep Scottish brogue.

I open my mouth to respond, but nothing comes out.

"What are you doing in my house?" he continues.

"I—I" I stammer.

Get it together, Sylvie. This was your idea. Don't let this giant oaf intimidate you.

"I was looking for my friend. She was here, but now…she's not," I reply, forcing my voice to remain steady. He's still holding my arm, his fingers pinching it so tightly it's starting to hurt.

"Your friend?" he asks.

I jerk my arm, trying to pull it free, but he won't let go.

"Yeah. She told me to pick her up, but I think she already left." I wave my phone to imply the girl has called or texted me. "So, I'll just…be on my way."

His brows pinch inward skeptically.

"So, you just barge into my house uninvited?"

"Yeah, I—"

When his lazy focus turns back to me, I notice a change in his demeanor. His eyes rake up and down my body before landing on my face and leaning in a little closer.

"Go on…" he mutters in a low, teasing manner. Goose bumps develop across my arms and neck. The man looks to be older than me, maybe midthirties. With long brown hair and a thick beard, all I can really see are his bright green eyes.

"I was just looking…"

"For your friend," he says, finishing my sentence.

"Yeah."

"I don't believe you," he whispers, his face so close I feel his breath on my cheek.

I jerk on my arm, but he still won't release it. "Then, let me go," I argue.

A wicked grin tilts the corner of his mouth. "I'm just starting to wonder…" he says with a note of sarcasm in his voice, "if you're here for the same reason she was. Perhaps you can pick up where she left off."

My blood runs cold, and I feel the heavy weight of fear settle in my stomach like I've swallowed a stone. Is he really implying that I'm here to sleep with him?

"Let me go," I mutter through my teeth.

With a few steps toward the wall, he slowly corners me against it. "Wh-what are you doing?" I stammer.

"This is why you're here, isn't it?" he asks.

"No!" I shout, putting a hand on his chest and trying to shove him away. Like a brick wall, he doesn't budge. There's a hint of humor on his face, and I can't quite tell, but I think he's teasing me. Saying all of this just to scare me. It's working.

"Then, why are you in my house?" he replies. His playful smirk fades, and it's replaced with something more sinister. "Are you spying for my sister?"

I flinch. "What? No."

When his eyes trail to the phone in my hand, his brow creases. I already know what he's about to do, so when I struggle to release myself from his grip, it's futile.

"Give me this," he growls, snatching the phone from my hand.

"Stop!" I scream.

Then, I watch in horror as he tosses my phone to the floor and stomps the heel of his boot on it so hard it shatters against the hardwood.

Finally, he releases my arm, and I gape at the broken phone on the floor. "You brute!" I scream, taking a swing at him. My hand lands disappointingly against the thick muscles of his arm, clearly causing him no pain at all.

"What did you do that for?" I shout.

He points a finger in my face. "You tell my bitch of a sister that she's not getting my house, and she can stop sending her little friends to spy on me. Now, get out."

His lips curl in a sneer as he points to the door. Then, he drops his arm and walks away, leaving me to blink in disbelief.

"Hey!" I call after him. "You need to replace my phone!"

Still walking away from me toward the back of the house, he doesn't respond to my shouting.

"Asshole!" I yell again. "I'm talking to you."

He chuckles as he enters a large living room. To the right is a bar with bottles of liquor displayed on glass shelves over a marble counter.

"Bold of you to shout at me in my own home. You're lucky I haven't called the police on you yet."

"I'm serious," I say, winding a stray curl behind my ear. "You broke my phone for no reason."

"I broke it for a very good reason," he replies with a sarcastic laugh. "You probably had pictures on it that could be incriminating, and my sister would just love that."

"Incriminating?" I reply. "I took pictures of the old typewriter in the library!"

"The typewriter?" He's uncapping a bottle of something that looks like whisky when he stops and glances up at me, bewildered. "Why the hell would she want pictures of a typewriter?"

I slam my hands down in frustration. "They're not for your

fucking sister. I don't even know your sister. I snuck in to find this stupid old typewriter that was apparently an heirloom in my boyfriend's family, you stupid ogre."

His eyes burn with anger as he sets the bottle down. "Let me get this straight. You walked into a stranger's home to take pictures of an old typewriter for your boyfriend?"

He glances around behind me as if Aaron is going to appear out of thin air. I roll my eyes. "Yes, and I was on my way out when you attacked me, threatened to defile me, and then broke my phone."

"Is this how girls behave in America?" he snaps in return. "Just barging into people's houses to take a picture of something you think belongs to you?"

I scoff. "To be fair, this is hardly a house."

"It's *my* fucking house."

"It's practically a castle. Why do you even live out here?" I ask incredulously.

"To avoid having to interact with people like you," he replies.

"You're really an asshole."

He simply chuckles in response. "What is your name?" he asks, taking a step toward me.

I take a step back. "None of your business."

"Tell me your name, and I'll replace your phone," he replies, teasing me.

Chewing on my bottom lip, I stare at him with hesitation.

"Sylvie," I say, taking another step away from him as he continues to close in on me.

"Sylvie what?"

"Devereaux," I mumble.

"Sylvie Devereaux," he says, my name sounding melodic and beautiful on his tongue.

My back hits a wall, but he continues toward me. I stop breathing for a moment as I stare into his haunting green eyes.

As he leans in, I catch the scent of his cologne and feel dwarfed by his intimidating size. He must be six and a half feet tall. As he places a hand on the wall over my head, I realize what an idiot I am.

I had my chance to leave, but now I've just gotten myself cornered by someone who's already proven himself to be volatile and angry.

His fingers delicately touch my chin. As he leans in, I shudder and try to turn my face away.

"Sylvie Devereaux, get the fuck out of my house."

My chest aches for air, waiting for him to back away enough to let me breathe. When he does, he lets out a menacing laugh.

"You asshole!" I choke out as I gasp for air.

Before he can crowd me again, I turn and run toward the door. I step right over my shattered phone on the floor, turning back to pick up what's left of it before bolting out the door I came in. The rain is still going strong as I stop and glance around for Aaron's car. He's parked just near the road, and I take off in a sprint toward him.

He's giving me an impatient expression and is clearly stressed as I tear open the passenger side door and climb in.

"What the fuck, Sylvie?" he shouts.

"Just drive," I mutter breathlessly.

"You're lucky you didn't get yourself killed."

"There was no one in there," I lie. "I just dropped my phone, so I don't have your pictures."

"You're fucking unhinged," he mumbles under his breath as he drives toward the road.

My heart is still hammering in my chest. As we reach the main road, I glance back at the manor in the distance, watching it grow smaller and smaller in my rearview.

At least I made it out of there unharmed.

And I'm never going back.

Chapter Two

"You could have gone to jail," Aaron mutters. He's sitting on the bed facing away from me, his elbows on his knees.

Rolling my eyes, I drop onto the bed and pick up my laptop. "Stop being so dramatic. I'm fine."

"Are you sure no one saw you?" he asks in a panic.

I drop my hands in a huff. "I told you no one saw me. Why do you care so much?"

"I have my image to worry about, Sylvie. I'm sorry *you* don't care about anything, but I do, and if I'm going to run for office someday, I don't need a criminal record in Scotland holding me back because my impulsive and careless girlfriend thinks she can just *do* anything."

"Technically, I *can* do anything," I mutter to myself as I open my laptop.

"Not without consequences, Sylvie."

I click on the cloud drive on my laptop and immediately scan through the photos. There at the bottom of the array of pictures of the Scottish countryside and Edinburgh's Royal Mile are the photos of the dusty old typewriter I nearly sacrificed my life for.

Aaron is still droning on and on about my actions and

consequences and how it's not technically my fault that my parents didn't raise me with any discipline.

Same shit, different day.

I decide not to show him the photos.

Instead, I open an internet browser. I type Barclay Manor.

Immediately, a photo pops up on a basic wiki page about the manor, the town, the family, and its history.

The auto-generated questions below list: Does someone still live at Barclay Manor?

So I click on it.

"Are you even listening to me?" he asks. I glance up from my laptop.

"My parents were incompetent. I'm not going to disagree with you," I reply noncommittally. He's absolutely right. They were incredibly incompetent as parents. It's not that they're stupid people. In fact, they are brilliant and could hold a steady conversation for hours about the contextual theory of Van Gogh through his Parisian era, but they generally sucked as a mom and dad.

They were never afraid of being so bold to explain to me that parental love was inane and subconscious, which wasn't always the warmest consolation as a child. Biologically, my mom loved me—because she had to.

Luckily for her and my father, they are both geniuses, and that talent paid for modern conveniences like full-time childcare, which made raising me nearly effortless.

"Yeah, well, you're twenty-five now, Sylvie. It's about time you start acting like it."

"Why are you being so uptight?" I reply with annoyance. "What happened to the guy who snuck backstage at the music festival with me?"

"That was three years ago, Syl. Grow up."

As he gives me a contemptuous glare, I sink into the bed, feeling the shame he's hurling at me like knives. He sulks into the bathroom, slamming the door closed, leaving me alone with my thoughts.

It feels as if we're growing in separate directions. He's so focused on his future, settling down, and growing up. He sees twenty-five as some mature magical age when we're supposed to suddenly have it all figured out. I don't feel anywhere near having it figured out.

He's on a speedboat, headed straight for dry land.

I'm floating on a breeze with no direction at all.

And for some reason, I should feel like shit about that.

I turn my attention back to the laptop. I click on the link there under the question Does someone still live at Barclay Manor? And right there on the screen is the man I saw today.

It's a handsome photo with an inscription underneath— *Killian Barclay.*

Of course, in the photo, he's dressed up. In a black jacket and green kilt, standing in front of some PR backdrop for a charity, he looks miserable and handsome at the same time. He appears a bit younger in this photo, and when I click on his name, it takes me to a screen full of photos of him.

Most are like this one—posed, strategic, flattering. But there are a couple mixed in that look more like bad paparazzi timing, drunkenly climbing into the back of an SUV. There's one where he seems like he's in the middle of a brawl at a party. And one where he's actively yelling at the cameraman taking the photo.

This guy clearly has anger issues.

Clicking on his name takes me to his Wikipedia page, and I read that he's almost thirty-seven years old. He's the oldest of four in the Barclay family and has been living in the manor since the death of his parents when he was eighteen. As for photos, there aren't many from the past ten years.

That's all the page really says about him, but judging by the lack of details, I assume he's unmarried without kids.

How strange it must be to live in that big house all alone.

I hear Aaron's muffled voice in the bathroom, and I glance up from my laptop to try and decipher what he's saying. I can't quite make it out, so I return to my internet search instead.

I find myself staring at Killian's picture again, replaying the entire interaction today. Something about it felt so off. Who was the girl who left before I walked in? A guy who lives alone in a mansion like that with probably millions and millions of dollars at his disposal would likely hire a sex worker instead of dating, right?

God, what would have happened if I hadn't gotten out of there? Would he have expected me to have sex with him?

If he wasn't such an ass, I might have. Not that I would cheat on Aaron. I just mean…if there was no Aaron, I might have let that six-foot-five rich Scottish jerk throw me around a little bit.

And what was up with the whole spying thing? Does his sister send spies in on him often? What is he hiding that would require spies?

That's weird, right?

My phone is still shattered and will probably stay that way until we find a store to replace it, but I have been dying to tell my best friend Margot about what happened today. So I pull up our text message thread on my laptop.

Hey. I miss you.
Almost got ravaged by a giant Scotsman today.
#noregrets
But don't tell Aaron. He's being a jerk about it.

I smile down at the message thread and wait for her to read it. Checking the time, I see that it's still midday in New York, even though it's late here. So she should be up.

My best friend doesn't have a sleep routine, or any kind of routine, really. She doesn't have a job or a partner. She's the only other person I know floating on the breeze with me.

I tell Margot everything. Her mom is an actress and model who became best friends with my parents back in the 1990s. Which means they basically raised us together. Margot took after her mother and pursued modeling, and she's flawless.

When she doesn't read my messages after about five minutes, I get a little annoyed. To be honest, I'm bored. Aaron is mad at me, and this whole fucking trip was for him. Now I just want to go home.

The bathroom door opens, and he walks in, shoving his phone into his back pocket.

"Let's get some sleep," he mutters quietly. "We have an early flight tomorrow."

As he tears off his shirt, my computer pings with a message.

He's probably just worried about you.

Her message annoys me. She's not supposed to take his side. Without responding, I close my laptop and shove it on the side table. Then, I roll over with my back to Aaron.

"Who were you talking to in there?" I ask.

"You were hearing things. I wasn't talking to anyone," he replies flatly.

He switches the light off, bathing us in darkness, and I close my eyes.

The sooner I fall asleep, the sooner we wake up for the airport. And the sooner this whole trip will end.

Chapter Three

"Dear Ms. Devereaux, my name is Monica Rodriguez, and I'm calling from First Financial. Your credit card payment is ninety days past due and currently in default. We have no choice but to send your account to collections and deactivate your credit cards."

Delete.

The voicemail disappears, leaving my inbox empty. That foreboding feeling of dread settles in my stomach. The message from my bank sucks, but not as much as what I have to do now.

When I reach the barista at the counter, I order my small black coffee and scrounge in the bottom of my purse for enough loose change to cover it.

"A name for your order?" she asks.

"It's a small black coffee. Just pour it into a cup."

The girl with a septum piercing and bright purple eye shadow gives me a condescending look. "A name for your order," she repeats.

"Sylvie," I say with a huff.

Then I turn away from the counter and find a quiet corner of the coffee shop to wait. Staring down at my brand-new phone, I pull up my contacts and hover my thumb over the button I really don't want to push.

My initial prediction was that I'd make it eighteen months with what I had in my savings account and on my credit cards when Mom and Dad told me I was cut off. Eighteen months—*if* I was conservative with my spending and didn't do anything drastic.

Like go to Scotland with my boyfriend.

And buy a new phone.

I made it four months.

"Sylvia," the miserable wench at the counter calls out, holding a small paper cup.

I roll my eyes as I approach her. "It's Sylvie," I murmur before taking the coffee.

"Sorry," she replies, her tone full of sarcasm.

When I leave the shop, turning right toward my apartment, I pull out my phone again.

I have to do this. I have to, right?

I can't just…survive without money. And getting a job right now isn't as easy as I thought it would be. The only places that are hiring are paying less than what it costs to live in the city, so what is the point?

"Fuck it," I mutter as I punch my thumb on my phone screen. It lights up with my mom's picture.

Calling Mom...

I wait as it rings, and rings, and rings.

"Hi, you've reached the voice mailbox of Torrence Devereaux. She is currently unavailable. If you are calling to commission or purchase a piece of art, please contact her assistant, Enid Hamilton, at 290-555-1004. Thank you."

Enid's voice grates on my nerves, but I stick through the greeting until it beeps.

"Hey, Mom. It's Sylvie. Your daughter. I don't know if you're still in Florence, but I'm just calling because I'm literally fucking starving. You can't just cut me off like this. I'm not sure what you expect me to do. Can't I just have, like, half of my allowance until I figure something out? You can't do this to me. Just call me back…please."

I hang up the call as I reach a crosswalk, waiting in a crowd of pedestrians as I try my dad's number. It rings and rings and rings just the same.

"Hi, you've reached the voice mailbox of Yuri Devereaux. He is currently unavailable."

"Fuck my life," I mutter to myself.

"If you are calling to commission or purchase a piece of art, please contact his assistant, Enid Hamilton, at 290-555-1004. Thank you."

Beep.

"Dad," I cry into the phone. "It's Sylvie. Please call me back. I'm just…" My voice cracks. "I'm having a really hard time lately, and I need your help. Just a little something to get me through the season. No one is hiring right now, and my credit cards are all maxed out. I'm not sure how I'll pay rent this month, and I'm scared."

My voice is thick with emotion, but my eyes are as dry as the desert. I can feel the curious attention of the nosy people around me glancing up from their phones to sneak a peek at me.

"Thank you, Daddy. I love you."

I punch the End Call button and pull up the last contact on my list. With a disgruntled sigh, I hit the phone icon next to her name. This time, she picks up after the first ring.

"Hello, Sylvie," she says without a hint of amusement in her voice.

"Hello, Enid," I mutter into the phone. "Are my parents still in Florence?"

She sighs. "They haven't been in Florence since May. What can I help you with?"

The light turns, and the crowd begins their walk across the intersection.

"I'm trying to get ahold of them."

"They're in the studio," she replies coldly.

In the studio is a phrase I've heard since the day I was born. *In the studio* could refer to a few hours or a few months. It is both literal and symbolic, a blanket statement that refers to some artistic zone my parents escape to—usually together—where they cannot be bothered, or else it would disrupt their delicate creative process.

They were often *in the studio* over my birthdays, the first day of school, a couple of Christmases, and once when I was seventeen and was in a bad car accident on the way to the Hamptons with some friends. They showed up at the hospital four days later.

The piece they were working on is now in the Guggenheim.

"That's fine. I was just checking on them. I haven't received my deposit in a couple of months, and I was getting worried. Maybe you could log into their accounts and send it over."

"Bullshit, Sylvie," Enid barks. "They cut you off four months ago. Are you really out of money already?"

My molars grind. "Fuck you, Enid. You've been sucking their teats since you graduated college."

"I do my job, Sylvie," she replies. Her voice is so fucking annoying. Nasally and posh. "You do know what a job is, don't you?"

"Oh yes, your job must be so hard," I argue. "Being at my parents' beck and call twenty-four-seven. On the yachts and at all the parties. Tell me, Enid. Are you there when they fuck each other too?"

"You're disgusting, Sylvie. No wonder they're so embarrassed by you."

My hand squeezes the phone so tightly I'm surprised it doesn't snap in half. I should relax. I can't afford another one.

"I'd rather be an embarrassment than a leech."

"Again," she snaps into the phone. "This is my job, Sylvie. You should consider getting one. Or are you still *working on your novel?*"

I can practically hear her doing air quotes around that condescending phrase, and the urge to toss my phone into the sewer, imagining it's her, is overwhelming.

"Fuck you, you ugly, uptight little twat."

With that, I punch the End Call button and let out a frustrated, growling huff. I want to scream. I want to hurl this hot coffee at anyone I can. Just once I wish I could really let go and express all of the things I'm feeling.

I bet Killian Barclay doesn't have to deal with shit like this. I bet he lets out his frustration all the time, and no one judges him for it. I wish I knew why my mind was constantly revisiting that day, but I have no idea. He burrowed himself into my subconscious.

Instead of turning right toward my apartment, where I know Aaron is waiting for me, I keep straight on 5th toward Margot's place. Unlike Aaron, she won't give me some condescending lecture about responsibility and maturity. He's never been supportive of my dreams anyway. He doesn't care if I finish my novel. He never even asks about it.

When I reach Margot's building, the doorman welcomes me with a smile. "Morning, Sylvie," he says.

I force myself to grin back at him regardless of my irritated mood. "Morning, Chuck. She's home, right?" I ask, turning back toward him once I'm in the lobby.

He nods, but there's a hint of something hesitant on his face. "She's in," he replies.

I don't bother asking him if everything is okay, but I hurry to the elevator anyway. Hopefully, that's not a sign she's on another one of her benders. Margot has a history of going off the deep end after a fashion show if she feels like it didn't go exactly the way she wanted. Or if a photo comes out that she finds less than flattering. She'll replace food with alcohol and socializing with sex for weeks on end until I scrape her off the floor and put her back together.

I can't watch her go through that again.

When the elevator lets me off on the eighteenth floor, I rush down to Margot's apartment and try the handle first. To my surprise, it's unlocked.

What the fuck is wrong with her, leaving her door unlocked in the middle of Manhattan?

Two steps into the apartment, I hear the unmistakable sound of her moaning chants. They're loud and high-pitched, and by the sound of it, she's being railed within an inch of her life.

Oh, fuck.

Before letting the door close behind me, I grab it and quietly ease myself out. My cheeks heat with embarrassment from hearing my best friend getting it on.

Stifling a giggle, I tiptoe out the door, thinking about how I'm going to give her shit about this later.

Then, my eyes catch on a pair of familiar shoes on the floor. They look exactly like Aaron's—the ones I got him for his birthday last year. This guy she's seeing has good taste.

But then my gaze lingers on the shoes, and I realize they are a little *too* familiar. Like they have the same wear marks as Aaron's. Still tied the same way he ties his, slipping them off when he gets home without undoing the knots.

I hear a familiar grunt from the bedroom.

And suddenly, it's like I'm frozen in time. Like everything is moving around me, but I'm stuck in one place.

Reality comes crashing in, and the rage I felt a few moments ago bubbles over like a pot of water set to boil for too long.

I step inside and let the door close before marching down the hall of Margot's apartment toward her room. As I reach the door, I stand there, coffee in hand, and watch as my boyfriend of three years pounds into my best friend from behind. His white ass is on display, and he's got a hand on her head, shoving it into the mattress. She's moaning loudly, and, honestly, it sounds a little fake and dramatic.

They don't even know I'm standing here watching them. I'm

gawking at them for far too long, but in my defense, I'm stunned.
I can't stop thinking about the fact that the last time Aaron and I
fucked, we did it in missionary position, and he ground on top of
me like a disgusting slug.

He slaps her ass, and she yelps in pleasure. "My dirty little girl."

My face contorts in disgust. *What the fuck?*

Am I in the right apartment?

Is this the right reality?

"God, I love you so much," he adds. "I love you so fucking
much."

His voice is strained, groaning out the words as he thrusts
into her. Suddenly I feel like I'm going to be sick. And I move
without thinking.

I flip the plastic lid off of my coffee, watching the steam rise
from the liquid. Then, I scream as I hurl it at his naked body. I
watch with delight as it lands against his back, singeing his skin
and making him squeal in pain.

"What the fuck!" he shouts, flailing onto the bed and rolling
onto his back, his face twisted in fear.

Margot screams, quickly covering her body with a blanket
and staring at me in horror.

"Sylvie?" she cries.

Aaron freezes and gapes at me as I stand in the doorway,
glaring at them both with my jaw clenched tight in anger.

My eyes bore into Margot, my best friend, as she tries to catch
her breath. For the first time today, my eyes brim with tears, but
I don't say a word. Not to either of them.

I just turn on my heel and barrel out of her apartment.

All I can think as I reach the door, rushing past Chuck and
onto the street, is that I spent my last five dollars on that coffee.
And while it was worth it, I have no fucking clue what I'm going
to do now.

Chapter Four

WALLOWING IN SELF-PITY DOESN'T PAY MUCH. OR ANYTHING. Whenever you hit rock bottom, people love to say, *There's nowhere to go but up*, but they don't exactly specify when that will happen. Because I've been scraping the bottom of this barrel for two weeks now, and I'm not sure how much longer I'll last.

Aaron moved out ten days ago. When he tried to come home that night with second-degree burns on his back and tears in his eyes, I threatened him with a kitchen knife. He called me a bitch, grabbed his phone charger, and left.

Margot tried to call me. She left me a seven-paragraph text message about how I've never been that great of a friend and somehow managed to pin this all on me, explaining how my never consoling her over her breakups led to her spreading her legs for my long-term boyfriend. I don't know. I didn't really read the whole thing, if I'm honest.

She did claim that they were in love and had been for a while. Maybe *she* should have gone to Scotland with him. She could have chased around his ancestor's bullshit for three weeks.

There's been a red eviction notice on my door for the past three days, but I've been ignoring that too. I'm working on a theory that if I just ignore literally everything in my life, then the universe will just work itself out.

I mean, what are they going to do? Carry me out?

I've sold enough of Aaron's shit to feed myself over the last two weeks but not enough to pay the rent. He took the really good stuff.

Lying on my couch, bored and depressed, I scroll through the pictures on my phone, deleting every single one of me and Aaron. They just feel like lies now. Why did he ever bother to look happy with me?

There's a knock at the door that I ignore.

Ignore everything.

Nothing matters anyway.

I turn my attention back to my phone, discovering a dirty video Aaron and I made over a year ago on Halloween when he filmed me sucking his dick in my Alice in Wonderland costume. He was the Mad Hatter.

I won't delete this one just yet…

"Ms. Devereaux," a woman calls through the door, and I wrinkle my brow as I stare at it. There's something familiar about the way she said my name. Melodic and enticing.

It reminds me of…

"My name is Anna Barclay. Are you home?"

Barclay?

"What the…?"

My voice trails as I climb off my sofa and walk silently toward the door. Without a sound, I squint through the peephole and see a well-dressed woman holding a manila envelope standing on my welcome mat.

"Hello, Ms. Devereaux," she croons. "I see the light through the peephole. I know you're there."

I pull my head back in a snap. "What do you want?" I ask with skepticism.

My mind is reeling, trying to figure out why this woman is

here. Is this because I broke into their house? I mean…*broke in* is hardly accurate. I just walked in. Did that brutish asshole tell on me? Can I still be arrested?

"I'd like to speak to you," she says. "I believe you already met my brother."

Her brother?

So is this the sister that sends spies into his house? Maybe that's what she's looking for now? Would she pay me to spy on him again? I'd gladly do it.

Curiosity gets the better of me, and I unlatch the dead bolt and turn the brass knob on the door. As I peel it open, I stare at the woman waiting there. She's very pretty. With long brown hair and large green eyes, she looks to be in her mid to late thirties. I can see the resemblance between her and the man who nearly attacked me. She's tall too, but not as tall as him.

"What do you want?" I mumble through the gap of the doorway.

"Can I come in?" she asks.

"For what?"

"I have something to discuss with you. A…business proposal, if you will."

My brow lowers as I stare at her, glancing down at the envelope in her hands. A business proposal? She *does* want me to spy on him.

I quickly glance behind her to see that she's alone before I slowly open the door and allow her to come in. She scans my apartment, possibly noticing how immaculate it is. I might be broke, depressed, and lonely, but I keep my space clean, always.

Leading her down to the dining room, I point to the table. "Would you like some coffee?" I ask hesitantly.

"Coffee would be nice," she replies.

As she takes a seat at the table, I move into the kitchen and grab the coffeepot from the machine. "So, how did you find me?" I ask as I fill it with water.

"My brother told me your name. I saw your face on the security footage. Then, I looked you up. Read an interesting article in the *New Yorker* about you. You were listed as a potential rising star in literature. Your parents were mentioned too."

I glance down as I continue making a pot of coffee. That piece came out nearly two years ago. I was fresh out of college and had impressed enough professors to get a spot on the *ones-to-watch* list they publish every year.

It felt like a gold star at the time.

Now it feels like a festering wound.

"Are you looking for a freelance writer? I don't really do that sort of writing," I say before switching the machine on. It whirs to life as I take down two mugs from the cabinet.

"I'm sorry, but no. I'm not interested in hiring you as a writer."

Ouch.

"Then what is it?" I ask from the kitchen.

"Why don't you come sit down, and we can discuss it? It's… sensitive in nature."

My cheeks grow hot as I stare at her. Possibilities flit through my mind, but nothing sticks or makes any sense.

Pulling out a chair, I sit down and face the woman, waiting for an explanation.

"Ms. Devereaux, what I'm about to offer you is unconventional and a bit strange. I'll warn you now."

"Okay…"

She opens her manila folder. Inside is a stack of what looks like very official papers. There's even a fancy crest at the top.

"You should know a little about my family before I continue."

I don't respond as she turns the papers toward me. I stare at her inquisitively.

"I have three brothers. Killian is the eldest. Then, Declan. And Lachlan. Then me, between Killian and Declan."

"Okay…" I say again, waiting for the part where I come in.

"My brother Killian, being the eldest, is the heir to our

family's estate, Barclay Manor, which you have recently visited. He chooses to live there, regardless of our family's wishes. Our parents have sadly passed away."

"Why does your family not want him there?"

Her spine straightens. "Killian is…eccentric. He's turned our family's estate into a house of debauchery and parties."

"Sounds fun," I mutter to myself. Behind me, the coffeepot beeps, and I quickly turn away from Anna's judgmental glare. "Cream and sugar?"

"Just cream, please."

"Got it," I reply, going to the fridge for the cream. "So, Killian won't leave your family's castle," I say as I prepare our coffees. "What do you need me for?"

"That's the strange part."

As I carry over our cups, she purses her lips and waits for me to sit before speaking again.

"I'll cut to the chase, Ms. Devereaux."

"Please," I reply, setting my cup on the table.

"I'd like you to marry my brother."

Suddenly, it's as if the entire dining room of my apartment cants to one side, and my coffee cup tips over, spilling the hot contents all over my lacquered table. Anna quickly lifts her papers, to avoid the coffee staining them.

"Oh shit," I mumble, rushing to grab some paper towels from my kitchen and quickly cleaning up the mess. She waits patiently as I dab it up.

"I'm sorry…what?" I stammer, sitting down and staring at her in shock. The wadded-up paper towels are still littered all over my table.

"It's quite complicated, but the only way for my family to access the ownership of the manor is if it's transferred out of our brother's name. And the only way for it to be transferred out of his name is if he remains married for at least one year. At which point, ownership of the home would be granted to his wife."

"One year?" I stutter.

"Or until they have a child."

My eyes nearly bug out of my head.

"I don't expect you to do that," she adds.

"Oh, good," I reply sarcastically. "You just want me to marry a complete stranger for a year so you can con your brother out of his home. Okay. Well, that's good because, for a moment, I thought you were out of your mind."

She lets out a sigh. "Before you paint us as the villains, you should know that Killian's reasons for staying in the manor are not to his benefit. He did not handle the death of our parents well, and after he spent his twenties in a drug- and alcohol-induced haze, he has secluded himself in that house since. We discovered recently just how out of hand his lifestyle has gotten. We're doing this for his own good."

"Have you, and I'm just tossing out ideas here, thought to talk to him about it?"

"For seventeen years," she replies flatly.

"Seventeen years?" I snap.

"My brother needs to move on with his life. He needs a nudge."

A laugh bursts through my lips. "A nudge? You flew halfway across the world to ask a complete stranger to marry your brother, and you call that a nudge? Why on earth would I agree to this?"

"Ten million dollars."

My body freezes, and I stare at her in shock. She said that so calmly that it took me by surprise more than the actual amount.

"Of course, we would support you during the year. You'd live at Barclay with Killian. You'd be taken care of with whatever you require. There are some serious stipulations to the contract, such as you'd be required to make public appearances with Killian. Neither of you could be adulterous, or else the contract would be nullified."

"Wait, wait, wait," I say, holding my hands up. "Why would he agree to this?"

"He thinks it's a ploy to improve his reputation in order to get his family off of his back and let him keep the house."

His reputation. I know a bit about that from what I read online the day I saw him. Killian Barclay had made a name for himself as a playboy and partier.

"Why couldn't he just improve his reputation?"

"We've convinced him that if he is seen settling down, the family might be more inclined to allow him to stay in the house without a fight."

Leaning back in my chair, I cross my arms over my chest. "So…what's to stop me from just keeping the house to myself after the year of marriage, if, like you said, I will have ownership of it?"

Her lips purse. "Because there would be a very strict contract that states you will sign the deed over to my family or face a hefty fine worth more than the cost of the manor itself."

"This is some manipulative shit," I reply with a laugh.

"Like I said," she mumbles. "It's for his own good."

"Why me?" I ask, narrowing my eyes at her. "Out of everyone on this planet, why me? You don't even know me."

"I know you were bold enough to walk into our house uninvited that day," she says with a scolding expression. "I know you were raised in a wealthy environment. You're well-educated and accustomed to a certain level of comfort. And I know that your parents recently cut you off."

My head tilts in surprise. "How do you know that? That's not something you'd find in a Google search," I say skeptically.

"No, it's not," she agrees, implying that this lady is even more manipulative than I first assumed.

The dining room grows silent as we stare at each other. My mind is spinning as I let the entire thing play over and over. It's unbelievable and sort of hilarious.

"So…" she mumbles over the top of her coffee cup. "What do you think?"

I let out another laugh. "I think you're fucking bold. How many unsuspecting American girls are you bombarding with this offer?"

She takes a sip and sets down her cup. "You are the only person we're asking."

I tug my bottom lip between my teeth. "Well, I'm sorry you wasted a trip. Be sure to see the Statue of Liberty while you're here. Thanks for a good laugh and a hilarious story I'll tell someday."

"Why don't you think about it?" she asks as she stands.

"Yeah, sure," I reply with a chuckle. "I'll think about dropping my entire life here to marry a stranger in Scotland."

"Here's my card." She sets it on the table and gives me a tight smile. "Thanks for hearing me out."

I don't have anything else to say, so I stand in silence as she walks to the door. She gets to it and puts her hand on the knob before I realize something.

"What did he say?" I ask. "About me."

She stops and turns toward me with a crooked grin. "He said you were the rudest, meanest, most infuriating woman he'd ever met."

"And that made you think I'd be a good fit for this?"

"No," she replies with a shake of her head. "But he did."

With that, she opens my front door and disappears out of my apartment.

I'm left standing in silence, confused and shocked and wondering what the fuck just happened.

Chapter Five

THE ONE PERK OF HAVING SLIGHTLY FAMOUS PARENTS IS THAT sometimes I know exactly where they are going to be and when. As I stride through the lobby of their gallery uptown, I smile at one of the security guards and thank my teenage flirting skills I used years ago to get him on my good side.

And being the daughter of the artists means I don't have to have a ticket or reservation.

I just have to get past Enid.

The gallery is in a brownstone on the Upper East Side, which means there's not a lot of space for me to hide from their bitch of an assistant who will no doubt usher me out if she sees me.

Two steps into the ground floor gallery space, I spot my mother on the opposite side. She seems thinner than I remember. Almost skeletal. Her thinning red hair is styled with wide curls that rest on her bony shoulders.

She's holding a glass of wine and speaking to a group of people gathered around one of her oldest paintings.

"Of course, the style in those days never quite allowed for introspection. Everything had to be expressed in moderation," she says in her sophisticated tone that makes my spine tense.

There is a wall between my mother and me. Not literally, of course. A real wall I could climb over. But this one is unscalable. I don't know where she keeps her emotions, because they are not available to me. Instead of showing me love, empathy, or compassion, my mother appraises me—finding every single flaw or room for improvement.

Once upon a time, she heralded me as her greatest piece of art, but as I grew and stopped being just a pretty thing to look at, I started to feel more like the mess left over from whatever piece of art she was making. The dried paint under her nails. The watercolor stains on the table. The stench of acrylic chemicals.

I was never the masterpiece she once assumed I'd be.

And when her eyes land on my face across the gallery, it's obvious, and it feels like a gut punch.

"Excuse me," she says politely to her friends or admirers. Then, with her lips pressed in a tight line, she hurries over to me. "What are you doing here?"

My throat burns, so I clear it. "You don't return my calls."

"Well, are you calling because you want to talk to me, or are you calling because you need money?" Her voice is so low I can only make out her words by the movement of her lips.

"No, I'm not only calling for money," I reply, averting my gaze as I talk.

She crosses her arms. "Then, what is it, Sylvie?"

Just then, an angry pair of heels click against the hardwood as Enid approaches from the next room. "What are you doing here?" she whisper-shouts.

"Talking to *my* mother. I didn't realize that was a crime," I argue, throwing my hands up.

"Well, after the shit you pulled last time you were here, Sylvie, it is technically a crime. You've been served a restraining order."

My jaw drops, and I feel the eyes of the other people in the gallery scoping toward us. "A restraining order?"

My mother sighs. "Against the *gallery*," she says, giving Enid a serious expression. "You really shouldn't be back here, Sylvie."

"That was over a year ago. I've changed."

Enid crosses her arms now. "Oh really, how have you changed?"

Avoiding the question, I glance around the building. "Where's Dad?"

"He's in the studio," my mother replies.

I let out a defeated sigh. If anyone is likely to give me a moment of pity, it's him.

"Can't we just…talk? Somewhere? Anywhere. *Alone*." I say to my mother, not bothering to glance in Enid's direction.

Her breathing is heavy, and her expression is cold. "Come on," she says without sounding the least bit welcoming.

I follow my mother up the stairs of the gallery to where I know the office is. When we reach the second floor, I spot a piece on display in the middle that makes my heart fly up to my throat.

It's an acrylic portrait on canvas that was obviously ripped to shreds before being sewn back together. The hazel eyes in the painting haunt me, and I find myself pausing to stare at it. Tears prick behind my eyes, and my mother notices me standing there, frozen in place.

"We've made the best of a bad situation," she mutters quietly before urging me into the office.

I quickly blink back the tears before they can show. Then I follow her into the office.

She closes the door behind me before crossing the room toward her desk. "Go ahead. What is it you want to tell me?"

Everything feels stuck. As if I'm still standing in front of that painting, still ripping it to shreds, still hearing her tell me how disappointing I am, still reading the inscription, still crying in the back of a cop car.

I came here to ask for money. The plan was to beg and appeal to her nonexistent nurturing side, but even I knew that was futile. So what the hell am I doing here? Why do I even bother?

She's staring at me with a harsh expression as she waits. "Sylvie…" she mutters with irritation.

I look up from the floor and stare into her eyes. "I'm getting married," I announce.

Her brows shoot upward, and she looks momentarily surprised. "It's about time," she replies, her tone a bit lighter. "You and Aaron have been together for years."

"It's not Aaron," I say, tainting his name with bitterness.

"Then who is it?" she asks, letting her brows crease.

I swallow down my nerves. I'm not committing to anything yet. I'm just telling my mother. That hardly counts.

"His name is Killian. He lives in Scotland."

My mother laughs, and the sound of it is so patronizing I double down. "He's very rich, actually. Lives in a manor."

She's smiling as if this is all a joke. "And how did you meet this…Killian?"

"While I was there last month," I reply. "We just…ran into each other and kept in touch. His sister was actually just here visiting, and we've been setting everything up. I'll be leaving soon."

She laughs again. "*You're* going to Scotland? What about Aaron?"

"He's been fucking Margot for months."

She gasps at the vulgarity of my language, but I get some pleasure from shocking her.

"Killian loves me."

God, even uttering those words out loud makes me feel like an idiot, even though I'm the only one in the room who knows it's a lie.

"When is the wedding?" she asks, and I can no longer tell if she's taking me seriously or not.

"I'm not sure, actually. But I'll be going soon, so I just wanted to let you know…" I lift my face, meeting her gaze. "I don't need anything from you. Not anymore."

The weight of the stare between us makes the air hard to

breathe. I keep waiting for her to let this grudge she's holding go, but she won't. Her expression stays tight and guarded.

"Okay," she replies coldly.

I have to fight the urge to cry. "Aren't you going to…wish me well or at least come to the wedding?" My stupid, weak voice cracks.

She shifts her weight and rolls her eyes. "No, because I don't believe for a moment that you're really marrying some rich man in Scotland. Seriously, Sylvie."

My gaze darkens. "I am."

Her scoff is dramatic and hurtful. "This is just what you do, Sylvie. The moment you don't have attention, you come in here with some elaborate scheme or dramatic story. It's all so childish."

"I literally never have your attention," I argue, unable to keep the emotion from my voice now. My vision grows blurry with moisture pooling in my lashes.

"Oh, don't be so immature. Just grow up."

When I shake my head, a tear falls. "I am getting married, Mom. It's true. I'm moving to Scotland, and I'll be gone."

Looking unimpressed, she just gives me a shrug. "Fine, Sylvie. If that's what you want me to believe, then I'll believe it. Best of luck."

"That's it?" I mumble.

"What else do you want me to say after everything you've done?"

After a shuddering breath, I wipe my tears away. "That's all. Bye, Mother."

Without so much as a hug or a handshake, I turn and bolt out of her office. I pass by Enid on the main level as she's talking to the same group my mother was.

"Bye, you greasy cunt," I call out to her, pleased to hear the gasps of horror as I dash out the front door.

As I huddle against the brisk night air, I pull my cardigan around me and force myself to breathe. With each pain-riddled inhale, I feel the dam break, and my tears form. By the time I reach 57th and Park, I'm crying in earnest.

Everything hurts from that interaction with my mother, but the thing that digs the deepest is her not believing me. Why does that one part feel as if it's swallowing me whole? She doesn't care if I stay or go. She doesn't care that I never feel loved by her. She doesn't care about me at all, but the fact that she didn't believe me…that makes my breath quiver, my lip tremble, and the tears flow.

Well, I'll show her. I wasn't lying. I will marry that Scottish man, and I will move to Scotland, and I will be taken care of for the rest of my life. I don't need her anymore.

As soon as I get back to my apartment, my face is a mess with tears. I scramble through the drawer of my desk, looking for the card I left there. For a moment, I panic, thinking I might have thrown it away.

But my heart hammers in my chest when I spot the name on the glossy forest green card—*Anna Barclay*.

With a nervous gulp, I pull out my phone and dial the international number. Then I check my time and realize it's already early morning there. Maybe even too early for her to be awake.

But after two rings, she groggily answers.

"Hello?"

"Anna," I say, feeling frantic and unsettled. "This is Sylvie Devereaux."

"Hello, Ms. Devereaux," she replies in her calm and collected manner. "Have you given some thought to my offer?"

I'm doing this. I'm really fucking doing this.

"Yes," I say with confidence. "I'll do it. I'll…marry your brother."

"Very good," she replies with a squeak of excitement in her voice. "I'll have the contract drawn up and sent over today. We can arrange for a crew to put your things into storage for you, and the fees would be covered. We should be able to get the typical waiting period waived and Marriage Notice processed quickly. Would you be ready to leave in, say…a week?"

My heart is pounding so hard that I feel like I might pass out. I glance around my apartment at the various things that I have collected over the years. It's all just things that have no real meaning to me anymore. No friends to say goodbye to. No family to see me off.

The sooner I'm out of here, the better.

"Yes. Next week is perfect," I reply.

"Wonderful. I'm very excited, and I know Killian will be too."

The mention of his name makes my blood go cold. I'm going to see him again. I'm going to *marry* him.

"Thanks," I mutter.

"See you next week then," she says.

"See you next week," I echo.

When the phone line goes dead, I plop down on my couch and stare at nothing in particular.

What on earth did I just do?

Chapter Six

ANNA IS STANDING IN THE AIRPORT, WAITING FOR ME AS I WALK out of the terminal. She greets me with a smile, and I force one in return.

Somewhere between the neurotic night I agreed to this, and the moment that airplane put its wheels down on a runway in Edinburgh, I completely talked myself out of this wild scheme.

But here I am anyway. Because I want to be? No.

Because I have a point to prove? Yep.

"Ms. Devereaux," she says in a polite greeting. "How was your flight?"

"Please, call me Sylvie," I reply. Anna is probably only a few years older than me, but she talks like she's Scottish royalty, and we're all in some historical romance simulation. "It was good. Thank you," I say, hoisting my backpack higher up on my shoulder.

"I hope you were able to get some rest. We have a busy day ahead of us."

"Yeah, actually, I did." Which is true, thanks to those first-class sleeping pods they flew me in. I bet the folks back in coach are feeling a different way right now.

She starts walking briskly toward the exit. "We'll be heading straight over to the house today," she says in a straightforward, businesslike sort of way. "You can meet Killian a bit more properly now."

My stomach tightens at the mention of seeing him again.

"It's about an hour to the manor from here. We can go over some of the terms and rules in the car."

I nod as if this is completely normal business and not the most unhinged, reckless thing I've ever done.

After we get my baggage from the carousel and our driver carries it out to our car, Anna and I climb into the back seat together. She offers me some water and something to eat but doesn't waste any time before getting down to business.

"Now, I trust you've gone through the contract you signed, so none of this should come as a surprise to you."

I nod, taking a gulp of water.

"But there are some important stipulations to the agreement that I feel we should reiterate."

"Okay…" I mutter, waiting to hear them. I *did* read the contract, but contracts are contracts, and the language was superfluous enough to be confusing and vague. So I signed it.

"The term of marriage must reach one year from the date the certificates are signed in order for you to receive your payout."

"Got it," I say. Easy enough.

"After you've reached one year, you will sign the deed to Barclay Manor over to our aunt Lorna, who will handle the estate from there. Your marriage will be annulled, and you can return to America with your ten million dollars."

I force myself to swallow. She makes it sound so simple, but this part of the bargain has me feeling dizzy. I hope by the end of the year, it will be so easy to just take this man's house from him and go home as if nothing happened.

"Both you and Killian must remain faithful to each other for the duration of the twelve months in order for commitment to be considered maintained."

"Both of us?" I mutter as I pick up a piece of meat from the tray of snacks she gave me when I climbed in.

"Yes, both of you. This is important, Miss Devereaux."

"Why should I lose out on my ten million if he can't keep his dick in his pants?"

I don't bother to tell her that I failed to keep my *real* boyfriend loyal, let alone my *fake* husband.

"This is part of the rules in the trust, Sylvie. It's not something we can negotiate. If anyone is caught stepping outside of the marriage, the union is considered void, and none of the legal propagations stand."

"What kind of rule is that?" I stammer. "If a wife is loyal to her husband, but *he* cheats, she loses out on her house? Fuck that."

Anna purses her lips and gives me a stoic glare. "Life is rarely fair."

I stare out the window of the car as we drive down the busy city streets, wondering how the hell I'm supposed to keep a man like Killian faithful to me when we're not even in a real relationship.

The rest of the drive is more boring talk about the contract. It starts to feel hopeless by the time we reach our destination. As I approach the manor for the second time in my life, I stare at it, amazed that anyone can truly live there. It looks like something out of a historical novel, not the twenty-first century.

I know from experience that the inside isn't quite like the outside. The interior has been renovated, the kitchen opened to the sitting room. The walls aren't dark and foreboding but white and airy.

"Welcome home," Anna says with a smile as our driver opens our door.

As we step into the manor, memories come flooding back. I pick up the same cologne and spice scent I remember from the first time I was here.

But something is different this time. Unlike last time, there is a heavy beat of music playing somewhere in the house.

"What on earth?" Anna mumbles.

Then I hear the unmistakable giggle and moan of a woman upstairs. My cheeks heat and I bite my lip as I turn my attention toward Anna to gauge her reaction. I know the sounds of sex when I hear them. The last time I walked into a scenario like this, it was my boyfriend. This time it's my soon-to-be husband.

"Excuse me," Anna says to me as she stomps angrily into the house. "Killian!" she calls with fury.

I hang back in the entryway for a moment.

The girl upstairs giggles even louder.

When Anna reaches the living room, she lets out a scream. Her hand flies to her mouth, so I hurry to catch up, curious to know what has her so bothered.

As I turn the corner into the large sitting room, my jaw drops when my gaze lands on a completely naked woman scurrying to cover herself on a dark-green upholstered sofa.

"I'm so sorry, miss!" the young woman stammers as she rushes to get dressed. "My apologies."

"Killian!" Anna shrieks as she takes off toward the stairs. Her heels click loudly against each one.

I stifle a laugh, biting my bottom lip as I turn away from the naked woman and follow Killian's sister toward the stairs.

Killian's loud footsteps echo through the house as he rushes to meet his sister's rage-fueled attack. A moment later, there's a heated argument between them, and I stop in my tracks. I'm about halfway up the stairs, eager to listen to their fight but not interested enough to get involved.

"You can't just barge into my house!" Killian bellows.

"Will you *please* put some clothes on?" Anna shrieks.

"I'll do whatever the fuck I please," he replies, that deep Scottish accent bringing back memories of the day he yelled in my face. It should scare me, but it doesn't. It just activates my anger.

Heavy footsteps pound against the floor. I take a few more steps, peering over the railing to see Killian's white ass as he disappears into one of the bedrooms.

Anna turns back toward me, looking flustered. "I'm sorry about this. I told him to expect us today."

I shrug. This entire scheme is growing more futile by the second. The likelihood of me making it more than a few months is dwindling by the second.

Twelve months? Impossible.

"You realize there is no way this is going to work, right? He's not going to keep his dick in his pants, and I'm sure as hell not going to—"

Feeling his anger-laced green eyes on my face, I slant my head to see a now-dressed Killian watching me from the bedroom.

"Yes, he will," Anna mutters heatedly. "There is too much on the line."

Another young woman comes bounding out of the bedroom. Her cheeks are still flushed, and her hair is messy with knots and tangles in the back, which is a pretty good indicator of what they were just up to.

That explains all those giggles.

"Excuse me," she murmurs sweetly to Anna and me as she scurries past us, still buttoning up the top of some sort of black shift-dress-style uniform.

Anna glares at Killian, and then she glances softly at me. "Don't worry, Sylvie. We'll be hiring a new cleaning staff."

I press my lips together. Somewhere in the distance, I hear a door closing.

Which means I'm now alone with my soon-to-be husband and his sister. Killian saunters out of the bedroom, running his fingers through his long brown hair as he pulls it into a bun at the back of his head.

"You again," he says to me.

I square my shoulders as I turn to face him. "I was invited this time," I reply.

"I'm surprised you came."

"Well, I'm just full of surprises." I cross my arms in front of my chest and glare up at him.

"We'll see about that."

His green eyes are so fierce it becomes hard to stare at them for too long. His heavy brows hang over his eyes in austere contemplation. It's almost like I start to shrink under his gaze, and it grates on my nerves to feel that way.

But I don't back down. Soon, we're in a heated staring contest, and it's Anna who finally breaks it up.

"Killian, get this mess cleaned up. I'm going to show Sylvie her room, and we'll meet downstairs for tea in thirty minutes. I expect you to be there. We have some things to go over."

The corner of Killian's mouth lifts in a crooked smile. "I look forward to it."

Without a response, I turn away from him and follow Anna down a long hallway to the left, opposite from where the giggling girl emerged. The entire time she gives me a tour, I try to shake the feeling of irritation from that short interaction with Killian.

I realize he was trying to get under my skin. He was trying to assert dominance by mocking me and making me uncomfortable. I won't give him the satisfaction.

The truth of the matter is, I want this money. I *need* this money. Which means I have to make this work one way or another. Whatever this family plans to do to Killian when all of this is over isn't any of my business. I don't care about him or the house he wants to keep.

I'm in this for *me*.

Which means over the next twelve months, I'm about to become this man's worst nightmare.

Chapter Seven

"There will be a full staff on hand...once we replace them," Anna says as she pours hot water into my cup. I pick up the string from the tea bag and dunk it a few times as she continues.

It's still so odd to me that she is so involved in her brother's life. He's thirty-seven. Why is she even here? My parents practically wrote me off once I turned eighteen. Pushed me right out of that nest, and I would never expect them to put this much effort into getting me to fix my life. The only effort they've ever shown is by calling their accountant to have them cease my allowance deposits. I'm sure that took a phone call. It's so endearing to think they took the time to do that for me.

"What kind of staff?" I ask as I reach for the sugar.

"You'll have a cook, someone to clean, and a driver if you need to go anywhere."

"Seriously?" I ask with a perplexed expression. "So there will just be people here all the time?"

"Not all the time," she replies. "They keep basic hours, and they don't live here. But if you need them, they're available. There is a groundskeeper who lives in one of the houses on the property."

"Can't I just…drive myself?"

I see the corners of her jaw click as she presses her teeth together. "You can go anywhere you'd like. I'm not holding you here, but for your safety, we'd prefer if you'd use the driver."

My hand stills mid-dunk. I'm not an idiot. I know what she means by my *safety*, and it means I'll be watched. Wherever I decide to go will be everyone's knowledge. The reminder that I'll be someone's wife, regardless of how *fake* it is, makes me shudder with apprehension.

I'll be someone's property.

I mean, not literally. But suddenly, it feels like I'm living by some pretty archaic rules. I'm in a fucking manor that is staffed like it's *Downton Abbey*, and I have to live with a real-life chauffeur like I'm some sort of princess. It feels like prison bars made of gold.

Ten million dollars, Sylvie, I remind myself. I can do just about anything for one year. One year of actual luxury, and then I'll be set for life.

"Who will know it's not real? The staff?" I ask, wondering if I really need to sell this marriage all the time to everyone.

Anna places her hand on the table in front of me and leans forward. "No. No one can know the scheme. The only people who know are myself, my siblings, and our aunt. That is all. The public, the staff, and *especially* our extended family must believe that it's real."

I force down a gulp. A moment ago I figured the marriage was just a contract we had to uphold for a while, but now I have to actually convince people for a very long period of time that I'm in love with Killian Barclay. I think I might have bitten off more than I can chew.

Speaking of the devil, he bounds loudly down the stairs and into the sitting room, where Anna and I are stationed around a small table, each with a cup of tea in front of us.

"Join us for tea," she says to her brother.

He seems freshly showered. His hair is still a little wet at the tips, and he's in clean clothes. He's wearing a pair of dark jeans, brown boots, and a white knit Henley.

Is he *trying* to impress me with those sculpted shoulders in that tight top? It's like he's showing off, and it's cheesy and gross. Killian is a chauvinist, and I *hate* chauvinists.

Without giving him much attention, I focus on my tea, lifting it to my lips for a sip.

"No, thanks," he replies as he crosses the room toward the bar against the wall. He pours himself something, and I watch his sister for her reaction. There's a flinch in her stoic, brave expression which reveals something more similar to heartache. Just a subtle flinch of pain.

Killian drops onto the sofa lazily with his drink in his hand. "So, when's the wedding?" he asks. "I need to know when to plan my stag do."

I make the mistake of glancing toward him, and he gives me a quick wink, making my blood boil, so I look away again.

The incentive to talk business makes Anna sit taller and look a good deal more in her element than a moment ago.

"There will be no stag do, Killian. And I think it's best if we do a private ceremony at the church—"

"No church," he barks, cutting her off.

"Killian…" she pleads.

"I told you. The wedding has to be here, or I'm not doing it."

Anna lets out a surrendering sigh. "Fine. We'll have the wedding here and make the official announcement to the public next week. That would be the easiest and most efficient solution."

"What do you mean *official announcement*?" I ask, tightening my grip on my teacup.

"The family puts out statements to the public through the newspaper, but more recently on social media and through our family's bulletin. Next month, the two of you should attend an event in town, so people can see you together."

I notice the way Killian grimaces.

Meanwhile, I'm too distracted by the promise of an announcement. The thought of everyone I know seeing that, especially my parents, makes me giddy with excitement.

"Wait," I say, realizing something that makes my skin crawl. "You said the staff will all have to believe we're really married. Does that mean I have to sleep in his room—"

"Och, no," Anna answers, cutting me off.

"Oh, yes," Killian says at the same time. He's wearing a cunning smile, and it's handsome and alluring, like the devil's. He could lure women to their deaths with a smile like that.

"No," Anna says again, side-eying her brother. "There are no physical requirements in this agreement." I notice the way her cheeks blush, and her fists clench on the topic.

"Unless you want to," Killian adds with a wink.

"I won't," I quip.

"Of course, in public," Anna adds, "you would need to be convincing as a couple."

I let out a sigh and grind my molars at the thought. I can do that. For a few hours, I can at least pretend that he's not a complete pigheaded asshole.

"You can handle that. Can't you, darling?"

I glance at Killian, wondering if he can read my mind.

"How hard could it be?" I reply with a forced smile.

Every time Killian and I speak to each other, I notice Anna's discomfort grows. She's clearly recognizing just how poorly he and I get along and that this might actually be a terrible idea, which for the record, I tried to warn her about.

"Killian, why don't you take Sylvie for a little walk around the garden? Spend some time getting to know each other. You two can discuss your personal terms, and I'll just wait here, looking over some paperwork."

I turn my attention to Killian on the couch and notice the way his eyes burn with skepticism. I suddenly remember how, on that day I broke into the house, he kept insisting I was a spy for his sister. What on earth does he really think she's going to do while she's here? I mean, she's already walked in on his orgy. What more could he be hiding?

"I think that's a fantastic idea," he says as he stands from the couch. His tone is dripping with sarcasm. "Come on, darling."

With a roll of my eyes, I stand from the chair and look at him, waiting for him to lead the way.

Looking miserable, he walks toward the large French doors that lead to the garden behind the house. I never saw this part when we drove up over a month ago. Plus it was raining then, so I missed the gorgeous view.

Barclay Manor sits in the middle of a sprawling countryside. The garden behind the house is expansive and mostly flat before it leads to a large body of water with rolling hills and trees in the distance.

For a girl who grew up in Manhattan, this feels epic and overwhelming. The world felt much smaller in the city. We could only see as far as the building in front of us. Even in the high-rise apartments and rooftops, it felt like my view was limited to the edge of town. Breathtaking nonetheless, the views in New York are nothing like the views here.

It makes me feel even smaller. One puny human in the grand scheme of things. Insignificant and useless.

"Come on," Killian says with a growl as he makes his way down the stairs to the manicured garden below. "It's not raining today, so we better make the best use of it before it does."

I let out a cynical laugh. "And what exactly would be the best use of it?"

He directs an arched brow toward me. "We're supposed to be gettin' to know each other, remember?"

"Okay, so what would you like to know?" I ask.

He stops and stares down at me. "Why the fuck would you agree to this? You must really be out of your mind."

I scoff. "Why would *you* agree to it? Your sister told me you thought I was rude and mean."

"Oh, you are, darling," he says with a chuckle.

"Then why me? Why would you agree to marry me if you hate me so much?"

He steps toward me, crowding me toward the gray stone wall. His tall frame blocks the sun from my eyes, casting him in a shadow.

"Because as soon as the year is up, I don't want to have a wife anymore. As soon as my family sees that I'm a changed man, they'll leave me be, and I can stay in my house without them meddling in my business.

"So, I'd rather marry a selfish, rude, ugly, entitled cow like you so I never have to worry about hurting your feelings or wanting to make you happy. We stay our separate ways and get through the next twelve months without having to see each other much. Do we have a deal?"

My blood has never been hotter.

"Deal," I mutter through my clenched teeth.

As he turns away to continue our stroll through the yard, I add, "You do realize you can't keep fucking the staff if we're married, right?"

He huffs, letting his head hang back with an amused grin as he turns back toward me. "I'll fuck anyone I please, and you'll keep your mouth shut about it, or you'll risk us both losing what was promised to us."

"Oh, so you get to have your fun, but I don't?" I argue, stepping up to him. I don't care that he's almost twice my size or that he could bend me in half with one hand. I refuse to let this giant brute manipulate me or have his way while I'm stuck asking for a ride and being watched like a child for the next year.

"And what are you going to do about it, darling?"

"Stop calling me that," I spit.

"I'll call you whatever I want."

I take another step closer to him.

"One thing you should know about me," I say, poking him hard in the chest. "I'm stubborn, and I don't back down in a fight. And I really fucking want that money, so if you think I'm going to risk losing because you wanna get your dick wet, you're wrong. I can make your life hell if want to try to blackmail me into staying quiet."

"You really are a conniving little bitch, aren't you?" he replies, but the insult doesn't even sting.

"Yes, I am," I say with pride. "And you're right. We are going to stay our separate ways over the next year, and then we can easily split and take what's owed to us. I won't ruin it for you if you don't ruin it for me."

"Is that a threat, *wench*?"

I glower at him. "Sure is...*brute*."

Moving around him, I continue my stroll down the gravel path, waiting for the moment when he finally moves from his spot and picks up his pace behind me.

I don't feel bad that all of this is just his family tricking him out of his home. If he wants to be a rude and uncultured brute, then I won't feel bad at all.

Chapter Eight

THE WEDDING IS NOT REALLY A WEDDING. ESPECIALLY CONSID-ering I haven't spoken a word to my soon-to-be husband in two days. Not since that day on our walk when he tried to bully me into thinking he could do whatever he wanted and I had to abide.

I don't abide. Ever.

I spent most of the last two days trying to recuperate from my jet lag without much success. Last night, around three in the morning, I heard some cursing and stumbling down the hall where Killian's room is, but there were no other voices to be heard, so I didn't bother much about it.

Now, I'm standing in front of a plain white dress, trying to work up the courage to put it on. I feel so stupid for doing this. I don't have a friend or family member here. I'm going to stand up in front of some strangers and say my wedding vows to a man I can't stand and wouldn't marry even if I did like him.

Vows mean nothing. It doesn't matter if I make them. It doesn't matter if I'm not being genuine.

Vows aren't something I can spend or eat or live in. Money

is though. Money can buy me a car, one I can drive by myself wherever I want to go, preferably far away from anyone else.

Money can buy me a beautiful house in a strange city where I can start a new life.

Money can get me whatever I want, so anyone who says money can't buy happiness is probably poor and bitter.

A knock at the door pulls me from my thoughts.

"Sylvie, are you ready?" Anna calls from the other side of the bedroom door.

I heave a sigh. "Almost."

Standing up, I grab the white dress from the hanger and toss it over my head, shoving my arms into the sleeves and shifting it down around my breasts and waist. My long wild hair cascades over my shoulders, so I grab a clip from the vanity and pull it into a French twist. Tiny wisps hang over my ears and on my forehead, so I comb them back into the curls, spraying a little hairspray to keep them in place.

When I turn to face the full-length mirror, I pause at the reflection.

I'm not much for weddings. I don't believe in marriage. And I've never pictured myself in a white gown before like so many of my friends did growing up. The sight of myself in a white dress with lacy shoulders and rich, ornate fabric shouldn't really affect me, but it does.

I look like a grown-up, happy version of myself. Like this version doesn't suffer from a strained parental relationship and reckless life decisions. This version of myself did everything right. Found a nice partner, fell in love, and is moving through life's little rites of passage without fumbling at every turn.

There's another knock at the door. "Coming," I call after one last look.

When I open the door, Anna is standing there waiting. She's in a deep-green dress that looks lovely with her warm chestnut-colored hair.

"You look beautiful," she says without even looking at my dress. I realize as we start our walk down the hall and to the car that she's likely to be the only person to tell me that today.

As I descend the stairs, I see Killian waiting by the front door. He has his back to me as he looks down at his phone. His hair is down—deep-brown locks the same color as Anna's. His come just to his shoulders.

He has on a granite-colored wool jacket and a green and orange kilt. I bite the corner of my lips as I stifle a smile. I've never seen a man in a kilt in real life, and I'm a little annoyed with myself for how intrigued and aroused I am by the sight.

The kilt stops just above his knee and was probably specially made for him since he's built like a tree. His legs are sticking out of the bottom, thick and covered in hair. Then there's the long white socks and a pair of black shiny shoes.

It's honestly not fair how handsome he looks, even from the back. But let's be honest, that kilt is doing the heavy lifting. His personality makes it very hard to find him the least bit attractive.

When he hears us coming, he turns, and our eyes meet. For a split second, he's not wearing a rueful expression. For just a hair of a moment, he looks as if he's admiring me. As if he might be the slightest bit nervous about today too. Which would be nice to know since I'm feeling nervous as hell too.

"Let's get this over with," he grunts before painting the hatred back on his face where it belongs. Then he opens the door and marches out to the makeshift altar outside in the white gazebo in the garden.

Anna gives me an apologetic expression. "I can handle him," I mumble to ease her worries.

There is a crowd of people gathered near the gazebo, including the priest in his green robes.

When we approach the small group set apart from the rest, I notice that one of the men standing there looks like a younger cleaned-up version of Killian. Another man next to him doesn't look as much like Killian, but he's wearing a scowl like Killian, so maybe there's a gene for bad attitudes after all.

Anna leads me over to them.

"Declan, Lachy, this is Sylvie."

The first one to smile and greet me is the short-haired Killian clone. "Lachy," he says as he reaches out a hand. "It's so nice to meet you." His accent is thicker than his brother's.

"Nice to meet you," I reply warmly.

Then I turn to the other brother, who gives me a curt nod. "Declan," he says flatly.

"Hi…" I stammer uncomfortably. "Nice to meet you."

"The rest are mostly aunts and uncles and a few prominent people from the town. You'll get a chance to meet them more at the reception later," Anna says. I respond with a nod.

When I feel a heavy hand rest on my shoulder, I flinch. Feeling Killian's touch and proximity is a little unsettling, but then I realize the priest is watching us, and when he sees my fiancé sidling up to my side, he smiles.

"Let's get married, then," Killian says, and I turn to see the fake smile plastered on his face. It's not very convincing to me, but the priest seems to be buying it.

"Of course," the priest mutters as he shuffles toward the center of the gazebo. Everyone takes their seats, and I walk down the aisle on Killian's arm. It all feels very messy and rushed, but as long as everyone is buying it, I don't care.

When we reach the front, I notice Lachy smiling, and I keep my eyes on him. He looks to be closer to my age and much more like the guy I'd be dating than Killian.

My hands start to shake as I turn to face Killian. The moment our eyes meet, I feel the tremble subside. He's not scowling at me or giving me some hate-filled expression. I don't feel so alone as we stare at each other. He's in this too and hates it as much as me, and something about that is comforting.

The priest recites all the traditional things he's supposed to say at a wedding, but I'm drowning it all out at the moment.

Ten million dollars, I tell myself. *Set for life.*

That's the incantation that gets me through the next few minutes. Briefly, as Killian and I stare at each other, I replay the conversation we had the other day. About avoiding each other for the next twelve months. And I wonder to myself if this would be easier if we didn't seem to despise each other so much. Would I be dreading this the same way I am now if I could see Killian as a friend? Does it even matter?

He squeezes my hand and nods his head to the priest. "What?" I mumble.

"Say, 'I do,'" Killian whispers.

"Oh, I do," I say, feeling a chill work its way down my spine.

The priest says the marriage vows before Killian replies, "I do."

"Have you the rings?" the priest asks.

I turn toward Anna, who hands us a set of gold bands. I glance down at the one in my palm. A simple gold ring for Killian.

When he reaches a hand out for me, I place mine in his, and he slips the ornate diamond ring over my finger. "With this ring, I thee wed." He spits the words out with a hint of bitterness, and I look at the priest to be sure he didn't catch that.

He smiles at me to signify that it's my turn. Still trembling, I reach for Killian's hand.

The moment he places his large hand in mine, I stare down at it. For some reason, I'm enthralled by it. It's soft against my fingers, and I find myself admiring the size difference between mine and his, letting myself explore the palm before flipping his hand over to slide the ring over his fourth finger.

I don't let go right away. Feeling his gaze on my face, I lift my eyes to his.

"Here before God, and in His name, I now pronounce you husband and wife. You may kiss your bride."

My breath hitches. *Fuck.* I forgot about this part.

Killian doesn't waver. He places a hand around my back and tugs me to his ginormous body. My spine bends as I stare up at him. I'm barely even on my feet when he cradles my head and presses his lips to mine.

It's brutal and harsh, and I squeeze my eyes closed as his rough beard scratches my face.

The kiss is over as fast as it began. The next thing I know, my feet are back on the floor, and I open my eyes to see Killian's brothers and sister staring at us with a mixture of smiles and unamused expressions. Anna claps softly, and I touch Killian's arm to steady myself.

Then, he walks back down the aisle, and I follow him, holding tight to his gray wool jacket.

Killian marches right toward the house. I'm practically dragged behind him.

"Wait! We need photos!" Anna calls.

Killian stops in his tracks and stares at his sister expectantly.

"Here, next to the gazebo," she says, pointing to the structure.

Killian grabs my arms and hauls me to stand next to the white brick. Anna gets her camera out and points it at us.

"Smile!" she calls.

When it's obvious that Killian and I aren't willing to do much more than stand next to each other without touching and refuse to smile, she heaves a sigh and gives us both a steady glare.

"Fuck it," he mutters. Then, he slings an arm behind my back. We hold hands in front and stare at the camera. When I see him grinning, I can't help but smile too.

This all feels incredibly strange and awkward, and I have to keep reminding myself this is a fake marriage and not a real wedding, so I don't have to bother being disappointed.

Chapter Nine

AFTER THE WEDDING, EVERYONE COMES BACK TO THE HOUSE. Once it's filled with guests and food and music, it feels like a different place.

I'm a feather in a hurricane, blown frivolously from one end to the other, never landing. Killian is rarely by my side, and for that, I'm grateful. Most of the day is spent being introduced to relatives and friends by Anna. They ask about my family, how I met Killian, how I like Scotland, how many babies I want to have.

Every time I get my hands on a glass of wine, I gulp it down as fast as I can, as if it will soften the blow of this god-awful, miserable day.

There are moments when families laugh together that make the absence of mine feel debilitating. Then there are moments when they are obnoxious and overbearing that make me grateful mine are not here.

It's nearly two hours after the start of the party, and I manage to slip out the back door of the house and onto the stone veranda. Once there, I scurry down the stairs to escape the eyes of anyone at the party.

I desperately need a break.

But as soon as I reach the gravel pathway below, I nearly run headfirst into the last man on earth I want to see—my husband.

"Oy," he says with a groan when he spots me interrupting his escape. His large hands engulf my arms. "Watch where you're going, wench."

"Let me go, Killian," I argue.

He releases my arms, and I step away from him, fixing my dress.

"What are you doing out here?" he asks. I pick up the scent of something smoky on his clothes.

"Getting some air," I reply, turning my back on him. "What are *you* doing out here? That's *your* family."

"Aye, but they don't like me much. That's the whole reason you're here. Make them like you, and then they'll like me." He reaches into the small leather pouch tied around his waist and pulls out a pack of cigarettes. I screw up my nose and turn away from him, wrapping my arms around myself to keep warm in the cool fall air.

"Disgusting habit," I mutter quietly as he lights up.

"Thanks for letting me know," he replies. "Since your opinion does matter so much to me."

I scoff, spinning back to face him. "How do you expect your family to like me when you clearly despise me so much?"

"Och, you'll fit right in," he replies with a sarcastic chuckle. "You're selfish and entitled, just like them."

"You are literally the rudest and most entitled person I have ever met!" I shriek.

"Well, when your family conspires against you to take your house, how kind and gracious would you be? What's your excuse?"

"Ugh!" I stomp away from him, not getting far before my retort comes flying to the forefront of my mind, so I turn back his way. "You do realize that all you need to do to get your family off your back is take care of yourself, get your life together, and be a responsible adult? You don't need me here at all."

He chuckles around his cigarette, and I quickly look away from that siren song of a smile. "It's my fucking life. I can live it however I want. They have no rights to *my* house or my privacy. But don't worry. You won't be here long, darling. I predict you won't make it a month before you're boarding a plane back to America."

I take a slow step toward him. "Technically, it's your family's house, Killian. It's not wrong of them to want to preserve it before you burn it to the ground. And second, I will make it the year because as much as I hope your family does get that house from you, I want the money they're offering me more." By the time I finish, we're practically toe-to-toe, but I have to crane my neck to see his face.

We're in the middle of a stare-off when I hear a set of footsteps on the veranda. I don't pull away before Lachy spots us standing so close together.

"Uh-oh. What am I interrupting?" he asks with a charming smile.

"Nothing," Killian mutters as he finishes his cigarette and stubs it into the ground with his shoe. Then he storms back up the stairs without another word, and I'm left alone with his younger brother.

"Don't mind him," Lachy says with a crooked smile. There are deep dimples on both sides of his cheeks, and I never truly understood the power of good dimples until he aimed that beaming grin in my direction.

"Oh, I don't," I reply, looking off into the distance. It's nearly dusk. The sun has set, but there's just enough light left in the sky to give the world a sepia filter. Light without the sun is eerie, like we are caught in between two days.

And maybe that's what my life is right now. A mystic dusk. Not quite day and not yet night; just stuck in the middle. A yearlong dusk.

Once this whole thing is over, I'll be free. No longer living in my parents' shadows. I won't need them anymore, and it'll finally give me the peace to just be happy.

"Everything all right?"

I've nearly forgotten Lachy was standing there when he interrupts me from my thoughts. I tear my gaze away from the misty glen in the distance and turn my attention to him.

"Yeah, I'm fine," I lie.

He scrutinizes me for a moment before he speaks. "Listen, I know this whole thing is just…a farce. But you'll be around, part of the family, for the next twelve months. And I know you have your own reasons for doing it, but I just want you to know that you're really helping him more than you think."

"Helping him?" I ask, astounded.

"Yeah. It sounds strange, and I'm sure you think we're terrible for lying to him, but there's so much you don't know about Killian. He needs this."

I kick some gravel with the toe of my shoe. "It's a bit elaborate if you ask me."

Lachy laughs. "I know. But when I tell you we've tried everything, I mean it."

"Is it really that big of a deal to you that he moves out?"

Lachy's face falls. "It's not about the house. Not to us. If Anna made it sound that way, it's because Anna is pragmatic."

I raise a brow as I take a step toward him. "Then, what's it about?" I whisper.

Lachy clenches his jaw, and his eyes dart out to the horizon. He looks a little uncomfortable with the question. "Anna really hasn't told you much, has she? I mean about Killian."

I shake my head.

"The truth is…" he mumbles quietly. "We don't think Killian has left the house in nearly ten years."

My jaw drops. Suddenly, I'm replaying every interaction I've had with him. The argument over the wedding being at the house instead of the church.

"Why wouldn't Anna tell me that?" I say, staring straight ahead, unfocused and in shock.

He shrugs in return. "Don't be mad at her for that. Like I said, she just…thinks in black and white. To her, getting the house away from Killian is the same as getting Killian out of his grief."

"From your parents' deaths?"

He gives a noncommittal shrug. "In a way, yes."

"In a way?"

Lachy laughs uncomfortably. "This conversation is too heavy for a wedding."

"I deserve to know these things. I'm about to be stuck in a house with this guy, and I don't even know him," I argue, stepping closer to Lachy.

He puts up his hands in surrender. "Hey, I don't want to overstep, but I can assure you that you're safe with Killian. He might act like a brute, but he's not really one."

I take a step back and shake my head. "Anna told me we're supposed to make a public appearance next month. How does she expect any of that to happen?"

Lachy heaves a sigh. "Wishful thinking," he replies with a tight smile.

It suddenly feels like I'm going to have to work harder than I thought for that ten million.

"Ugh." I let out a groan, suddenly remembering our argument the other day when I ridiculed him for being able to go wherever he wanted without a driver while I was stuck here. I feel like an idiot. "Everything makes so much sense now," I mutter quietly to myself.

Not having a car for myself must be Anna's way of ensuring that I don't abandon him here. Maybe she's hoping that Killian and I can go places together or that having me with him will give him the strength to leave the house.

"Listen…" Lachy says carefully. "I don't want to tell you Killian's business, and I think there's a lot that Anna is hoping he'll tell you himself. But I do want you to understand that my brother is a good man. He's just…been through a lot. He's hurting, and there's nothing any of us can do to help anymore. But I think having you around might."

"He hates me," I reply without turning toward him.

"Killian hates everybody," he laughs. "But I don't think he really hates anyone, ye know?"

I let my eyes drift closed, and I force a few deep breaths into my lungs. Because I know exactly what Lachy is trying to say. But I also know what it's like to hate everyone. He's just sweet and naive, so he might not understand what it's like to be so filled with hate that it blooms like flowers in your bloodstream.

He might not think Killian truly hates anyone, but I think it is quite possible he does.

Because I do.

"I better get inside," he says with a nervous laugh. His footsteps crunch in the gravel as he walks toward the stairs that lead to the veranda.

"I'll be in in a minute," I reply.

When Lachy is gone, I open my eyes.

And just like that, dusk is over.

Now it is night.

Chapter Ten

My feet ache, and the lace of this stupid dress has rubbed a patch of skin under my arm raw. When everyone except for Anna and a few other stragglers have left, I escape up to my room.

My bedroom is large, the second-largest room in the house, Anna said. It has an en suite bathroom, a giant closet, and its own small balcony that overlooks the garden.

Everything in the room is dated and ornate, save for the few random modern things like the flat-screen TV mounted above the dresser and the wireless charger on the nightstand.

When I drop my phone on the charger, my arms are so tired, it lands in the wrong spot and falls to the floor in the space between the table and the bed. With an exhausted sigh, I kneel down and reach for the phone on the floor.

Just as my fingers brush the device, my gaze lands on something strange. It's a black leather strap fastened to the post.

"What the…?" My fingers touch the strap, grazing along the frayed edge, where it was clearly cut. I quickly stand up and inspect the rest of the bedposts, but they don't have the same leather strap.

Furrowing my brow, I try to imagine which of the Barclay children was likely to stay in this room with its kinky black straps.

Inwardly, I laugh at the idea that little miss uptight Anna would have a wild side.

After tearing my dress off and tossing it in a pile on the floor, I go to the bathroom and run a scalding hot bath with a big fat scoop of rose-scented bath salts. As I lower my body into the tub, I let out a sigh of relief.

This isn't so bad. I can do this.

Technically, all I have to do for the year is get through each day and somehow manage to keep Killian Barclay from screwing anyone else. Knowing now that he never leaves the house, my job actually got a little easier.

It doesn't state anywhere in my contract that I also have to help turn this man's life around. It's not up to me to get him to heal from the loss of his parents or get over this fear of leaving his house. I'm not a spiritual healer. Or a therapist. Or a miracle worker.

My job is simple. Stay married to Killian for a year and get ten million bucks for it.

What am I stressing about?

"Sylvie." Anna's voice calls through the door of my bedroom.

"I'm in the bath. Don't come in," I call back in a lazy monotone drawl.

"We're just leaving. We've put Killian to bed. He…had a lot to drink today. I'll stop by tomorrow to check on things."

"Good night," I grumble back in a low call.

She hesitates. "Good night."

Her heels click against the floor as she retreats from my door. A few minutes later, I hear the front door close in the distance.

Then, the house is quiet. *So* quiet.

It's an eerie sort of silence that makes me uncomfortable. Like the silence before a scream or the blast of a bomb. I can't stand it.

It's the sound of being alone with him. Even if he is sleeping in his own room down the hall. This silence means everyone is gone. There is no buffer between us.

Snatching my phone from the counter next to the tub, I open

the music app and start playing something upbeat and melodic. Only a few minutes in, I realize it doesn't fit with the moment, so I find something slower and more relaxing. When I've picked the perfect playlist, I drop the phone on the counter and let the sound echo against the walls of the giant bathroom.

I sink deeper into the tub and try to just melt into the relaxation. I wish I could turn my mind off, but I can't. I just keep going back to the events of the day. The wedding. The feel of Killian's enormous hand in mine. The fake smile he wore for the pictures. The way he stared into my eyes as we said our vows. The smell of smoke on his clothes as he stepped up so close to me.

So far, he is nothing more than a montage of moments to me. Most of them are harsh and unpleasant. Is this how the year will be? Will I ever truly know and understand him? Will I grow to like him?

No. I've never grown to like anyone, not really. I grew to like Margot once and look at how that ended.

It's best I don't try with Killian. Keep him at arm's length. Never dive too deep. Don't look too close.

I don't know how much time passes as I sit in the hot water, letting my mind drift quietly through my thoughts. Maybe six songs have gone by when I hear a crash out in the hallway.

I jolt, my eyes popping open as I sit upright and watch the door to the bathroom. I left it open, but I'm almost positive I locked my bedroom door.

Didn't I?

What if Killian breaks in? What if he thinks that now that I'm his wife, he can just barge in and take what he wants?

My heart hammers in my chest as I listen for another sound. In the distance, I hear a string of curses, mumbled and slurred. Then another loud *thunk* that sounds like furniture falling over.

The sounds are growing distant, which is a good sign.

When I don't hear anything for a while, I sit back in the bathtub and try to relax again. Maybe he fell down the stairs and cracked his head open. If he bleeds to death, do I still get my money?

Or go to jail for murder?

Yeah, definitely the latter. There's no way they wouldn't suspect me of killing him if ten mill was on the line.

"Shit," I whisper to myself. I really, really don't want to go down there. But if he is seriously hurt, that could come back on me.

"Stupid fucking Scottish asshole," I mutter to myself as I climb angrily out of the tub, water sloshing to the floor. Grabbing the towel, I wrap it around me and quickly dry off before snatching the fluffy white robe from the hook.

Just as I tighten the belt of the robe around my waist, I open my bedroom door—which was unlocked. The round glass table on the second-floor landing is covered in water, and the large ornate vase knocked over and cracked down the middle.

Fresh-cut red roses are scattered all over the table and floor. I pick one up and set it on the surface before glancing around for Killian. If I can at least get some confirmation that he's alive and not bleeding to death, I can go back to bed and lock my door this time.

"Killian," I call in a flat, unamused tone.

He doesn't answer.

I tiptoe down the stairs. Reaching the front of the house, I turn first toward the living room in search of him there, thinking he might want to watch TV down here. But it's empty. There's an unopened bottle of whisky on the floor by the bar, and one of the upholstered green chairs is tipped on its side. That must have been the sound I heard.

When I try the kitchen, I stop and stare in shock. It looks like a tornado swept through the room. Broken glass on the floor. Whisky spilled on the counter. And when I ease in further, I recognize a pattern of red drops on the floor leading to the dining room.

He's bleeding.

"Fuck," I whisper.

As I turn the corner into the dining room, I let out a shriek when I spot Killian slumped over on the floor with his back against the wall, and his legs extended out in front of him. He's in nothing more than a pair of tight black boxer briefs. His long hair hangs forward, draped over his face.

My eyes catch on the muscles of his shoulders and the patch of dark hair on his chest that leads down over his stomach and into his boxers.

Leaning against the wall with a half-empty glass of whisky in his hand, he looks passed out cold.

Standing in my bathrobe, I stare down at him for well over a minute. When I see movement in his chest and shoulders, I breathe a sigh of relief. There's still no sign of where the blood came from. He didn't step in broken glass.

Inching forward, I lift his hair enough to inspect if the blood is from a head wound. Luckily, it's not.

Lifting up his left hand, I first see the gold band on his ring finger. The sight of it feels like a bucket of ice water being poured over me.

I put that ring there. He's *my* husband.

I have a matching one on my hand now.

When I flip over his hand to inspect his palm, I find the source of the blood. There is a long clean slice over his entire hand. Blood seeps freely from the wound, pooling on the floor.

My first thought is…*Can someone bleed out from a hand wound?* Eventually, his blood would clot and stop him from dying, right?

Even with that much alcohol in his system though? Doesn't it thin the blood?

Maybe if I just elevate it? I could grab a chair from the dining table and rest his arm on it to help stop the bleeding.

This is his problem. I mean…three days ago, I wouldn't have even been here to help him.

I could have been sleeping upstairs in my room, so really I'm not at fault if I don't do anything. He chose to drink too much. He chose to be a clumsy, reckless idiot.

With a sigh, I stand up. Grabbing a chair, I pull up next to him and lift his arm so it's propped up. Blood still drips from the gash but not as steadily.

He's fine.

Turning on my heel, I tiptoe out of the dining room and back toward the stairs, watching for blood or broken glass. My conscience is clear. I helped him, and let's be honest, he's lucky I did that much after the way he's treated me.

It's clear Killian wants to be alone. And part of being alone and relying on no one is taking the risk of not having anyone around to help him when he needs it. That's on him.

He obviously doesn't want me here, so I'll pretend I'm not here.

If he bleeds out on the dining room floor, then he probably shouldn't have chosen to be so reclusive and ill-tempered.

I make it almost halfway up the stairs before I stop and squeeze the banister in my grip.

If I wake up in the morning to find him dead, then that's a whole mess I have to deal with. Not to mention, I doubt I'd see a dime of that money. Being married to him for one day is not the same as being married to him for one year.

I do *not* care about Killian Barclay. I don't.

But I do care about not going to jail and losing ten million dollars. So I spin around on the stairs and walk to the bathroom. Rifling through the cabinet, I find what I'm looking for—gauze, bandages, and antibiotic cream. After shoving them into the pockets of my robe, I grab a washcloth and run it under the warm water of the sink.

Taking them back to where I find Killian positioned exactly as I left him, I pull the chair away and kneel on the floor next to him. Placing his large hand in my lap, I feel a wave of relief when I notice that the bleeding has almost stopped.

Using the wet washcloth, I wipe away as much of the blood as I can. A lot of it has dried against his skin. His hand is heavy in my lap, and I softly stroke each finger, straightening them, just watching them curl back into a relaxed position.

Once the wound is clean, I take the gauze out of my pocket and begin wrapping it firmly around his palm. When it's covered, I use the bandages to hold it in place. I test my work by squeezing his hand to see if it will bleed through, and he stirs.

"Ugh…" he groans. His head tilts back, and he glares at me through half-closed eyes. "Not *you*."

"I'm helping you," I reply.

"Fuck you, cow." His words come out raspy and slurring.

As I finish cleaning up his hand, I feel his drunken gaze on my face, wondering if he sees the hurt in my eyes from his cruel words. I don't bother arguing with him. I could call him a brute or an asshole or a lazy drunk, but I don't.

Maybe if I don't sling back his insults, he'll see for a moment how hurtful his words are.

The next time I look up at him, his eyes are closed, and his breathing has grown loud as he sleeps.

I swallow down the sting of resentment.

After bandaging his hand, I go to the kitchen and find some towels to clean up the drops of blood on the floor. The cleaners will have to do a better job tomorrow, but I can at least wipe it up now while it's still wet and hasn't stained the hardwood.

It takes me a while to wipe up the mess around where he's still sleeping. Once I'm done with that, I get the spots he dripped from the kitchen. As I clean up the shards of broken glass on the floor, I find the culprit. The entire bottom half of the glass is still intact on the floor, and there is a ring of blood around the top. He must have been holding it when it broke.

After I find the broom, I carefully sweep up the kitchen and discard everything into the trash bin. There is a bottle of antibacterial spray in the cupboard, so I might as well use that while I'm at it. Next thing I know, I'm mopping the entire floor, moving the mop around Killian's sleeping form.

I don't even know what time it is by the time I've finished clean-ing. Killian stirs again. I can hear him groaning while I'm picking up the fallen chair in the living room. When I rush over to see what's wrong with him, I nearly collide with his giant bare chest.

My hands fly up, my palms pressing against the patch of soft black hair on his chest. He scowls down at me as he sways on his feet.

"Move," he mutters in a low growl.

"Try *excuse me*," I reply with attitude.

"Fuck off."

He attempts to shove me away and stumble past me but quickly loses his balance and goes careening into the wall, hitting it with a loud thud. His face screws up in anguish as he reaches for his shoulder.

I let out a disgruntled sigh. "Let me help you before you kill yourself."

"Don't touch me," he replies, taking another staggering step forward.

I put up my hands in surrender as anger boils in my blood-stream. "Fine!" I shout. "Take care of yourself then, Killian. Cut your whole fucking hand off next time. I don't care."

"What are you shouting about?" he groans.

"Just what a royal asshole you are."

I cross my arms over my chest. He stops in his floundering retreat and turns back toward me. "I'm an arsehole? What about you? You don't want to help me. You just want your precious money because you're a selfish little bitch."

"I just bandaged up your hand, you dick! You should be thanking me!"

"If it wasn't for you, I wouldn't even be this fucking drunk. But after I realized I married such a heinous bitch, I couldn't wait to get properly smashed."

My teeth are clenched, and my nostrils flare as I stare at him. For the first time since I arrived here, I'm starting to wonder if I can really do this. Can I get through the next year with this insufferable pig? How am I possibly going to make it that long without killing him?

"Go to bed, Killian," I mutter coldly.

He sways in his stance, staring at me angrily, and for a moment, I swear I catch a glimpse of disappointment on his face. As if he wanted me to argue back. Instead, I relented. I let him call me a heinous bitch without calling him an ignorant troll in return.

"I'm too tired from cleaning up your whole fucking mess to argue with you right now, so please, just go to bed and leave me alone," I say in quiet surrender.

His face tenses in frustration. "Gladly."

He barely makes it to the stairs, and when I envision him tumbling down them and breaking his neck, I hurry behind him. Without a word, I lock my arm around his and pull him up the stairs.

I feel his rueful gaze on my face as I help him, but I don't look back. I don't want there to ever be a moment of weakness between us. No sliver of kindness or compassion. Not a hint of attraction.

As we reach the top of the stairs, I let Killian go and watch him as he stumbles to his room, slamming the door once he's safely inside. Once I'm alone, I take a deep breath and let my exhaustion sink in.

Today was the longest day of my life.

One down. Three hundred and sixty-four to go.

PART TWO

Killian

Chapter Eleven

My new wife and I have relaxed into a bearable routine. The only time I have to look at her is at dinner, when we sit on opposite sides of the table. A time or two, I've caught her glancing up in my direction.

She has watchful hazel eyes and the world's fiercest resting bitch face. A slightly downturned mouth, big, full pouty lips, and a brow line so straight, it frames her face in a perfect scowl.

I knew from the moment she stumbled into my house that Sylvie was the perfect girl for the plan my sister was so enthusiastically orchestrating. She didn't just break into my home uninvited like some entitled brat, but she dared to challenge me at the same time.

I had never met a more infuriating and bold woman in all of my life. If I was going to let my sister win this battle and find me a bride for a whole year, then it couldn't be some dainty waif of a woman. She couldn't be polite or delicate. I didn't want to worry about hurting her feelings or being rude to her.

Sylvie is perfect.

It's been nearly a month since she arrived. I've picked up on her routine. She starts each day with an ungodly amount of coffee.

Then she goes into her room and takes the world's longest shower. After which, she watches the trashiest reality television and eats nearly everything she can get her hands on in the kitchen.

Some days she asks the driver to take her somewhere, usually insisting he pick the place based on her requests. *The best bookshop in town. The coziest coffee shop. The seediest pub.* Then she leaves for a few hours, and I'm free to roam my own house without worry.

But for some reason, I find myself spending those hours in restless anxiety. The walls start to close in. The house is *too* quiet.

I *could* go into town too. I could easily walk into a pub or head farther south and go into the city. I just don't want to. It's too crowded and noisy, and people are daft idiots. Why would I want to spend my days there when I have so much space and comfort here?

It's not that I *can't*—it's that I don't want to.

When the front door closes in the distance, I listen for the footsteps. If they are clunky boots on the hardwood, then it's Sylvie. If they are furious-sounding heels clicking, it's my sister.

A disgruntled sigh escapes at the sound of heels.

"Killian," Anna calls.

I could escape to the garden. Busy myself with the roses or tend to the bees, but she's too quick. I'm barely out of my chair when she enters.

"Oh, there you are," she says in a rigid tone.

"Here I am," I reply.

"Where is Sylvie?" She glances around the room as if my wife and I would just be sitting together like a regular couple.

"How the fuck should I know?"

Anna rolls her eyes as she proceeds farther into the sitting room, dropping her purse on the table.

"How are things going with you two?" she asks.

I shrug. "Barely see each other really."

She lets out a frustrated-sounding sigh. I briefly wonder what it might be like if my sister wasn't perpetually disappointed in me. If, for one moment, she could just see things the way I do.

"You've been married for a month now, and no one has seen you together. The honeymoon period is over. So it's time for you and Sylvie to make a public appearance."

"Fuck that," I groan, making my way to the bar for a shot.

"It's barely past noon, Killian. Must you really start drinking already?"

"What else would you like me to do, Anna?" I reply before immediately regretting it. I just gave her an opening to meddle even more.

"Help me plan this outing for you and Sylvie," she implores.

"I don't want to go on some stupid fucking outing. What is the point?"

"So people can see you together, and our aunts and uncles believe in this marriage, Killian. Take her to a rugby match. Post some photos online. That would make them happy," she says. I reply only with a deep sigh. Her heels click softly as she inches toward me. "When was the last time you went to a rugby match?" she asks delicately. "Or a football game?"

Her voice carries that worried tone that grates on my nerves. I hate that she worries over me. Especially when I'm perfectly fine here.

"I'm throwing a party," I reply.

In my periphery, I see her shaking her head. "No, Killian. No parties."

"Not that kind of party," I mutter lowly. "I'll just invite some of my old mates to stay at the house. A dinner party. Nothing too wild."

It's mostly true. My mates and I are still capable of having *normal* parties. Things might have gotten out of hand in the past, and word might have gotten around as to just how out of hand, but it doesn't have to be that way anymore.

"Your uni mates? Are you sure that's a good idea?" she asks.

I set the bottle of whisky down without pouring myself a glass. Anna wants to see I'm changing, and if that's what I have to do to keep my house, I'll do it.

"Most of them are married now with kids." I turn toward her with an air of confidence I have to constantly force with my sister. Or else she'll walk all over me. "If we're going to do this, Anna, we're going to do it my way."

She relaxes her features and lets out a sigh. "Fine."

We're interrupted by the sound of the front door closing again. That familiar echo of boots on the hardwood causes the corner of my mouth to twitch. Instead of going up the stairs toward her room, Sylvie makes her way down the long hallway to the sitting room at the end, where my sister and I are currently standing.

When she enters the room, she's gazing down at her phone with her earbuds in. When she looks up, she flinches, clearly surprised by the two of us standing here, watching her.

"Oh, hey," she says nonchalantly to Anna and me.

"I'm glad you're home. We have something to talk to you about," Anna says, taking a seat on one of the large upholstered chairs. Then she glances up at our new housekeeper, Martha. "Could we get a pot of tea, please?"

"Of course, ma'am," she replies before rushing off toward the kitchen.

Sylvie pulls out her earphones. "What's up?"

Anna gestures to one of the chairs. "Killian and I were just speaking about you two making a public appearance as husband and wife."

Her eyes dance toward me and back to my sister as she sits. "Where at?"

"Here," I reply with a low hum.

"It would be a dinner party with some of Killian's old friends. They'd likely stay the weekend. We have over sixteen guest rooms in the house."

"Fifteen," I correct her.

"Och, yes. Of course," Anna replies. "Since Sylvie has taken one, we now have fifteen available guest rooms."

"What do I need to do for this party?" Sylvie asks, glancing back at me.

"You two will need to appear as a couple. Which means you'll need to be affectionate as well as *talk* to each other."

Sylvie rolls her eyes and purses her lips. "Tell him he needs to learn his manners and stop being such a pompous asshole."

"I will as soon as you stop being an inconsiderate little cunt."

My sister gasps. "Both of you! Stop it!"

Sylvie doesn't give up that easily. "What did you call me?" she shrieks as she bursts out of her chair.

"You heard me," I reply.

"I'm here helping *you*," she cries.

I huff with a chuckle. "For how much?"

"You are such an ignorant pig!"

My lips stretch into a smile as the blood pumps faster through my veins. It's invigorating how easy it is to rile her up and get her going.

"See, we look married already," I reply with a laugh.

"I'd rather eat dirt than pretend to be married to you," Sylvie shouts. "I'm afraid I'll have to miss your little party."

Just as she starts to stomp out of the room, my sister stands. "It's part of the contract, Sylvie," she calls, stopping Sylvie in her tracks.

I watch with pleasure as her hands clench into fists. She spins around angrily. "Then tell him to stop talking to me like that!"

Anna lets out a sigh. "Killian…please."

I put up my hands in surrender. "Fine."

"You two will need to be believable as husband and wife, or none of this will work." She grabs her purse off the table.

"Where are you going?" Sylvie asks, looking terrified.

"I can't help you with this part. I suggest you two learn how to talk to each other and figure it out. This party will be the true test. If you can't convince your guests that you love each other, then this whole thing has been for nothing. And we've failed."

My sister leaves just as Martha walks into the room with a pot of tea on a tray and three mugs. I fucking hate tea. And I know Miss America over there loves coffee, but I feel bad for having the staff make it for nothing. So, I thank her as she sets it down and leaves.

Sylvie lets out a huff when she sees me preparing myself a cup. With an obstinate expression, she walks over and plops down on the chair opposite me. I pour her cup and sit back in my seat, crossing my ankle over my knee.

"Look at us being civilized," I joke as I hold the cup up to my lips.

"Your sister is right. We have a lot on the line, and we need to figure this out," she replies grumpily.

"All right, darling. What do you suggest we do?" I ask before taking a sip.

Sylvie glares at me over her cup. I love to see the fiery hatred blazing in her eyes. It makes me so grateful I chose a little firecracker like her. This whole thing would have been so boring with some acquiescent young woman.

"Surely we can just fake it in public, right?" she asks.

"Of course," I reply with a smirk.

"What are we going to say if they ask how we met?" Sylvie kicks her boots up and lays them on the coffee table. The sight of it would make my sister faint, but I find it fascinating. Much like the time she paraded through my home as if she owned it, Sylvie has this infuriating sense of entitlement. As if rules don't apply to her. As if everything around her is absurd, and she stares right into the face of the absurdity.

It makes me hate her even more.

With a smile, I shrug. "What's wrong with the real story?"

Her eyebrows bolt upward. "You want to tell your friends we met when I broke into your house?"

"Sure. Why not?"

"Because it makes me look like a criminal," she argues.

My eyes narrow. "But you are a criminal." I set my teacup down. "Besides, it's exactly what my friends would expect from me."

The moment the words leave my lips I regret them. And judging by the creeping smile on Sylvie's face, she's about to tease me about it.

"Did you just admit that I'm your type?"

"No," I reply with a growl.

"Careful, darling. You wouldn't want your wife to suspect you of catching feelings."

"Shut up." With a grimace, I avoid her gaze.

Sylvie giggles playfully, and the sound is annoyingly sweet. "We'll tell them it was love at first sight. You were head over heels the moment you saw me traipsing through your house. Most men would have tried to kill me, but not you… You were in *love*."

"That's enough, cow," I bellow.

Sylvie bites her bottom lip as she smiles at me from the opposite chair. "You know, you can't call me a cow at the party. Or bitch or cunt."

"And you can't call me a pig or a brute or an arsehole."

"Deal," she replies. "I'll just call you darling."

I screw up my face in disgust. "No."

Her lips twist, and she closes one eye in a look of contemplation. "What about…honey or baby?"

I make another expression of revulsion.

"Fine," she laughs. "What is Gaelic for *my love*?"

"Mo ghràidh," I reply in a deep rasp.

Her face falls as she stares at me. I watch as her lips part, and her eyes settle on my mouth. She attempts to repeat the phrase, stumbling over the second part with her American accent so it comes out as *mo ger-eye*.

Quickly, she sits upright and recomposes herself. "No, don't use that."

My smirk turns into a scowl. "Why not?"

"Because it's too…"

"Too what?"

"Nothing. Just say darling."

"I don't want to say *darling*," I argue.

"Why do you always have to be so difficult?"

"You're the one being difficult…mo ghràidh," I add that last part with a hint of humor.

"Ugh!" In a fit of frustration, she bursts out of her chair and stomps angrily out of the room. Just before I hear her footsteps on the stairs, she hollers back, "This is sure to be a disaster, and it will be all your fault!"

I can't help but laugh as I lean back in my chair, teacup in hand, propping my boots up on the table the same way she did.

Chapter Twelve

"BARCLAY!" I HEAR THE SOUND OF MY OLDEST MATE, LIAM McNeil, just as the front door opens. He ignores the valet at the door taking jackets, and he comes barreling toward me with a laugh.

"McNeil!" I reply with a wide grin. He throws his arms around me and pounds his fists on my back in a brutal hug.

As we pull away, he grabs my face. "I haven't seen you in months. You got uglier."

"I felt bad for taking all the ladies. Had to even the playing field for you."

He lets out a boisterous laugh. "How kind of you."

I lead my oldest and closest friend into the sitting room, where a few of our other guests are already waiting. Most of them are coupled. Friends from uni who have all grown up together. We still have the same old parties we had when we were young. They've just changed…a little.

The only truly single ones left from the old crew are McNeil and me, but he's about to learn that I have technically left him as the only stag at the party.

This is the first time my friends have visited since I stopped throwing wild parties. Nearly two years it's been since then, and already I can feel their eyes and expectations. This won't be like it was before though, or so I keep telling myself.

What I promised my sister was true. This weekend will not end up like one of those parties.

Sylvie is still up in her room, and I'm starting to get nervous that she's really not coming. Should I go up there and check on her? I'll drag her out if I have to.

The rest of my friends greet Liam with enthusiasm as my eyes keep scanning toward the staircase at the foyer, waiting for her to make her way down.

"Let me get you a drink," I tell Liam as I lead him to the bar.

"Thanks, mate," he replies. I pour two fingers of Macallan into a glass and pass it to him.

"It's good to see you again," he says with a crooked smile before lifting the drink to his lips.

"You too," I reply.

I notice out of the corner of my eye that Liam's gaze tracks carefully around the room, but he's not focusing on the people. It's almost as if he's looking for something.

"What are you looking for?" I ask with a chuckle.

"What the hell are you up to tonight? You ain't got any of that kinky shite going on, do you?"

I nearly spit out my whisky. "I told you already. I'm done with that shit."

He smiles wickedly. "That's right. You're a married man now." He shakes my shoulders, and I hold up my left hand to display the ring there. After dropping his hands from my shoulders he adds, "But being married doesn't mean you can't still be that kinky fucker we once knew."

"Jesus," I mutter. He doesn't understand that I've got my family breathing down my neck, threatening to take my house away from me. But I'm not getting into that with him. "For me it does. None of that will be happening tonight. It truly is a quiet weekend getaway."

"Fair enough," he replies, putting the glass to his lips. "But if I remember Killian Barclay, then I know a few whiskies in you will get you to do just about anything."

He lets out a hearty laugh as he slaps a hand on my back. I force a smile in return.

My head perks up at the sound of footsteps on the stairs. I don't know why my heart suddenly starts hammering in my chest. Maybe because I'm about to introduce my wife to all of my oldest friends. I've never done this before.

When Sylvie appears in the room, my jaw nearly hits the floor. In my mind, I was expecting her in her usual style. Black jacket, loose-fitting top, tight jeans, and thick black boots.

But that's not what she's wearing tonight. She's in a thin green dress, deep cut and hanging from her delicate shoulders. Judging by the thin straps and the sight of her perky nipples under the satin, she's not wearing a bra.

Suddenly, my throat is dry, and my cock gives a twitch.

And I'm glaring angrily at her.

"Fuck me," Liam whispers. "Is that…?"

As he pauses with his lips against his glass of whisky, I let out a groan.

"That's my wife," I say with a disgruntled sigh.

Liam gapes. "Holy shite."

Just then, Sylvie spots me across the room. Slowly she makes her way toward me, and I notice how miserable and nervous she looks. Her full lips are set in a delicate pout, and her normally fiery eyes are sullen and emotionless.

And it pains me that I won't be able to call her a heinous bitch all night. I'll miss the rise it gets out of her.

When she meets me at the bar, she hesitates for a moment. She goes in for an embrace but pulls away nervously. Trying to ease her discomfort, I throw my arm around her shoulders and drag her lithe body to mine.

Sylvie is so much smaller than me. The top of her head doesn't even meet my chin. She makes me feel like a giant, and touching her even slightly has me worried I'm going to break her.

"Sylvie, darling, this is my old friend Liam McNeil. Liam, this is my wife, Sylvie."

Liam makes a dramatic show of putting his glass down and turning toward the both of us.

"Killian Barclay, you can make a better introduction than that. This is your wife," he shouts.

All of the chatter in the room dies, and just like that, all eyes are on us.

Turning Sylvie toward the rest of my friends mingling around the room, I make a proper announcement. "I know you've all seen the announcement online and in the paper. I'd like you all to meet my wife, Sylvie Barclay."

Just then, her face turns up toward mine. Perhaps it's the sound of her full name now that we're married. My friends' reactions are loud and excited, clapping and murmuring to each other.

But I'm too busy staring at her. It's not like the day of our wedding, when she was still a stranger, and there was nothing in the eye contact between us.

Now, she's staring up at me with cold, lifeless eyes. It's the insignificance in her gaze that pains me. As if she doesn't care about me at all.

I much prefer the hatred.

"Mo ghràidh," I add so softly no one can hear it but her. I throw in a smirk and a wink.

It causes her eyes to squint angrily and her hands to pinch my sides, struggling to push me away, but I don't let her move an inch. Instead, I haul her closer and press my lips firmly against hers.

My friends whoop and holler at the show of affection. Sylvie keeps up her struggle, and it only encourages me more.

Without meaning to, I slip my tongue between her lips. She immediately stiffens, letting out the smallest whimper. Instead of pulling away or ending the kiss, I deepen it. This only makes my friends grow louder, urging me on as I scoop her tighter to my body and kiss her with heat and passion.

Our tongues tangle, and our teeth nibble, and somewhere along the way, she stops fighting and simply melts in my arms.

When we finally part, she gives me a fiery wide-eyed stare. Her angry gaze stays affixed to my face as Liam jerks me away and pats me hard on the back.

"Let's fucking celebrate," he shouts before the sound of a bottle of champagne popping jerks Sylvie out of her reverie. We're each forced a flute of bubbly into our hands, and the next thing I know, we're toasting with my friends.

But I'm in a daze. I'm too focused on her, her reaction, her attitude. Even when she fakes a smile and laughs with my friends' wives, she hides her discomfort under the surface. I want to drag it out of her.

After the first bottle is gone, I start to worry that this party is off the rails already. Just then, Martha walks into the room and announces that dinner is ready. So the party files into the dining room where the large table has been set with a modern arrangement.

The group mingles around the table, and Sylvie ends up on the end opposite me. It grates on my nerves to have her so far away. We're supposed to be proving to everyone how in love we are. It's hard to do that when I can't even reach her.

Which means it relies on our abilities to talk to and about each other, something we've failed at miserably up until now.

We don't even make it through the first course when one of the wives at the table asks, "So, how did you two meet?"

My gaze flits to Sylvie, who stares back with a challenging expression.

Here goes nothing.

"Well…would you believe this little criminal broke into my house?"

With hooded eyes, she glares at me from across the table.

"Broke into your house?" my friend Greg laughs from the opposite end.

"I did not *break* in," Sylvie replies defensively. "The door was unlocked."

"I was just out of the shower when I heard footsteps on the stairs. I come out to find a beautiful American woman standing in my foyer."

I catch the way her throat moves when she swallows.

"What were you doing?" someone asks.

"My boyfriend at the time wanted to see something inside the house but was too scared to walk in. I happened to see a woman leaving through the back, so I just...slipped in."

Holding my glass in my hand, I lean back in my chair. How have we not talked about that day since Sylvie moved in? I completely forgot about the woman who left that morning. I couldn't remember her name if I tried.

But I sense a hint of jealous pride on Sylvie's face at the mention of the girl. I like the way it looks on her.

"You just...slipped into someone's house?" Liam asks with a laugh.

"I knew from that moment I would marry her," I say proudly from the head of the table.

Sylvie rolls her eyes and shakes her head, biting back her smile. "What he means is he knew from that moment he would trick me into marrying him."

"They trick us all into falling in love with them, don't they?" one of the women at the table says with a grin.

Sylvie stares at me. Her bright hazel eyes are all I can see. "I was definitely tricked."

Everyone laughs, and I join in. I know she's saying it all for show, and none of this is real. I know deep down she still despises me. It's fun though. I'll admit that. To see her coerced into being nice to me. She hates every second, and it brings me more pleasure than anything I've ever done. And that's saying a lot.

Chapter Thirteen

AFTER DINNER, THE PARTY MOVES TO THE BAR. WE'RE ALL SITTING around the living room, and I'm too drunk already. I can tell.

It feels as if Sylvie is a moving target I can't seem to keep focused on. Every time I turn around, she's moved. One moment, she's sitting next to Greg's wife, whose name I can't remember, and then when I blink, she's outside on the veranda, staring out at the infinite darkness over the garden.

I'm sitting on the sofa next to Liam with an empty glass in my hand. He knocks my shoulder.

"That is one hell of a wife, Barclay. How the hell did you manage that?" he slurs.

I laugh and rub my brow. "Fuck if I know," I reply. I have to keep my answers vague and noncommittal. I'm too fucking drunk to answer anything specific.

"She's hot as fuck. I bet she's fire in bed. Tell me all the dirty details, please. I hear American girls are wild."

I give a chuckle, avoiding the sour taste in my stomach. "I don't kiss and tell."

"You arse," he replies with a laugh. "I haven't shagged anyone in months. I miss your parties. I'm fucking desperate. Does she have a sister?"

I smile at the ceiling without answering. Does she?

No. She's an only child. I think.

Fuck, I'm an arsehole.

The group of us are all scattered in a circle. Angus is across from me, the smartest mate in the crew. He and his wife, Claire, have been married the longest. Next to him is Greg and his wife…Emma? Then there's Nick and his longtime girlfriend, Theresa, to our right.

We started partying hard here every month a few years back. That's about the time I stopped leaving my house. Stopped doing a lot of things. As my eyes scan the group, I let myself imagine I could have ended up like them. I could have gotten married, moved to the city, and had a few kids. Lived a normal life. Instead of burying myself in the past.

They seem happy. But then again, none of them had gaping wounds of grief and regret to cure with alcohol and women.

Sylvie walks in from outside. She has her arms wrapped around herself as she shuffles toward me, taking a seat at my side, leaving a foot of space between us.

"Let's play a drinking game," Liam announces before going to the bar to retrieve a fresh bottle of wine. He sets it in the middle for us. When he notices Sylvie doesn't have a glass, he gets one and fills it for her with a wink.

My molars grind, and I don't understand why I can't just relax.

"Never have I ever…" he says. A few people around the group give a positive reaction, but I personally hate this game. It somehow only makes me drunker and feel like a piece of shite. Not to mention, if I want to keep this party under control, a drinking game is not the way to do it.

I feel the weight of Liam pouring whisky into my glass, and I force a smile toward him. "Thanks."

"Killian…why don't you start?" he says as he drops into a seat next to me.

I let out a groan. Then I glance at the woman to my left. "Never have I ever broken into someone's house."

Sylvie gives me a stern glare as she lifts her glass to her lips. The people around us break out in laughter, but no one else takes a drink.

"Your turn," I say to her as she wipes her lips.

"Never have I ever been so drunk I sliced my hand open without even knowing it."

I try not to give much of a response. I just lift my hand, revealing the still-healing scab, and take a sip of my whisky.

Sylvie stares at me for a moment, looking not quite proud but not quite apologetic either. The game goes around the circle, most of the questions staying innocent and fun. That is until it comes around to Liam.

"Never have I ever fucked two chicks at once."

"Of course you haven't," Greg teases.

Sylvie's eyes glance toward my face. This one isn't too bad. The guys here know me, so it's not like I have anything to hide. I lift my glass and take a small sip as everyone reacts with laughter and cheers.

When I bring my glass back down, I do my best not to look at Angus's wife across the room.

"Your turn, Barclay," Liam says, prodding my shoulder.

Fuck, I'm tired of games. I used to love shite like this, but now it feels targeted and dangerous.

Aren't we getting too old for this?

"Never have I ever...been cheated on."

I don't know why I say that. It's a risky and strange thing to say in this crowd, considering what happens every time we're together. But I figure it's the only one I know I can say, mostly because I've never had a real relationship to cheat on. To my surprise, quite a few people drink—including Sylvie.

Something about that irritates me.

Angus doesn't drink though. I do notice that.

Again, I force myself not to look at his wife, Claire.

When Nick's girlfriend notices Sylvie drinking, she asks, "I assume it wasn't Killian."

Sylvie shakes her head. "No. My stupid ex. Caught him fucking my best friend."

"Oh shite," someone replies.

"What did you do?" one of the women asks.

Sylvie sits up proudly. "I threw scalding hot coffee on his back. Gave him second-degree burns."

The corner of my mouth lifts in a smile.

After about three rounds of that game, it becomes glaringly obvious that we are not in our twenties anymore. We're all smashed. After I get up to use the restroom, I come back to find Liam sitting closer to Sylvie than I was.

He's laughing, clearly toasted. She's wearing a forced, hesitant smile that makes me want to scream.

"Sylvie," I bellow. They both turn to stare at me. "It's time for bed."

Her brows pinch inward, clearly surprised at me trying to tell her what to do. But if I drink anymore, I'll end up passed out on the floor again, and I can't leave her down here with Liam in this state.

It takes her a moment of my harsh gaze before she realizes that she can't stay down here without me. As she stands, I take her arm in mine. She glares up at me with frustration.

"We're off to bed," I tell our friends. "Everyone sleep well, and if you need anything, the staff will be here bright and early."

The crowd says good night as I practically drag Sylvie out of the room and toward the staircase.

"Let go of me," she whispers as we reach the stairs.

I let go, although I don't want to.

When we reach the second floor, she goes left, so I grab her arm again. "You're sleeping with me tonight."

She rears back and stares at me with ghastly shock. "The fuck I am," she replies in a hasty whisper.

I drag her closer until my mouth is near hers. "I'm not leaving you alone. Liam is too drunk, and he has eyes for you."

"I don't care," she replies with disgust. "I'll lock my door."

"We're supposed to be married, Sylvie. What will they think if they see you sleeping in a separate room?"

I don't know why I'm so desperate about this. I truly am worried about Liam. I've known the man a long time, and as wild as things get at our parties, I've never known him to be the kind to hurt or violate someone. But with the way he was talking about her tonight, I can't stand the thought of her and him together.

Sylvie lets out a sigh. "You're not going to give this up, are you?"

I shake my head.

"Fine." She jerks her arm out of my grasp and moves toward her room. When I grab her again, she looks back at me in shock. "I have to get some pajamas. I'm not sleeping near you naked."

The thought of her naked in my bed has my cock twitching again. It's been over a month since I've seen the least bit of action, and it has me thinking irrationally.

Sure, Sylvie is infuriating and stubborn. I may hate her personality, but her beauty remains, and my cock doesn't care much about personality.

She emerges from her room a few moments later with pajamas and a toothbrush under her arm. She closes her door behind her before following me to my room.

Once we're both inside, I close the door and lock it. Sylvie turns back to see my face after the lock clicks into place. Something about being in a locked room together makes her uncomfortable—I can tell.

"Sorry," I mutter as I unlock it.

She closes herself in the bathroom, and I hear water running and the toilet flushing as I sit on the side of the bed. I've sobered up in the past hour, but I still feel numb and reckless. Like I could say anything on my mind. I could do anything.

Normally when I'm drunk, I'm alone or with friends. Being with someone like Sylvie when I'm wasted is dangerous. It makes me want to spill my secrets, and that's a very, *very* bad idea.

The door opens, and she comes out in a pair of dark-blue satin pajamas. Her wild strawberry-blond curls are piled on top of her head and wrapped in a satin ribbon. She's wiped every ounce of makeup from her skin, leaving her cheeks spotted with freckles and her lips bare of color. I'd like to kiss them again to feel what they'd be like without the makeup covering them. Her eyes are so much rounder and brighter without the black lines and shading.

I'm staring for too long. Quickly, I stand up and rush into the bathroom. In there, I douse my face with cold water, brush my teeth, and empty my bladder. I don't own a pair of pajamas, so my only choice is to sleep in my undergarments and white T-shirt.

When I come out of the bathroom, Sylvie is already curled up on her side, facing away from the middle. I laugh to myself at the row of pillows she's placed between us. As if pillows could protect her if I wanted to touch her. Which I don't.

I climb into bed and click off the lamp on the nightstand. I roll away from her, and the room is bathed in silence. It's so quiet, I can hear her breathe. It's choppy and shallow. And I can feel a slight quiver on the bed.

My stomach aches with dread.

"Are you really so afraid of me?" I whisper.

"I'm not afraid of you," she replies defiantly. I let out a sigh before replying.

"I can feel you trembling."

Silence engulfs us again, and in the silence is the harrowing truth staring at me like a mirror held up to my face. It tells me that I'm too harsh. Too cruel. Truly a brutish monster, as she's pointed out repeatedly in the past month.

"I'm not," she argues before punching her pillow and settling back down into the mattress.

We don't say another word, but even as her breathing settles into a sleeping cadence, I stay awake. I can still feel her shaking.

Chapter Fourteen

When I wake, Sylvie is gone. Her side of the bed still shows the indentation of her body and carries her soft, flowery scent.

I hear movement downstairs, but I don't stir for a while. Staring at the ceiling, I replay the events of the last twenty-four hours. This whole fake-wife arrangement is so strange. Only a month has gone by and we still have eleven to go.

What will we be like in a year? Will she still hate me? Will she hate me even more?

Can I truly go a full year without sex? Surely at some point, she and I can reach some sort of arrangement where we keep our extramarital affairs between us.

Last night I actively tried to keep her away from Liam, but what if something did happen between them? It would give me the leverage I'd need to do the same. Tit for tat. A secret between us. The contract stays in place, but we still get to have our fun.

Deep down, I hate the idea, but I know it would be better for me in the long run.

It was wrong of me to bring her to my room. The last thing I need to do at this point is treat my wife like…my wife. I don't need her getting the wrong idea about me. When this is over, she has to leave. One year, and then I'm on my own again. Besides, I promised her we'd spend this time separately, not with me dragging her to my bed.

When I do finally get up, I hear shouting outside, so I peer out of my large window. Liam is on the vast grassy field outside, shirtless, with a rugby ball under his arm. When he sees me watching, he waves.

"Get your ugly arse out here!" he bellows.

I laugh, spotting Greg, Angus, and Nick on the field as well. They turn to see me, each of them waving. Briefly, I wonder where the women are. Should I be nervous about Sylvie being alone with them, especially Claire?

I shake the thought away. It's not even ten in the morning. I doubt they'd be sharing stories this early, anyway.

After hurriedly getting dressed, I jog down the stairs. Heading straight out the door to the field behind the house, I greet the ladies, who are all sitting around a table with cups of tea in front of them.

Except for Sylvie, who's sipping what I assume is her third cup of coffee. She glances up at me over the steaming liquid. Before jogging out to meet the guys, I hesitate.

I'm supposed to treat her like my wife, aren't I? What would a husband do in this scenario? I imagine Greg or Nick would kiss their ladies. Sylvie's eyes narrow at me over her cup as I hesitantly make my way over.

"Mornin," I mutter as I press my lips against her forehead. The other women at the table ooh and aah over the gesture, but Sylvie barely reacts. With a cold expression, she softly mumbles, "Morning."

"All right, two on two!" Liam bellows from the stairs of the veranda. "Let's go, old man."

He tosses the rugby ball at me with force, and I catch it against my stomach. It nearly knocks the wind out of me, but I keep my smile.

Before he and I rush off to the field with the other guys, I notice the way his gaze lingers on Sylvie.

My idea from earlier resurfaces.

If I could get Sylvie to sleep with Liam, it would clear my conscience for the rest of our marriage. He's a good-looking guy. Built, tall, rugged. He has more of a clean-cut look without the beard, and he makes a lot of money. I know that's important to her.

The four of us play a slow and painful match of rugby, all putting in far more effort than we have at our ages. Nick takes a hit that he almost doesn't get up from, which we all tease him about since he's the oldest by four years. The ladies come out and cheer us on a bit, taking pics and laughing at us as we fall over.

It's nothing like it used to be when we played in uni nearly fifteen years ago. But it's fun.

Not once in the past decade have I thought about what I was missing—until now.

After an hour, we are all sweaty, muddy, and starving. Angus ambushes Claire with a disgusting hug, making her squeal as he wraps his arms around her. Sylvie gives me a pointed glare.

"Don't you dare," she mutters. I laugh, wanting to hug her just to piss her off now.

I choose not to and walk beside her instead.

Liam strides beside me. "So, Sylvie. You're not taking this big Scotsman to America, are you?"

She glances up, first at me and then at him. "No," she replies, shaking her head. "I'm not going back."

"Ever?" he asks.

She gives him a shrug. "I don't have much reason to. My parents and I don't get along well, and I like it here."

"I read something about your parents," Claire says from behind us. When we all turn, she gives us a sheepish grin. "I hope you don't mind me bringing that up, but I saw it online when Killian's family made the announcement. That your parents are famous artists or something."

My gaze darts toward my wife, waiting for her reaction as the entire group meets the gray stone steps of the house. My sister mentioned something about Sylvie's parents being artists, but I never gave it a second thought. I didn't care much, and technically, I still don't. It's just curiosity.

Sylvie smiles at Claire. "It's okay. They are pretty famous in the art world. They have paintings in museums all over the globe."

"But you don't get along with them?" Angus asks.

Softly, she shakes her head. "No. They're just…fucking assholes."

This makes the group laugh, but my mouth doesn't move toward a smile.

Sylvie has been calling me an arsehole since she arrived, and I'll admit…I *am* an arsehole—to her. Are they? What could they have done to warrant that sort of reaction?

"Well, you turned out all right," Liam says with a wink. She gives him a soft smile.

That's a good sign.

"Let's get inside and get cleaned up," I reply, breaking up the moment.

Once in the house, we all scatter in different directions. I jog toward my room while the rest of them move toward the guest rooms, which are mostly on the third floor. After taking a quick shower, I step out of the bathroom and dress in a rush. My growling stomach has me hurrying. Whatever Martha made for lunch smells delicious all the way up here.

Just as I burst out of my room, I nearly knock someone over in the hallway. It takes me a moment to register that the petite woman isn't Sylvie.

It's Claire.

My hands fly from her shoulders, where I held her to keep from bowling her over.

"I'm sorry," I stammer.

"It's okay," she replies uncomfortably.

"I didn't see you there."

"I was just…poking around," she replies. Her eyes stay on my face as I back against the wall, putting as much space between us as possible. Then I quickly scan the periphery of the hall to realize she and I are alone.

My lungs hold my breath, my gaze raking over her face.

"How are you?" she whispers.

I force myself to swallow.

"Fine," I mutter quietly.

It's clear she expects me to return the question, but I don't. I shouldn't be talking to her at all.

"Sylvie is really lovely," she says, making casual conversation.

I glance around again, wondering where my wife is at the moment.

"Where is she?" I mumble.

"She's downstairs," Claire whispers so softly I can barely hear it. "Everyone is."

My eyes lift to her face again. My feelings are so conflicted and hard to describe.

"Claire…" I start, trying to back away even more, but for some reason, she sees this as an invitation to step even closer.

"I've missed you."

I force in a deep breath. There's a part of me that's dying to tell her I don't think about her at all. And when I do, it's only when I'm drunk, and my demons show up to remind me what a liar and bad friend I am.

"What about Angus?" I murmur in question.

"I love Angus," she replies as if it's obvious. "But there will always be a part of me that…"

She reaches out and rests her fingers against my chest.

Fuck. Fuck. Fuck.

"Angus can't please me the way you do, Killian."

I can't breathe.

"I told you it was over," I reply softly. "You shouldn't be here. You're married to one of my best friends."

She takes another step closer. "I thought this was why you invited us."

"I invited you all here to meet my *wife*." If only I could just tell her the only damn reason I had this fucking party at all was to prove to the world that I'm not a fucking mess and that I have a happy marriage.

I can't even pretend I'm all right.

"Besides," I add. "I won't do that to him again—"

A creak on the stairs makes the both of us jump back. We barely do it in time before I turn to find Sylvie staring at us skeptically.

"It was good catching up with you," Claire says to me with a polite smile. Then she turns toward the stairs, passing Sylvie as she goes. "You two are such a lovely couple," she says to her before she disappears down the stairs.

I'm left alone with my wife, who is staring at me with that cold, lifeless expression she so often has. "What was that?" she asks with a scrutinizing gaze.

"Nothing," I grumble before pushing past her to go down the stairs.

She grabs my arm. "It didn't look like nothing."

Frustration builds inside me, and I turn back toward her, ready to blow with anger. I put my face in hers, muttering in a low, angry growl. "I said it was nothing."

"I don't care what it was," she replies, stepping up, her neck craned to see my face. "Just keep it in your pants so I don't lose what's owed to me."

"You think I would fuck my friend's wife?"

She tilts her head with a cynical smirk. "Of course not, Killian. As you said...that was *nothing*, right?"

"Fuck you, cow," I growl.

She shakes her head with a roll of her eyes. Blowing me off, she squeezes past and walks to her room. "You won't be fucking anyone." Then she turns toward me and gives me a fake smile. "Darling."

As she disappears into her room, I have to fight the urge to punch a hole in the wall. Instead, I head downstairs to be with my friends—the *real* people in my life.

Last night, it was kind of me to remove her from the situation and spare her from Liam's advances. Tonight, I won't be so kind.

Chapter Fifteen

THE DAY GOES BY IN A BLUR OF LAUGHTER AND CONVERSATION. My friends leave tomorrow, and already I'm feeling like a real ass for staying out of touch for so long. We reminisce about uni, catch up on each other's lives, and make plans to definitely do this again soon. Like this.

I manage to avoid Claire for the rest of the day, never even daring to look in her direction over lunch or the walk around the grounds later in the day. At the same time, I also manage to avoid Sylvie as well. When she is with our group, she keeps her distance from me, blending in nicely with the ladies so it doesn't seem strange that she and I aren't speaking or touching.

The plan tonight is to throw an old-fashioned rager. Everyone wants to get piss drunk, and I'm feeling uneasy about it. I can't let things get out of hand like they used to.

I'm the first one down for dinner, and I can't ignore the sour feeling of anxiety gnawing at my gut. Something about what happened today with Claire and Sylvie isn't quite sitting right with me.

What do I have to feel bad about though? I've called off things with Claire.

I'm certainly not going to feel bad about it now. And the last person I'm going to explain myself to is Sylvie.

To my relief, the next person downstairs for dinner is Liam. I'm standing near the bar in the parlor when he walks down and finds me deep in contemplation.

"What's on your mind?" he asks with a smile as he crosses the room.

"Not much," I reply nonchalantly.

As he pours himself a drink, he nods toward the hall. "Where's that hot wife of yours?"

I chuckle. "Still getting ready, I think."

Liam whistles with a shake of his head. "If that were *my* wife, I wouldn't let her out of my sight."

It's not the first—or even second—time this weekend my friend has commented on the beauty of my wife. This is exactly what I want, but for some reason, it bothers me.

"I couldn't control her if I tried," I reply with a smirk.

"It's not *her* I'd be worried about."

Glancing out the side of my eye, I wonder exactly what Liam is talking about. Is there another man in this house I should be worried about? What is he implying? Sure, my friends can be flirty, but none of them would truly touch my wife in my own home. Would they?

Suddenly, I see an opportunity. And I'm not proud of myself for it.

"Well, you know…" I mumble quietly. "Sylvie and I…we keep things *open*."

Liam's head pops up, and he stares at me for a moment as if he's trying to put something together. "You mean…"

I nod.

When he picks up on what I'm implying, a smile stretches across his face. "You're still a kinky fucker."

"Shhh… Keep your voice down," I mutter. Trying to keep things casual, I smile at my old friend. "She knows what she's getting herself into this weekend. I let her do what she wants, and she lets me do what I want."

He scratches his head. "I don't understand you married guys. Doesn't that bother you? For other men to touch your woman?"

My jaw clenches, but I bury the rising hesitation. "It just means I get to remind her who she belongs to when she comes back."

Liam's eyes widen. "Good point."

I shoot back my drink, hoping the alcohol will cool the buzzing heat in my blood. I hate the way this feels, and I really shouldn't give a shite. I barely know Sylvie, let alone have any romantic feelings for her. Hopefully, she's into Liam, and this could all work out in my favor.

What happens at the house this weekend stays here.

When I look up, I spot a mess of reddish-blond curls. My eyes collide with Sylvie's. She's wearing that same cold, dead expression she always seems to wear around me.

Liam still has his back to the room and has no idea she's on the other side. "So...does that mean you wouldn't mind if I—"

I knock him with my elbow, nodding toward my wife. Liam spins to find her there, quickly putting a fake smile on his face. "Sylvie!"

Sylvie stares at us in contemplation for another minute before turning silently on her heels and walking into the dining room. I'm willing to bet my wife will be glad when this weekend is over, and she can go back to her solitary routines.

Liam and I laugh for a moment before the rest of the crowd files down the stairs. Most of us have been drinking already so the party is already rowdy as we head in for dinner. The first thing I notice is that Claire sits right next to Sylvie at the table. I take the seat at the head again, but I can't get Sylvie to even look at me. And it's bugging the hell out of me.

The group is rowdy. As soon as we're all seated, Angus clinks his fork on his glass to make an announcement.

Standing up, he stares at me with a smile. "Thanks for invit-
ing us, Killian. It truly is great to be back with old friends again.
To you and Sylvie and your happy marriage. And to get fucking
bladdered tonight."

The group erupts in raucous cheers as everyone shoots
back their drinks. Even Sylvie gulps down the contents of her
wineglass.

As soon as the food is served, the dinner conversation turns
vulgar and inappropriate.

"Okay, be honest," Nick says as he glances at me. "You guys
have fucked on this table, haven't you?"

Everyone laughs.

I look at Sylvie. She tilts her head to the side and stares at me
as if waiting for my response.

"Twice," I say around a bite.

The group cheers.

Nick's girlfriend laughs. "Yeah, this is a nice sturdy table,
perfect for fucking."

The ladies chuckle along.

Then it's Greg's wife's turn. "God, I miss the honeymoon
period. I bet you two are still fucking like animals."

Sylvie clenches her jaw but glances at me again. I don't know
what's holding me back. I could easily lie and tell stories about
how raunchy our nonexistent sex is. But the words won't come.

So Sylvie chimes in. "He's the one who struggles to keep up
with me." A hint of a smile tugs at the corner of her mouth, and
I bite my tongue.

"It's the age," Theresa replies playfully. "Once they hit thirty-
five, they lose their stamina."

"Hey!" Nick complains.

"My stamina is just fine," I reply heartily. "Tell them." I glance
expectantly at Sylvie.

Everyone looks at her too.

After a moment, she shrugs. "His stamina is just fine."

"How many times a day are you two fucking? Living alone here at this manor, I bet it's like five times a day."

Sylvie's throat moves as she swallows.

"What is it now, darling?" I ask, drawing her attention. "Three times a day?"

"At least," she replies with a challenge in her expression.

"Your new wife must know everything about you, Killian," Emma says, with a drunken slur in her voice. "That you have some wild and kinky tastes."

My skin grows hot as I stare at Sylvie to gauge her reaction. There isn't much of one.

It's funny to think she knows nothing of my sex life at all, and I know nothing of hers. People around this table would be shocked to know that. They're already imagining us fucking in ten different positions in every room of this house.

"Well, does she?" Claire asks, holding her glass of wine in her delicate fingers.

I freeze as my gaze settles on her face. She wouldn't…

"Let's just say…" Sylvie says, filling the awkward silence. "Don't go snooping through drawers or under the beds."

Everyone laughs, and my head tilts as I stare at her across the table. It almost felt as if she was covering for me, and I don't understand why.

After dinner, the party spills into the parlor. It's darker than last night, and Liam has figured out how to work the speaker system. Music blasts through the built-ins. After the very first beat drop from some twenty-year-old song from our younger days, people start dancing.

I'm not drunk enough. I wish I was drunker. I keep going for the whisky, but something is stopping me. I can't stop watching Sylvie.

"Come on, Killian," Emma whines as she tugs on my arm. "Let's dance."

She drags me into the middle of the room.

"Dance with your husband," I reply with a lighthearted laugh.

"Boring," she drawls.

I don't really want to dance. I feel too old for this shit. It's songs from my younger days, but I don't feel like that man anymore. It's not a fun time to relive.

But I play along, letting her grind against me as another random mismatched couple starts to dance behind us.

I can already tell this will be trouble before long. Everyone is too drunk.

Wait. What the fuck am I saying? I love parties like this. I love nights that go off the rails. I want the mistakes and the sex and regrets and the fun and the reckless abandon.

Suddenly, I feel myself leaning into it. This is what I want.

Going to the bar, I crack open a new bottle and pour my glass with far too much. By the time I turn around, I notice Liam is sitting next to Sylvie. He's touching her arm.

So far, she's giving him the cold front of greetings, but when he says something to make her laugh, she tugs her bottom lip between her teeth and actually blushes.

I'm suddenly dying to know what he said.

Instead, I throw back another glass of whisky, waiting for the alcohol to numb my system.

Another song on the makeshift dance floor.

Another full glass emptied.

Then, another.

And another.

The room is starting to soften into shades of blue. It's dark and hazy, but the alcohol isn't kicking in as much as I'd like. It's like I can still see too much too clearly.

Everyone around me is obviously wasted.

I'm dancing with someone. Her fingers are under my shirt, and she's laughing. I glance over her head to see Theresa on Angus's lap, and I know in the back of my mind that image is wrong. She's Nick's girl.

Two years ago, it wouldn't have been wrong at all. This is what we did. We blurred all the lines and we fucked without abandon. We were wild and untamed.

But I've changed. This party wasn't supposed to end this way. Where is Sylvie?

I pull away from the woman with her hands up my shirt and stumble out of the room. The hallway feels long, and I stare down it toward the staircase on the opposite end. A feeling of dread crawls up my spine.

Are Sylvie and Liam up there?

That's what I want.

But I don't.

These feelings war inside me, and no matter how hard I try, I can't seem to tear them apart.

I stumble down the hall toward the stairs just to see for myself. I make it about two steps before another pair of soft hands wrap around my waist.

Sylvie.

"Come here," she whispers softly, tugging me into a dark room. It's a storage closet, but before I can argue, she's pulling my mouth down to hers, kissing me with passion and need.

I surrender to the kiss, letting the intensity sweep me out to sea. Her lips feel so good, and I'm so focused on the fact that she's supposed to be somewhere with Liam, but she's not. She's here with me.

Fuck, that's not what I want. But I can't seem to stop it.

"God, please touch me. I need you," she whimpers into my mouth. It sounds wrong.

But I'm too drunk to stop it.

Her hand takes mine, and she drags it between her legs, shoving my fingers against the moist center of her panties. She's so wet for me, I let out a growl when I feel it.

I don't understand these feelings for Sylvie. This hate-fueled desire. This need to own her, dominate her, force her to submit, make her mine. I don't want her. I don't care about her. I just *need* her.

My cock is rock hard behind my slacks at the thought. It's never felt so full of life before, a fire blazing in my groin at the idea of fucking my headstrong, stubborn wife into submission.

Before I know what I'm doing, my finger is inside her. She's clinging to my arm, moaning and whimpering. And suddenly, I realize that this is all too easy.

Something is missing.

She's supposed to fight with me.

"I missed you so much," she mutters. "Please fuck me, Killian."

I yank my hand from under her dress. "Bloody hell," I groan as my back hits the wall, and I realize what I've done.

"Wh-what's wrong?" she murmurs.

"Claire?"

"Yes, of course. Who else would it be?" she asks, her voice cracking with emotion.

My heart fucking shatters.

"I have to go," I stammer as I tear open the door and nearly fall out of the closet and into the hallway. There are moans and cries of sex from the parlor.

Where the fuck is Sylvie?

I take one marching step toward the stairs when I hear voices from behind me. I turn to see two silhouetted figures outside through the open doors. Two bodies pressed together, practically as one.

Rage boils inside me as I inch closer to the door. The only reason I'm not barreling out there is because a part of me needs to know. Would she really let him touch her?

In the back of my mind, I remember that that's what I want, but I can't fucking remember why.

In the silhouette, I see her hands pressed against his chest. He has her crowded toward the low wall. He leans his mouth toward hers.

"I can't," she says with the cool defiance only she can pull off.

"Come on, baby. I'll make you feel so good," he murmurs.

Rage cracks inside me like dynamite. I've never felt such anger. Suddenly I can't keep the slow pace. I'm practically running. Grabbing Liam by the collar, I yank him away from Sylvie.

"What the *fuck* did you just say to my wife?"

He holds up his hands in surrender, shock on his face. "Whoa, man. I thought you said it was cool."

"She said no," I snap.

"Okay, okay," he stutters.

"Killian, stop it." Sylvia tugs on my arm. "We were just talking."

"You were not just talking, Sylvie. He was trying to fuck you."

"I can handle myself!" she snaps.

"Go upstairs," I growl in her direction.

She looks offended for a moment. "You can't tell me what to do."

With my teeth clenched, I drop Liam's collar and turn my attention toward Sylvie. I'm too filled with anger to think clearly. My hand encircles her arm, and I drag her back into the house and all the way down the long hall. She's digging in her heels the entire way, slapping my arm and screaming.

"Let go of me, you fucking brute!" she shrieks.

But I don't stop. All I can see is her letting Liam put his hands on her. Letting him take what should be mine. Making a fool of me.

When we reach the bedroom, I toss her inside and slam the door behind me, locking us both in.

She swings her arm back and lets her hand come flying across my face. I don't even feel it.

"What is wrong with you?" she screams. "Everyone was having a good time, and *you* had to ruin it! You're so fucked up, Killian!"

"You were about to let another man fuck you in *my home*," I argue, my voice so loud it's practically shaking the walls.

"Everyone is down there fucking, Killian! You think I can't tell what kind of party this is? You think I couldn't see the way you were pushing me toward him? I know what you told him, Killian! That we have an open marriage. I know deep down you were *hoping* I would fuck him because you think that would be your free ride to fuck whoever you want!"

"You're delusional!" I shout in return, meeting her level of anger.

"I'm *delusional?*" she retorts. Her eyes are wild with rage, and I don't want it to end. I love the fire in her expression when we fight. "You are so manipulative and ignorant! God, I fucking *hate* you!" Her voice is a screaming pitch now, and there's no way our guests can't hear us.

I'm still drunk, but something about her fired-up state has me wanting to touch her. Not in a sexual way, but in a desperate way. Reaching toward her, I grab her arm again and haul her toward me. She immediately puts up a fight.

"Get your hands off me!" she shrieks, trying to tear her arm from my grip.

I tighten it and lean in, sneering in her face. "You are my wife, and I will put my hands on you as much as I want." I say it only to fuel her rage. It's too easy to do.

Her nostrils flare, and her molars grind as she glares into my eyes. Deep down, she's silently wondering how much I'm truly capable of. "Touch me, and I swear you'll die in your sleep," she mutters with vitriol.

"Being dead would be preferable to being married to an ugly, selfish cow like you," I say. It's like a game. One insult is traded for another until we're both satisfied. "You mean *nothing* to me."

"Good!" she snaps. "Then I'll just go back down to Liam."

She tries to move away, but I yank her back toward me. When I do, I spot a hint of moisture in her eyes. Something I said hit a nerve.

"Over my dead body," I bellow. She swings an arm out toward me. I snatch it at the wrist before it can make contact with my face.

"That's what you want, isn't it?" she shrieks. "You want me to fuck your friend so you can be free of me. Just keep living the way you always have, Killian. So nothing has to change."

The more she screams, the more we struggle. Until the only way I can calm her is to force her to the bed, draping my body over hers. Taking her wrists in my hands, I pin them to the bed over her head.

Suddenly, with our faces only inches apart, she stops yelling, and we are caught in silence. The way her body feels under mine is visceral. I feel so large in comparison to her, but I know I'm not crushing her. She can handle my size and anything else I give to her.

Again, I notice the moisture in her eyes. When she blinks, a tear rolls down the side of her face, disappearing into her hair. What could I have possibly said that would truly hurt her feelings?

"Why do you care so much about what I do?" she asks, her tone dripping with hatred.

"I don't," I reply.

Her vibrant eyes hold mine for a moment. We're staring at each other as our breathing returns to normal. Finally, she mumbles, "Get off me, Killian."

Carefully, I release her hands and roll away from her body.

Without another word, she stomps toward the bathroom, slamming the door behind her.

I struggle to keep from passing out as I wait for her to come out. When she does, she's wearing the same pajamas as last night. Giving me the silent treatment, she marches to her side of the bed and climbs in. With her back to me, she huffs as she punches her pillow again.

I stagger as I tear off my clothes down to my underwear. After switching off the light, I climb into bed next to my wife.

I know I should feel bad for how I handled this tonight, but I don't. Honestly, I'm still a little confused. I don't understand if things went right or things went wrong. I just know that wherever this woman is concerned, I'm often more confused than not.

PART THREE

Sylvie

Chapter Sixteen

THE FAMILIAR CLICK OF HEELS ON THE HARDWOOD PULLS ME from my book. Lounging on the chaise in the library, I turn my focus back to my current read and wait for Anna to find me. The rain is really coming down outside, and it's been doing this all week, throwing me into the worst seasonal depression I've ever felt. I haven't seen the sun in days—or is it weeks now?

"There you are," she says in a forced chipper tone as she enters the library and hovers near the door as if she's waiting for me to greet her.

"Hey," I mumble, looking back at the page I was just on. "What's up?"

"Where's Killian?" she asks.

My head slants toward her. "How the hell should I know?"

I haven't seen him in days. I know he's here in the house. I feel and hear his movements around me every day. But we don't acknowledge each other or talk. We begrudgingly cohabitate.

In fact, I don't think I've even made eye contact with him since that night two months ago when he pinned me to the bed like a territorial ape. It was that night that I knew I *really* had to keep my distance from Killian. Not because he's dangerous or cruel but because we could easily teeter into treacherous territory.

When our arguments grow particularly intense, it's hard to tell what is hate and what is passion. This thing between us is like a spreading fire, and every time we light the match, I never know where it will end. The desire to punch him and the desire to kiss him feel the same.

"How is my brother?" Anna asks as she lowers herself into an armchair.

I drop my book on the table and sit up, staring at her impatiently. "You realize he's not really my husband, right? I have no clue how he is, Anna. We don't talk. We're not even friends."

She waves me off, and I get the feeling she's trying to ignore the truth sitting right in front of her. "I know that. I just mean… has he left the house at all?"

Letting out a frustrated sigh, I scowl at her. "No. And while we're on the subject…" My tone is exasperated as I clench my hands between my knees. "Why didn't you tell me about that? He hasn't left the house in *ten years*?"

Anna puts her face in her hands. "I wasn't sure. None of us were. We had our suspicions, but how could we know?"

"What the hell happened? How could you *not* know?"

She bursts out of her seat, pacing the room. "Our parents were killed in a car accident when Killian was just eighteen. The rest of us went to live with our aunt and uncle, but Killian stayed here. He became a different person after they died. He used to be so…happy and ambitious. Then, it was like…he fell apart. He went to uni and partied all the time. Drank too much and stopped coming around."

Leaning forward, I hang on to every word, trying to ignore the gnawing feeling of regret in my stomach as I think about Killian in such pain. Alone.

"So why are you doing this now? Why are you trying to take his house away?" I ask.

Her eyes squeeze shut, and I see the pain etched in her features. "It's my aunt who really wants him out."

Anna sits down again, and I can see the discomfort in her eyes. "Two years ago, my brother Declan discovered just how out of hand Killian's parties had become. I won't go into detail, but he turned our family's house into…" Her voice trails as her cheeks begin to blush.

"Into what?" I press.

"It doesn't matter," she responds, waving the answer away. "The point is that my aunt doesn't want to see our family home treated like some sort of…sex club."

I press my lips together. I swear, every time this woman opens her mouth, I get more and more irate with what she says. What kind of family treats each other this way? How can they claim to love him so much but want to hurt him at the same time?

"It's *his* house," I argue, a touch too loudly. I slam my hand against the arm of the sofa. "Legally, it's his, right? So he can do whatever he wants with it. It's *just* a house. And so what if he doesn't leave it? It might be the only thing in his life that brings him comfort, but here you are, the people who are supposed to love him, and you're trying to take that way. Killian might actually be hurting, and you only want to hurt him more! What is wrong with you people?"

"What's going on in here?" a deep voice bellows from the doorway. Sylvie and I spin around to find Killian standing there, watching us with an expression of anger.

"Killian," she says softly as she stands up.

He ignores her and turns his eyes toward me. "Why are you yelling at my sister?"

"I—" The words get stuck on my tongue. Why *was* I just yelling at her?

"It's okay, Killian. She was just sticking up for you."

"I was not," I argue.

He snickers as he crosses his arms over his chest. My blood is still hot with anger that I don't understand.

"The holidays are coming up," Anna declares. "Auntie Lorna would really like to see you both at the Hogmanay party."

"No," Killian replies before she's even done speaking.

"What is that?" I ask.

"New Year's Eve," he replies in a disgruntled tone.

"Will you just think about it, please?" Anna implores.

His eyes find mine, and I see the warring thoughts written all over his face. This is part of the deal. It's not about just staying married for a year. It's about proving to his family that he's settled down. That he has every right to keep the house.

Of course...to *him*, that's the plan.

To everyone else, it doesn't really matter if he's settled down or doing better. It's about getting the rights out of his hands and into theirs.

"Fine," he mutters. "I'll think about it."

"Thank you," Anna replies, looking relieved.

Before Killian leaves the room, he lets his gaze rest on my face for a moment. I nearly forgot how intense his eyes could be.

"Now, stop talking about me," he says before disappearing out the door.

The room is bathed in silence as I sit on the chaise lounge with my book still on my lap. There's a lingering anger deep in my bones from my conversation with Anna.

We wait until we both hear the front door close, letting us know Killian has left the house before either one of us speaks.

"Don't you feel bad?" I whisper. "For what you're doing to him? Tricking him out of his own home with this fake marriage?"

"You wouldn't understand," she replies.

And I know that's probably a jab at my family and how little they care about me, but I'll never understand how lying to Killian about why we're doing this is their way of showing they care.

"Please, Sylvie," she mumbles softly. "Will you just try to help him? Talk him into going to that party, and I'll sweeten the deal."

My head perks up. "How much?"

"Ten thousand," she replies plainly.

"He's not going to listen to me," I argue. "He hates me."

When her eyes lift to my face, I'm surprised to find a hint of humor in her face.

"He doesn't hate you," she says. "At least not as much as you think he does."

I scoff out a laugh. "What makes you think that?"

"I see the way he looks at you. You two are more alike than you think. If he didn't like you, he wouldn't bother arguing with you. He's not afraid to hurt your feelings because he knows you can take it. He sees your strength, Sylvie. And I truly believe he will miss you when you're gone."

She picks up her purse from the table and walks toward the door. "If anyone can talk him into it, it's you," she says. And with that, she leaves.

Her words hang in the air after she's gone. I'm lost in contemplation, running through everything over and over and over as if I'm trying to pinpoint something on a map. How do I feel about this? This house. This marriage. Him.

My feelings are scattered and confusing. I've been in this house too long. I've been so deep in this for so long that I can't seem to find my way out anymore. The reward at the end doesn't glisten as brightly as it did three months ago.

———

Boredom settles in my bones like a sickness. Not for the first time in the past month, I consider picking a fight with Killian because at least it's something to do. But again, fighting with him has gotten dangerously heated. And that's a line I don't need to cross.

Fucking my husband would be a terrible idea.

I've tried working on my novel. But opening my laptop usually leads to opening a browser which leads to watching the lives of people I once knew and used to like flash by me like I'm stuck in some time travel simulation.

They're at Burning Man or at a resort in Bali. I'm wasting away in a nineteenth-century Scottish manor like I've been dropped in the middle of a Charlotte Brontë novel.

Nine months to go. I can do this.

I'm lying on the couch in the library, the fire crackling as I stare mindlessly at the hundreds of titles on the shelves around me. The words all fade together like meaningless stars in the sky.

The book I was reading grew too boring and political for me. It was supposed to be about a torrid love affair, and I wanted something salacious and dirty, but the author chose to delve into the inner workings of the Russian political climate after the war, and I gave up.

Nothing interests me now.

That is, until my eyes catch on a title that doesn't seem to fit with the others.

The Act of Submission.

I sit up and squint my eyes at the book title again. The spine is deep red, and the text is eloquent and flowery. It's between a book about beekeeping and a classic novel. Climbing from the couch, I cross the room and pull the book from the shelf. The image on the front is a pair of wrists bound together with a strip of red satin.

My eyebrows shoot upward. Quickly I check my surroundings to be sure he hasn't snuck into the room. Then I open the book.

Inside are illustrations and mostly text. The illustrations are sexual in nature without being explicit.

A man kneeling with his head bowed.

A woman staring up at another woman.

A naked woman hogtied and suspended in the air.

Does this book belong to Killian? Is he really into this? I mean, I found that leather strap on the bed frame, but that could have been anything. It could have belonged to someone else. Maybe Anna has a secret kinky side.

Suddenly my mind conjures images of Killian forcing me into

submission, and everything inside me bristles. Are these the kinds of women he likes? Was Claire like this?

This is why we would never work. I could never let him have that kind of control over me. I don't want to let him think he's won something.

Then I remember his weight on me that night. My adrenaline kicking up. My heart pounding. Arousal blossoming low in my belly.

Movement out of the corner of my eye draws my attention to the window. The first thing I notice is that the rain has stopped. A glint of light cascades across the panes, and something in me delights at the prospect of sunshine.

Walking to the window, I stare out at the wet trees of the fields behind the house. Then I spot Killian walking through the grass toward the house.

His hair is down, drenched from the rain and slicked back. His white shirt is tight against his body, wet and transparent. As he marches back toward the house, I find myself watching him with curiosity.

I've never met anyone like Killian in my life. He is tasteless and stubborn and so bold it's exasperating. But he knows exactly what he wants, and he takes it without apology. He truly cares about himself and no one else.

And if I didn't hate him so much, I might actually like him.

Chapter Seventeen

I SNATCH MY SCARF FROM MY CLOSET AND THROW IT AROUND MY neck. As I emerge from my room, I hear another door closing down the hall and look up to find Killian standing just two doors down.

We both pause and stare at each other for a moment. It's rare that we end up at the same place at the same time anymore, but when we do, it's always a little unsettling. His wild green eyes bore into mine for a moment.

"Where are you going?" he asks after his eyes rake down my body, noticing my winter boots.

"Into town to do some shopping," I reply.

He doesn't respond, only stares at me. So I casually add, "Wanna come?"

There's a flinch in his expression. Then he shakes his head. "Fuck no."

"What's wrong?" I ask, taking a step toward him. "Afraid of a little shopping?"

He tilts his head and gives me an unamused expression. His hair is pulled half into a bun at the back of his head, and I notice the rest falls past his shoulders. For some reason, I find myself reaching out to brush it with my fingers.

"You need a haircut," I say.

His eyes follow my fingers and then settle on my face, probably as confused as I am as to why I would *touch* it.

Naturally, he reaches out and tugs on one of my unruly curls. "So do you."

"Want to give each other haircuts?" I ask with a playful tone. *What is happening right now?*

He gives an uneasy chuckle. Even he's confused. We're standing here teasing each other in a casual conversation without slinging insults. I think finding that book yesterday has somehow morphed my perception of Killian. I'm not exactly sure how. It's almost like curiosity has overpowered the hatred.

"Okay, well…if you're sure you don't want to come…" I awkwardly head toward the stairs, and I swear I spot a hint of hesitation on his face.

For the first time in three months, I almost feel bad for leaving him here alone.

"Have fun," he mutters, leaving his back to me as I walk down the stairs toward the front door, where Peter, the driver, is waiting for me.

I carry that feeling of guilt with me during the entire drive into the city. And even as I shop, it's there. Nothing interests me. There's a street full of stores and restaurants, and along the center of the pedestrian road are stalls selling holiday things like baked goods and ornaments.

I was never much for Christmas back home. New York City makes it hard not to feel the spirit though. But this is different. There's no Rockefeller Center Christmas tree, but there is something more quaint and comforting.

After coming out of a clothing store, I stop at one of the stalls. It's handcrafted leather goods, purses, belts, and other things. My eyes catch on a very large pair of brown leather gloves. The leather is soft, and I pick them up, letting my fingers graze the surface.

I think about Killian's hands. I remember the weight of them as they rested in mine on our wedding day. And then again that night, bandaging the open gash across his palm.

Then I feel them around my arm—and around my waist.

It's a memory, but it's burnt into my mind like an iron brand. I can still remember how they felt as they pinned my hands to the bed. So much larger than mine. Capable of so much, but never used harshly against me. Even when he held me back, there was care in his strength.

"Would you like to buy those, dear?" the woman behind the booth asks.

I press my open hand to the gloves, noticing the size difference. The long fingers dwarf my tiny thin ones.

"Yes, please," I murmur as I look at her with a smile. Reaching into my purse, I pull out my wallet and hand her two bills to cover it. "Keep the change."

"Thank you," she replies sweetly. Then she offers me a bag for the gloves. "Happy Christmas, dear."

"Happy Christmas," I mutter in response.

The gloves don't replace the guilt still souring my insides. What the hell has gotten into me? Why would I feel bad for coming into town? It's not like he really wanted to come. If he wanted to, he could have said so. I literally asked.

Besides, he wouldn't want to come with *me*. I'm sure someday Killian will be able to get over his fear of leaving the house, and it will probably be to attend a rugby match with his uni friends. It certainly wouldn't be for shopping with an American girl he can't stand.

"Sylvie?" I glance up from the cobblestone ground to see a familiar woman standing near a storefront.

"Claire," I reply with hesitation.

As she smiles at me and crosses the passing crowd to hug me, I quickly try to decipher how I'm *supposed* to feel about this woman. Because my natural reaction is that I think she's a lying, cheating home-wrecker who tried to fuck my husband. But Killian is not really my husband, and that's not really my home.

Still, I hate her.

When she pulls away from our quick hug, she holds my shoulders and gives me a cheesy grin. "How are you?"

"I'm good," I reply, unable to meet her level of forced enthusiasm.

"How's Killian?" she asks, and my smile fades.

"He's fine," I mutter without emotion.

"Good." She draws out the response, clearly gauging my reaction to her speaking his name.

She has to know I don't like her. Why play these fake games? I caught her in the hallway with him. I heard the way she pulled him into the closet that night. I also know she didn't have him in there long enough for them to do anything—which means he turned her down—because of the contract, of course.

She doesn't know that though. In her mind, she must think that he loves me more, and that gives me a sense of smug pride.

"He's not with you today?" she asks, her eyes grazing the crowd.

My molars grind. "No. He stayed home." I emphasize the word *home*. Our home.

"Are you busy?" she asks. "We should grab a drink."

I don't want to grab a drink with this woman, but I do want to hear what she has to say to me. My curiosity always gets the better of me.

"That sounds great," I lie with a fake smile.

She leads the way as we walk down to a nearby pub. Once we enter, we hang our coats and scarves on the hook next to the door. Then we find an empty table and sit across from each other. The bartender brings us each a beer, and I keep Killian's gloves at my side.

We make small talk for a while. Claire tells me about her job in restaurant management. I tell her a little about my life in New York and how I'm working on a novel—that I haven't touched in over a year.

When there's a lull in our conversation, I feel her ready to pounce on a more scandalous topic.

"So…" Claire says after taking a drink. "I heard a dirty little rumor about you and Killian."

I take a long sip of my beer, waiting for her to elaborate.

"That you two like to…share. Is that true?"

I set down my beer and press my lips together. I know exactly why she's asking me this. She's testing me to see how much power she can use against me. It takes everything in me not to explode on this woman and call her out for being the meddling bitch that she is. Instead, I reply softly.

"You know…you can't trust rumors."

She laughs. "Surely, there's some truth to that one though."

"There's not." My answer is clipped. I meet her gaze, and while her expression is playful and happy, mine is cold and ruthless.

"Okay," she says with a laugh. "I was just asking."

"I'm sure you were," I reply. "Just curious, right?"

Her brows lift and her smile fades. "Did I do something wrong?"

I take another sip, letting her sit with that question for a moment, hoping it tortures her, waiting for the answer.

Deep down, I know I shouldn't care if she did try to sleep with Killian. It's none of my business…

Except it is. Because he is legally my husband, and if she did manage to fuck him that night, she could have cost me ten million dollars.

All of that aside…she tried to seduce *my* husband.

"You know, Claire…" I say, trying to keep my cool. "You may not be able to trust rumors, but you can trust your gut. And my gut is telling me that you tried to fuck my husband that weekend at my house."

"Sylvie—" she snaps, glancing around to see if anyone heard.

"My gut also tells me that you've fucked Killian in the past, probably when you were already married to Angus."

She leans forward, and I notice the tremble in her breath. "Stop it."

But I don't. The more I think about it, the more I'm starting to realize something. "Let me guess," I say with a tilt of my head. "Your little affair wasn't part of that kinky swinger shit you guys do at the parties?"

Her eyes half shut, which tells me I must be right.

"He told you about that?" she whispers.

"Killian is dealing with his own shit," I snap. "He doesn't need you fucking with his head even more."

Killian doesn't seem like the kind of guy who would screw his friend's wife. At least not without feeling like shit about it. Is that the prison he's locked himself in? One made of remorse and regret?

"It wasn't just my fault, you know?" she replies. "He's just as responsible as I am. I feel terrible for what I've done, and I'm paying for it with my own guilt."

That part pulls me out of my thought process. "Oh yes, so much guilt that you tried to screw him again?"

"Will you please keep your voice down?" she whispers angrily.

When I feel the curious stares from around the pub, I shrink down and keep quiet. Normally, I wouldn't care about attracting attention, but this isn't about me. This is his business, and the more people seem to meddle in it, the more fired up I seem to get.

I take another drink of my beer, desperate to calm my nerves.

"You know..." she says, scratching the back of her neck. "You're not at all what I expected for Killian. You two are so alike; I can't imagine how you're compatible."

"We're not that alike," I argue. That comment caught me off guard. I'm nothing like Killian. He's brash, rude, and inconsiderate.

When Claire doesn't respond, I swallow and look away.

"What? You think you're so much better for him?" I ask.

"I know what he needs," she replies smugly, and my blood starts to boil again.

"Oh yeah? And what is it he needs?" I'm asking to be defiant, but I'm also a little curious.

She rests her arms on the table and leans forward. "Killian doesn't need some headstrong brat who is going to make everything difficult for him. He needs someone who puts their trust in him. Someone who will let him have control and be the dominant man he is."

My face contorts into a sneer. I would never force myself to be something I'm not just because it's what he *needs*. But the more I let her opinion settle in my mind, the more *wrong* it feels.

"You don't know him at all," I reply.

She scoffs. "And you do? You've known him for what? Three months? If you think kinky swinger parties were the extent of it, then you don't know a damn thing."

Suddenly, I feel very confident that I know Killian far better than she does, even if she has known him for ten years. Hell, at this point, I feel like I might know him better than his own family. Maybe because he isn't afraid to be himself around me. He shows me the ugly parts—the parts he won't let anyone else see. I see when he's scared and frustrated and lonely and angry. All they see are fake smiles and rehearsed fronts.

I grab the bag, holding the leather gloves off the seat. The sudden desperation to be out of this pub and out of this city is overpowering. I just want to go home.

Standing up in a huff, I lean down toward Claire and force out everything on my mind, no matter how irrational it is.

"You don't know him, because if you did, you would know that's not what he needs at all. Killian doesn't need more control. He blames himself too much for that. What he needs is someone he can *trust*. Someone who will take away the decisions and the burden of having to make them. Someone he can truly let go with."

She lets out a sarcastic chuckle. "And you think that's you?"

I inch closer. "I know it is."

When her face flattens in anger, I resist the urge to throw the rest of her beer in her face or punch her in the nose. The old Sylvie might have done that, but I refrain. As much as I'd love to lash out at this cheater the same way I lashed out at Aaron, I don't.

Instead, I stand up tall and stare down at her.

"If you touch my husband again, I'll kill you."

Her eyes widen in surprise. And with that, I storm out of the pub, grabbing my coat and scarf on the way.

I realize as I march angrily into the now-dark city streets that threatening murder might not be a huge improvement in maturity from throwing drinks at her like a child, but it is an improvement nonetheless. And for that, I'm sort of proud.

Chapter Eighteen

MY MIND IS STILL REELING FROM THAT CONVERSATION WITH Claire as I storm down the cobblestone street toward where Peter dropped me off. I told him to pick up me around seven, but I realize as I glance down at my watch that it's well past eight thirty now.

Stopping in front of a closed store, I pull out my phone from my purse. I quickly find Peter's contact and notice the battery is down to one tiny sliver.

Shit.

Quickly, I punch out a message to him.

I need a ride—

The screen goes black.

"Fuck!" I bark as I squeeze the buttons again, hoping it will magically come back to life. Holding my useless phone in my hands, I glance up to check my surroundings. Surely there has to be a store around here that sells chargers.

But nearly every storefront displays dark spaces and locks on the doors. I forgot nearly everything in this town closes early.

Okay, okay. I'll just walk back to where Peter dropped me off. I'm sure that's where he's waiting. So I continue down the street toward where I think I'm supposed to turn. But when I reach that street, it's definitely not like I remember. Which means I must have made a wrong turn somewhere.

Panic starts to build inside me. I'm out of cash to call a cab, not that there are any on the streets for me to hail like I did in New York City.

I'm screwed.

Stop panicking, Sylvie. You've been in worse situations.

Shoving my phone back in my pocket, I continue my walk, waiting for any of these street names to appear familiar. But the night is so dark, and nothing looks like it did five hours ago. I never should have let Claire lead me away from the area I knew. I never should have walked off with her at all.

That conversation only frustrated and confused me more than I already am. I may not like Killian like she thinks I do, but I do sympathize with him. Everyone in his life seems to know what's best for him. No wonder he's locked himself away. Not a single person in his circle has actually offered to help him. They just want to control him.

And not in the way he needs.

I know that feeling. My parents want me to be someone else entirely. Everything I do and say disappoints them. To the point where I have alienated myself from everyone because it's easier to be alone than to be less than what someone expects.

But even that gets lonely.

So lonely.

I can only imagine what that's like for him. I meant every word I said to Claire. Killian just needs a soft place to land. A person who supports him for him. All the bad parts with the good. Someone who gives him room to be himself.

Hell, maybe that's just what I need.

Because now that I think about it, I never felt that with Aaron.

He never supported me without his own judgment. He was just as bad as Anna and Claire, claiming they can fix Killian.

Before I know it, I feel the moisture of tears pooling in my eyes. It must be from the panic of being lost in the city. Or the frenetic energy of that fight with Claire. But once I start crying, I can't stop. I'm wiping tear after tear from my eyes as I walk angrily through the dark city streets.

The only things that are open are bustling pubs and seedy tobacco stores. I could go in. I'd likely find someone or something to help. But I don't.

What is going back to the house going to help? I'd still be lost.

The screech of tires jerks me from my thoughts, and I let out a scream. Turning to stare into the bright lights, I back away from the black car, waiting for someone to emerge—praying it's my driver, Peter.

The door flies open, and I let out a gasp.

Killian's panicked expression has my skin tingling with goose bumps. "Where the fuck have you been?" he bellows. I've never heard him sound so angry. I take a step farther away.

"Killian?" My mind can't seem to catch up and process what I'm seeing.

"Get in the fucking car, Sylvie," he shouts in a growly command.

My expression twists in revulsion. "I'm not getting in there with you if you're going to yell at me like that."

As he slams the door and marches toward me, my eyes widen even more. "I told you to get in the fucking car, woman. You can either listen to me, or I'll toss you over my shoulder and put you in there myself." He crowds me against the building with an enraged snarl on his face. I can't help but notice the way his hands are shaking and his eyes are erratic.

"What is wrong with you?" I reply defiantly, but my tone doesn't carry the same livid heat it normally does. I'm too confused and shocked to be as angry as he is.

"For fuck's sake," he mutters as he reaches for me.

Before he can cause a scene and have the police take him to jail, I put up my hands in surrender. "Okay, okay!" I shriek. "I'll get in. Just…relax."

"Relax?" he howls at me. "You have had us worried sick. Peter came looking for you, but you didn't answer your phone, and he couldn't find you."

"I lost track of time. I'm sorry."

"Just get in the fucking car."

His chest is heaving in a panicked, shallow sort of way. I quickly move around him and rush to the passenger side, climbing in and forcing myself to relax. I didn't actually do anything wrong. I was just a little late. My phone died. It's not my fault for getting everyone worried.

As Killian climbs in next to me, I stare at him behind the wheel of the car. It's such an odd image for me. I've only ever seen him at the house. Something isn't right about him, but I can't put my finger on it.

"Are you okay?" I mumble delicately as he takes off down the cobblestone road.

His head snaps in my direction. "I'm fine," he grumbles.

He doesn't look fine.

But I don't push the subject. I still can't get over the fact that Killian is driving a car. He's not at the house. He…left.

"You're so…inconsiderate, Sylvie," he snaps.

I lift my head and give him a terse glare. "Inconsiderate? It was just an accident. I said I was sorry!"

"You had us worried sick." His hands squeeze around the steering wheel as my temper grows.

"Because I was a little late?"

"Because you don't think about anyone but yourself. Peter couldn't find you. And I don't like seeing my staff upset."

My gaze intensifies on him. None of this makes any sense.

We stay quiet for the rest of the drive. It feels as if there's a lump of something in my chest. Emotion I can't seem to swallow. Pain that won't go away. Guilt that rots inside me like a cancer.

He's angry at me because I worried him, and I can't make sense of it. I don't think I've ever felt someone's concern so intensely before. And I don't know if I like it.

When we reach the manor, I barrel out of the car, desperate to run from this feeling inside me.

He stomps after me, clearly not ready to let me go. I slam the door, but he quickly opens it and bounds inside before slamming it himself.

"Sylvie!" he roars after me. I'm halfway up the stairs when he practically chases me up them. There is a shake in my bones, and I don't know if it's adrenaline or fear or anticipation.

We are on the precipice of something big. I can feel it, and it terrifies me. Because it means I have to come out of the quiet, safe little bubble I've been living in.

I turn on my heel and shout back at him. "What do you want?"

"I want you to stop being an insolent brat!"

Stepping up another few stairs, he stops two away from me. I'm just barely as tall as him at this level.

"Why am I such a brat? Because I made you worry? That's not my fault, Killian! It's yours. I never told you to care about me."

I spin around, knowing full well what he'll do next. That familiar large hand wraps around my arm, hauling me back toward him. My hands go to his chest, but instead of pushing him away, I tighten my fists in his shirt.

We are chest to chest. I'm staring into his eyes blazing with fury as one of his hands grabs the back of my neck and brings my face close enough to brush our lips together.

"You make me so angry," he mutters.

I manage one desperate gasp before his mouth crashes against mine. The kiss isn't anything like our last two kisses. Those were performances. This is real.

Our tongues collide in a needy tangle of desire. He bites on my bottom lip, and I scratch his arm through the flannel of his shirt. The grip on the back of my neck tightens as he pulls me even closer, devouring my mouth and making me forget why I shouldn't be doing this.

I try to tell myself I don't like Killian. I *hate* him. But the argument is so weak. It fades away on a breeze in my mind while my body seems to be caught in a storm of passion.

Without breaking the kiss, he lays me on the steps and moves his mouth from my lips down to my jaw. I let out another gasp as the rough texture of his beard scratches my neck. His kisses are brutal, much like his attitude toward me.

He's not afraid of breaking me. He knows I can take it.

In a frenzy, he works off my coat and scarf. My fingers dig into his hair, dragging him closer as my legs part, allowing him space to settle between them.

The size difference between us is even more alarming in this position. My thighs are pressed as wide as they go while he grinds himself against me, and I let out a needy yelp.

I drag his mouth back up to mine and kiss him even harder. I don't want to think about anything. I just want to feel. I want to douse this fire that's been burning for so long.

He lifts himself from my body and moves his hands to the button of my jeans. Those large fingers work the zipper down, and I lift my hips, eager to shed my clothes. As soon as I feel the cool wood of the stairs on my ass, I shiver in anticipation. This is all moving way too fast. But I don't want to stop it.

My pants don't go far. They barely reach my knees before Killian moves downward and latches his mouth around my sex. I grab his hair again and let out a squeal of surprise. My arousal intensifies, exploding inside me as soon as I feel his warm mouth on my clit.

But this angle is too difficult, and I can't spread my legs for him, so he sits back up and starts tearing at my boots as if he's overcome with the need to get between my legs.

I pull at his shirt, and he takes a break from untying my laces to tear the long-sleeved flannel off. Touching his bare chest and shoulders with my hands is intoxicating. With every graze of his skin, I need more.

He finally works my boots off. Then he strips my pants off in one violent motion.

And then that's it. Just like that, I'm lying naked from the waist down on the stairs, spread bare for him like a meal on the table. It's unnerving and a little scary.

But my body is drunk on lust, so I reach for him. Without a second of hesitation, he drops to his knees a few steps below me and buries his face between my legs. Wrapping one arm around my thigh, he loudly devours me, sucking and licking every sensitive inch.

The other arm reaches up to my breast, tugging my shirt open enough to pinch the tight bud of my nipple. I suck in through my teeth, thrown off by the sensation.

My spine arches, and my lungs desperately try to suck in air, but it's useless. I'm helpless against him. I clench my fingers around the steps, and I close my eyes as I let him take my body.

I want to scream his name. I want to beg him not to stop. I want to look into his eyes as he pushes his tongue inside me, but I don't do any of it. Killian has his mouth in the most private, intimate part of me, and I'm not ready to face what this means.

I just want to come. I want to take the orgasm he gives me. And I want him to feel how much I love it.

Before I fly over the edge of pleasure, I grab the hand that's cupped around my breast, and I pull it to my mouth. I'm so caught up in the passion that I don't even know what I'm doing or why I'm doing it. I love the way his fingers feel in mine as I wrap my lips around the middle digit. Softly I suck and lick, mirroring his actions between my legs.

My climax builds so quickly that I barely have a chance to prepare myself. On a quick inhale, my body explodes in pleasure, and I bite down on his finger, hearing him howl against my sex. I only have enough air left in my lungs to groan out a feral sound of pleasure.

He tears his hand from my mouth, moving it to my throat and holding me there as I'm assaulted by wave after wave of sensation. I see stars as my body is rolled through the climax. Over and over and over again. It pulses through me for an impossibly long time until it feels like I can't take it anymore.

I collapse on the stairs when it finally ceases. He pulls his mouth away, and I can hear him gasping.

We both seem to surrender to the moment together. Neither of us speaks. Neither of us moves.

After a while, I slowly sit up. He's facing away from me, his elbows resting on his knees and his head hanging forward. My clothes are strewn over the stairs in a mess.

Part of me wants to reach for him, but that fear of facing the truth resurfaces, and I hold myself back. Instead, I quickly gather my things and quietly, without a word, tiptoe up to my room and shut the door.

Chapter Nineteen

I TOSS AND TURN ALL NIGHT. EVEN THOUGH I HAD MY RELEASE, I still feel strung tight. Everything between my legs is red and sore from the scratch of his beard. All night, I find myself touching it, exploring the sensitivity, and remembering what it felt like to have him down there.

The warmth of his mouth. The friction of his tongue.

It's all too much, like it's overloaded my system.

And one thing that keeps barraging my mind like a storm is the question of why. Why would he kiss me? Why would he touch me? Why on earth did he make me see stars on that staircase without wanting a single thing in return?

He had me feeling so guilty in the car for making him worry. And at the time I was feeling heated and defensive. Now, I'm seeing it clearer. Killian worried because he cared, and I have literally never felt such concern in my entire life.

Have his feelings for me changed?

Have mine?

Getting tangled up in our emotions is a bad idea. Killian still has no idea that being married to me will result in him losing his house. If I start feeling things for him, then I'll have to start dealing with things like guilt and responsibility. And I'd like to avoid those.

The space between us now feels so potent. Every single inch from my bed to his down the hall might as well be nothing at all. It's like I can just reach out and touch him, but I don't. The thought of tiptoeing into his room crosses my mind all night.

What would I even do? Crawl into his bed uninvited? Just climb on his dick like a cat in heat?

What we did today feels like peeking over a wall before quickly returning to our opposite sides. And I'm not going to lie. After today, I want to go back over that wall. I want more. Not just because the orgasm was great but because, for a moment, I didn't feel so alone.

But I won't. I can't. Getting physical is a bad idea if I want to keep my eyes on the prize. I need to get through this year and get my ten million so I can live the rest of my days in peace.

Don't do anything stupid, Sylvie.

It's sometime after three in the morning that I finally jump out of my bed, unable to take it anymore. I march angrily down the hall and burst into his room without a single idea of what I'm doing.

He's sleeping peacefully in his bed, lying motionless on his back. He doesn't even stir when I slam the door behind me.

I walk right up to his bed and poke him in the chest. "Hey!" I bellow.

He wakes with a start. When his eyes focus on my form standing near his bed, he lets his eyebrows fold inward with a scowl. Then he turns away from me and closes his eyes like he's going back to sleep.

"Killian!" I shriek as I shove him again.

"What do you want, wife?" he shouts.

I'm hot with anger, and I let it come flying out of my mouth. "Why did you do that?"

Turning back toward me, he holds his hands up. "Do what?"

"On the stairs," I reply, exasperated.

"What the fuck are you talking about?" he says as he sits up and rubs his eyes.

"We're not doing that, you know? We're not a real couple."

I hear myself. I sound flustered, but right now, I *feel* flustered. One moment Killian said I meant nothing to him, then he was yelling at me, and then suddenly, he was tongue fucking me. I don't know if this is what gaslighting is, but I certainly feel like I don't know my own mind anymore. He's infiltrated it with desire and passion, so I don't know where the hatred ends and lust begins.

He scrubs a hand over his face as he lets out a groan. "What on earth are you going on about? We're not doing what? It was just sex, Sylvie. Would you relax?"

"No," I snap. "Because I didn't know you and I were...doing that, and it took me by surprise, and I just want to know why. Why did you do that?"

"Why did I go down on you?" he asks, and my cheeks heat with embarrassment.

"Yes."

His expression is guarded as he stares at me through the moonlight. "Because I wanted to."

I feel unsatisfied with that answer, and I don't understand why. "Well, we're not doing this. Like I said, we're not really married."

"Yes, we are," he replies before folding his arms.

I let out a sigh of frustration. "I mean...we're not really a couple. So we're not doing the *just-sex* thing."

He scratches his beard for a moment, and I find myself zeroing in on his fingers, remembering the way they felt in my mouth. I wonder if I left a mark from where I bit him.

"Why not?" he asks.

"What do you mean, why not?"

He shrugs. "Why can't we have a physical relationship? We are married. We have a long cold winter ahead of us with nothing better to do."

Suddenly I imagine just how fun this house *could* be if I weren't constantly secluded in the library and living room.

But no. I just went over this in my head. If I get physical with Killian, feelings will surely get muddled, and that's a bad idea.

I quickly shake the thought away. "No."

"Is that really why you came in here and woke me up? To tell me we wouldn't be doing that again?" he asks, and I hear the skepticism in his voice.

"Yes," I reply, standing my ground.

To my surprise, he responds with a low, grumbly, "Come here."

My heart rate picks up. By the time I answer him, it's too late. "No," I murmur half-heartedly.

He lets out a growl. "Come here *now*."

My brow furrows, and I take an angry step toward him. "You can't talk to me like that! I don't have to listen to you."

In a flash of movement, he reaches out and grabs my hand, hauling me to the bed and flipping me over his body so I'm lying next to him. Then he rolls his large body on top of me.

"Killian!" I shout.

"You're all bark and no bite, my wee wife."

"Oh, I'll bite," I reply with fuming anger.

He chuckles down at me as he holds up his right hand. "That's right. You do. How could I forget?" As he shows me the red line across his middle finger, he uses it as an opportunity to flip me off at the same time.

Suddenly, I feel his heavy weight pressed between my legs. He's in nothing but a pair of tight boxer briefs, and I'm in a simple long T-shirt and a pair of panties. Which I'm realizing now was not wise to come to talk him in.

"You're telling me this wouldn't be nice?" he asks as he grinds his hips against my core.

By some miracle, I hold in the moan that wants to escape.

Because it does feel nice. It feels *very* fucking nice.

"No," I reply through clenched teeth.

"Don't lie, mo ghràidh."

"Don't call me that."

Ignoring my protest, he continues. "We could do this all winter. Fuck like animals all day long. With nothing better to do. You can still hate me. Call me a brute and an arsehole, and I'll call you a cow and selfish bitch. But with lots and lots of orgasms."

He grinds against me again, and I fail to hold in my reaction this time. A tiny whimper escapes, and I know I'm done for. Any argument is now weak and meaningless.

"I've been tested," he groans against my neck.

"So have I," I reply. "And I'm on the pill."

"See?" he murmurs. "There's nothing stopping us."

"I do hate you," I reply, my voice cracking on the high pitch.

The hard length of his cock slides against my clit, and I fight the urge to wrap my hand around his shaft just to feel the size of it. Based on what I sense now, it's impossibly large.

"I hate you too, darling," he replies, grinding again.

I whimper again.

Our eyes meet, and I stare into the green orbs, unable to deny that having messy casual sex with a handsome, rich Scottish giant isn't the worst thing to happen to me. I'd be a fool to turn him down.

He keeps up the grinding, and soon, I start to notice how heated and unhinged he's getting. His breathing is growing shallow, and his lips part with desire. The stiff cock in his boxer briefs is so hard it hurts as he rubs it eagerly against my clit. But it's a good pain. A needy, visceral pain that radiates through my entire body.

"I can still taste your cunt on my lips, Sylvie. I can't stop thinking about it."

His filthy words set me on fire. Any hope of turning back now is lost.

My back arches, and my head tilts backward. "Killian."

I moan his name like a plea.

"Tell me to stop," he mutters with his lips near my throat.

"Don't stop," I reply.

Reaching down, I rest my hand on the firm surface of his ass. It feels so weird touching him but also so good. How long have I wanted to press my palm to his backside? Squeeze it. Use it as leverage to pull him closer to me.

He grinds harder, and I start to wonder if he'll settle for this dry humping or if he'll take the opportunity to slip my panties aside and enter me. I don't know which one I want at this point.

I love this *almost-sex* feeling. Having him so close but still not quite where I want him.

My mind is already lost to the sensation. I'm supposed to be stopping this, but I can't remember why. I just want more.

So I wrap my legs around his hips and hold tight to his ass to grind him harder and harder and harder to a rhythm that makes my body tighten, and my blood flow hotter through my veins.

Angling my face toward him, he quickly latches his lips to mine.

I've already committed his kiss to memory. It's so different than the ones we have to fake. His real kisses are brutal and passionate, biting and nibbling and devouring.

"I'm gonna—"

The words fall off my lips as he kisses me again. When he pulls away, I see the look of ecstasy on his face—the near-climax expression.

"Let me see it again, darling. You come so pretty."

My hips are moving fast now, tilting and grinding, trying to keep up with the momentum of his hard cock. Two thin layers of cotton are all that separate us, and it feels like we're striking a fire with them.

I let out a high-pitched squeal when the pleasure seizes my body in an earthquake of sensation. My muscles clench tight around him, and I let myself drown in the feeling. It's not as potent as the one on the stairs, but chasing it is half the fun anyway.

His movements pick up speed until I look up to find him shuddering with a look of euphoria on his face. I feel the twitch of his cock against me as he comes, and I stare down between our bodies to watch the way it soaks the inside of his boxer briefs.

We freeze in our spots, him hovering over me. Lifting my fingers, I press them against the muscular planes of his chest. Softly, I touch the chest hair and wait for him to decide this is a terrible idea.

He doesn't.

He collapses next to me, staring at the ceiling as he catches his breath.

"See?" he mumbles in a quiet drawl. "This could be fun."

Fun. Fun until he finds out he's about to lose everything because of me.

"Sure," I reply softly.

He turns, jumping out of bed and going to the bathroom. I watch him through the darkness as he disappears inside.

"Don't move," he barks at me, and I roll my eyes at his order.

"When are you going to learn you can't just boss me around?" I reply.

He laughs to himself in the bathroom before coming out in a fresh pair of boxers and climbing into the bed next to me.

"You're still here, aren't you?"

I turn on my pillow to face him. "It's warmer in here with you," I say as an excuse for why I'm still in his bed.

"Sure it is," he replies sleepily. "Good night, darling."

"I'm not your darling," I reply.

"You still hate me, right?" he asks playfully.

"Yes," I lie. I *wish* I still hated him, but I have to be honest with myself now. I can't find a single reason to keep hating him.

"Okay, good," he says with a yawn. Before long, I hear his breathing change as he falls asleep with me in his arms.

I want nothing more than to sleep, but my mind is reeling. If we do go down this path, could we keep things strictly physical?

Sure, I may not hate Killian anymore, but I'm confident I could never come to love him. There are too many things about him I can't stand. He's controlling and ignorant, and most of all, I mean nothing to him. Nothing more than a warm body and a means to an end.

Yes, I believe we could keep things strictly physical.

Besides, I don't have any other choice. When Killian finds out that this marriage was just a scam to steal his house from him, then he'll *really* hate me.

As I lie here, I try to remind myself that I don't care what happens to him after this. We are not in a real relationship. In nine months, I will be gone from this place, and he will continue to mean nothing to me.

I'll be ten million dollars richer. I'll no longer be Mrs. Barclay. And everything will be as it should be.

Chapter Twenty

I FINALLY FALL ASLEEP, AND WHEN I DO, I SLEEP SO DEEPLY THAT I don't think I move all night. When I peel my eyes open, I'm almost surprised to see Killian's room. What a whirlwind the past twenty-four hours have been.

I turn slowly to face him and stare at his sleeping form across the giant bed. He's lying on his back, his dark-brown hair strewn across the pillow. His beard has grown longer and thicker since I first met him.

For a while, I just lie here and stare at every raw inch of his bare skin as if I'm not normally allowed to see him like this, so I have to sneak my peek when I can. Reaching out, I delicately run my fingers over the muscles of his shoulder and down his bicep.

What is he doing out there in those fields all day that helps him keep this physique? He has the body of a man who I assume frequents the gym, but as far as I know, there's not one in the house.

My gaze cascades down, over his pecs and abs until his body disappears under the dark green sheet covering his lower half. Last night I got a taste of what he's hiding in those boxers, and I can't help but be curious about it now.

Slowly, I lift the sheet and just take a quick peek underneath. All I can see at this angle are his dark boxer briefs and his thick, hair-covered thighs. Dropping the sheet, I find myself smirking.

Killian is really not my type—beefy, broody, and vulgar in every way. So why am I so attracted to him all of a sudden?

Maybe it's because I can finally enjoy a physical relationship without the worry of whether or not the other person likes me. I *know* Killian doesn't like me. It makes things easier. Less about emotions and more about sensations.

And even if feelings *were* involved—which they're not—how do I know what Anna and her brothers are planning isn't really for Killian's benefit? So what if they're meddling? They're trying to help him, which means I'm helping him too.

So, really, my conscience is clear.

As he stirs, I'm pulled from my thoughts and watch to see if he's about to wake to find me staring at him as he sleeps. When he doesn't open his eyes, I relax into the pillow.

Suddenly, I'm thinking about his sister and his aunt again. The Hogmanay party is next week. I never answered Anna back about Killian attending, so I assume she gave up on the idea. But I haven't.

She offered me ten thousand dollars to get him out of the house, and it really can't be that hard. Now that sex is on the line, I'm sure I can think of something to entice him to go to that party.

Trailing my fingers over his chest, I let them slide down his abs. Then I delicately run a soft line just above the waistband of his boxer briefs. He stirs again but doesn't wake. Very carefully, I climb over him, straddling his waist and settling my weight on his still-soft cock.

Seriously, what am I doing?

Twenty-four hours ago, I never would have entertained the idea of sleeping with Killian. Now I'm riding him like a horse while he's still asleep. I'm touching his body as if I have any right to.

He lets out a groan without opening his eyes. Sleepily, he

reaches down and grabs on to my leg, holding me in place as he grinds upward against me.

"Killian…" I whisper.

He's fighting it, keeping his eyes closed as I move slowly on top of him. I feel his cock hardening beneath me. With every passing second, I grow more and more desperate to touch it, feel it in my hand and about a dozen other places.

Being on top like this gives me a sense of power and control that I don't normally feel with him. He's so much bigger than me. But I know I could easily slip my hand into his boxer briefs right now and have him completely at my mercy.

That is until his eyes pop open, and he grabs me by the waist, flipping me until I'm on my back and he's between my legs again. I let out a scream as he does it, but the scream quickly dies as he buries his face in my neck and grinds his erection against me the same way he did last night.

I'm still sore from where his beard scratched my sensitive skin. I can feel it, but it's a delicious pain that only intensifies the pleasure.

"What a way to wake up," he groans into my neck.

His large rough hands caress my body, making my thoughts fuzzy. I was going to say something to him…wasn't I?

But then he lifts my T-shirt and kisses his way up my belly, latching his lips and teeth around the tight bud of my nipple. A breathless gasp escapes my lips as my eyes flutter closed.

What on earth was I going to say?

"Hog-a…something…party." The stuttered words slip through my lips like a plea.

Killian freezes before lifting up and staring at me in confusion. "What did you say?"

I have to recompose my thoughts. "The New Years party is next week…at your aunt's."

His expression turns to a scowl. "You're bringing that up *now*?"

"You're the one who threw me on the bed," I argue.

"Because you were riding my dick."

"Well, I think we should go," I say persistently. "To the party."

Scoffing, he climbs off of me and rolls onto his back. We lie there for a moment until he speaks again.

"Why do *you* care so much about whether I go to a stupid fucking party?" he asks, staring at the ceiling.

"Because your family seems to think you haven't left the manor in ten years." Slowly I turn my head toward him. "Is that true?" I ask softly.

"Of course not," he replies gruffly. I keep my eyes on him as he adds, "More like six."

I wince. *Six years.*

Turning on my side, I prop my head on my arm and stare at him. "Why?"

He mirrors my position and stares at me with a bemused scowl. "Why haven't I left? Because I don't want to. I don't like people. I like it *here*."

After a deep breath, I reply with a shrug. "Fair enough." I don't want to press Killian too much. That's what his sister does. That's what they all do. They push and prod and meddle and call it caring. But if he truly hasn't left the house in six years (before last night), then there must be a reason.

I genuinely wonder if any of them have thought to ask.

"So, let's prove them wrong and go to the party," I suggest.

"No."

I let out a scoff. "Come on."

When he doesn't bend, I reach out a hand and touch his chest, letting my finger drift around his pebbled nipple. "I'll sweeten the deal."

"Oh yeah? How will you do that?" he asks with a mischievous smirk.

"I'm sure you can figure it out," I reply, giving him a light shove.

He rolls onto his back. "Whatever you're thinking, you were probably going to do anyway."

As he folds his hands under his head, I let my jaw hang and shoot him an offended glare. "Don't be so cocky, brute. I never wanted you."

He smiles at me, the dimples on his cheeks barely noticeable through his beard, and I have to press my lips together to keep from smiling.

"Yeah, you did. Don't lie," he says with so much charm it makes me hate him more.

Pounding the pillow, I scurry off the bed with a huff. "Well, unless you agree to go to that party, *nothing* is happening."

"You vindictive bitch!" he calls after me, but I don't reply. I march down the hall to my room, still biting back my smile.

I'm still upstairs, getting dressed in my room, when I hear Killian's brothers and sister coming in. It's Christmas Day, which isn't normally something I celebrate much at home.

Aaron and I rarely exchanged gifts. In fact, I don't think I bought him anything for Christmas last year, but immediately my mind returns to the leather gloves sitting in my coat pocket downstairs.

I'm not an idiot. I see what's happening here.

It only took three months, but somehow, I stopped hating Killian and started feeling things that look like—

No. I won't say it. Not even to myself.

That is simply not an option. Killian and I have no future. Come September, this marriage is over. I'll have my ten million, and I will have to move on with my life.

That is the thought that has comforted me since I arrived here, but suddenly, it makes me sick to even think.

As I descend the stairs, laughter echoes from the parlor. I can clearly make out Anna's voice as well as Lachy's and Declan's.

Rounding the corner into the room, I smile at the sight of Killian and his siblings gathered on the sofas, smiling and opening presents.

When Anna sees me, her face lights up. "Happy Christmas, Sylvie!" she shouts, coming toward me with a cone-like hat and a popper.

I laugh as she places the hat on my head and pulls me in for a hug. "Merry Christmas," I reply softly.

There's a spot on the sofa next to Killian, and I take the seat, carefully glancing in his direction. His arm casually slinks around me, which only strikes me as odd after I remember that everyone in this room knows our marriage is fake. There is no reason to pretend.

"Here, Sylvie," Anna says as she drops a present in my lap.

"What is this?" I ask nervously.

"Open it," she replies.

"I…didn't realize we were exchanging gifts."

She waves me off. "Don't worry about that. Just open it."

As I peel off the paper, I feel sick with guilt. Under the wrapper is a cardboard box, and I lift the lid to find a soft cashmere scarf folded up inside.

"This is beautiful," I say, pulling it out and letting my fingers slide over the silky weave. "Thank you so much."

When my eyes meet hers, she sends me a smile. "You're welcome."

"I didn't get anyone anything."

Killian squeezes my shoulder. "It's okay. Really."

It doesn't feel okay. I feel like an ass. How was I supposed to know that this was going to be a family occasion? I don't belong here. I feel like an imposter in someone else's home. It's just that my parents never did a conventional Christmas. We did events and parties, and our gift exchanges often took place in the early hours and for never more than fifteen minutes.

"I got you something, too, but you don't need to feel bad." Killian stands from the couch and crosses the room to the tree. He takes a small box out and brings it over. My skin grows hot with anxiety as he sets it in my lap.

When I gaze up at him, our eyes meet, and I feel that same pull I felt last night.

I quickly look away. The gift in my lap is wrapped messily, which means he must have done it. He wrapped a present for me.

With a tremble in my hands, I tear off the paper. Inside is a brand-new cell phone. Blinking, I stare at him in confusion.

"I figured I'd replace the one I broke," he says with humor. I swallow down the emotion rising in my throat, remembering that day all those months ago when I watched a complete stranger shatter my phone with his boot.

"I know you have a new one already," he replies casually. "But this one has a better battery life, so it won't die on you while you're out shopping."

Lifting my eyes to his face, I meet his stare again. The rest of the room is quiet, and I can feel them watching us.

"Thank you," I whisper to him. His lip curls in a subtle smirk. "I got you something."

Jumping up from the couch, I rush over to the entryway where my winter coat is hanging. Digging into the pockets, I find the leather gloves I picked up last night. Staring at the gloves, I instantly remember how things felt *so* different between him and me just twenty-four hours ago.

I carry them into the living room and set them on his lap. "It's not much, but I saw them yesterday and…"

My voice trails as his eyes lift to my face. I don't even recognize us anymore.

He reaches into the plastic bag and pulls out the brown leather gloves. I watch nervously as he gazes down at them, a smile tugging on the corner of his mouth. "I love 'em," he says.

As he slips his large hand into the glove, I bite back the emotion that rises to the surface. My obsession with his hands only grows stronger seeing them covered in that soft leather.

"Aren't those lovely," Anna says with a smile from the other side of the room. When I look up, I see that they're all watching us.

It makes my skin crawl. Like the walls are closing in.

None of this was supposed to happen.

Suddenly, I feel a strange sense of irritation. Killian has clearly tricked me into feeling something for him I never wanted to. Or maybe it was just from being stuck in this house for so long.

I need to get out. Clear my head.

In a rush, I burst up from the couch. I go into the kitchen, forcing deep breaths into my lungs to stave the rising feeling of dread, like a rat in a cage.

Trying to force myself into a sense of normalcy, I start making coffee, but I can feel the tremble in my hands. As I'm filling the pot with water, a warm hand touches my back.

"What's wrong?"

I shrug his hand off. "Nothing."

"I said thank you for the gloves," he replies defensively.

"I know you did. I said I'm fine."

"You don't seem fine." He leans against the counter and crosses his arms. "Is this about what happened last night?"

Glancing up at his face, I pinch my eyebrows together. "Of course not. We didn't even have sex, Killian. I'm not going to get all clingy on you."

Without replying, he arches a brow at me. Feeling his gaze on my face makes me even more uncomfortable.

"Stop staring at me!" I snap before taking the water to the coffeepot.

As soon as I set it down, I let out a sigh. It's like I can suddenly hear myself, and I sound neurotic.

Holding on to the counter, I let my head hang. "I'm sorry. I don't know what's wrong with me."

He responds with a soft exhale. "It's Christmas, Sylvie. You're homesick, and I've not seen you talk to your family once since you got here."

I let out a huff and laugh. "And I likely never will."

He takes a step forward. "No one? Not even a friend?"

"My best friend was sleeping with my boyfriend, so no. Not even a friend."

"Sylvie…"

I hate the pity in his voice. I hate the attention. It makes me want to scream.

"You have us. You're not alone."

"Yes," I bark, slamming my hand on the counter. Then I turn toward him and let out all of the frustration boiling inside me. "Yes, I am, Killian. You're not my family or my friends. You're not my husband, and you know it. So can we just *stop* pretending for one second?"

His expression of sympathy morphs into contempt. "Are we pretending, Sylvie?"

I glower at him. "Of course we are. None of this is real."

When he only responds with a patronizing nod, I fight the urge to slug him. Why is he trying to push my buttons on Christmas? Why must he be so smug and difficult and handsome and likable?

Who gave him permission to stop being that ignorant prick he was when I first showed up?

"Fine, Sylvie. I'll stop pretending."

He folds his arms in front of himself and the room grows silent as we stare at each other. There's something about the way he just said that that's making me doubt the sincerity.

"You were pretending…weren't you?" I ask carefully.

He takes a long menacing step toward me. "Of course I was. You mean nothing to me, remember?"

My teeth clench as I fight the sting of those words. Feigning indifference, I scoff loudly, but he only takes another step closer. "I don't believe you," I reply.

"And I mean nothing to you, right? That's why you bought me those gloves."

Pressing my hands to his chest, I apply force as I stare up at him in shock. "You're the most insufferable asshole—"

Ignoring my onslaught of curses, he pins my body against the counter. Taking my wrists in his hands, he holds them behind my back. No matter how much I struggle to get out of his hold, I can't.

What's worse is that I stop trying. Because I love the feel of his body against mine. I love the way he quiets my anxious mind.

And I hate how much I love it.

When his face is just inches from mine, he softly whispers. "I don't know what's going through your head, but you're out of your mind if you think all of this has been pretending. Even when we're alone. You *are* my wife, Sylvie. At the end of this year, you can try to leave, and if you piss me off enough, I might let you go. But I have a feeling you won't. Because I don't mean *nothing* to you, and you know it."

I struggle against his grip. "Oh, I will leave at the end of this. And just because there's a contract in place doesn't make me your real wife."

With one quick motion, he wraps his free hand under my thigh and lifts me until my ass is on the counter and he's squeezed between my legs. I let out a gasp when I feel the hard length in his pants grinding against my clit.

Still holding my wrists together behind my back, he dives forward and kisses me hard on the lips. It's embarrassing how quickly I melt into it. A small whimper escapes as his tongue invades my mouth, and my legs wrap around his waist.

"I could fuck you right here, and you'd let me. Wouldn't you, darling?" His warm breath against my lips makes it hard to think.

"You can't just fuck me into submission every time we fight." I mumble in response.

"Can't I?"

Just as he starts to fumble with the elastic on his loose sweats, releasing my hands, we hear footsteps approaching the kitchen. When I shove against his chest this time, he relents and backs away.

"What's going on?" Anna asks as she steps into the room.

Killian keeps his back to her, likely to hide his erection, and I play innocent, crossing my legs and staying on the counter as if he and I were just having a simple conversation.

"I was just making coffee," I say, nodding to the pot.

Her eyes sparkle with the excitement of the holiday. "Lovely. Well, you two have to come back out to the parlor. We have more presents to open."

"We'll be right there," he replies in a deep grumble. She scurries out of the kitchen excitedly.

With a smile, I hop off the counter and continue making the pot of coffee I was working on.

After hitting the Start button, I turn to face him. As I look into his eyes, ignoring that potent connection I felt earlier, I realize what I have to do to get through the rest of this year.

I need to shove aside all of my feelings for Killian. He is still an ignorant, rude, brutish, moody asshole who only cares about himself.

Eyes on the prize, Sophie.

All that matters to me is that ten million dollars at the end of it. I'm certainly not going to let a handsome Scotsman with a big dick and a charming smile get in the way of that.

As I brush past him, I notice the way his scowl curls into a mischievous smirk. He snatches my arm and holds his face near mine. Our eyes meet for a moment, but instead of acknowledging that connection, I ignore it.

We stare into each other eyes like it's a challenge. Then, he gives a shake of his head, and I know he understands. We both got too close to feeling things we shouldn't. And it's best we just go back to the way things were.

"Happy Christmas, wench," he mumbles with a teasing smile.

I jerk my arm away from his hold. "Happy Christmas... brute."

And with that, I walk away, feeling as if a heavy weight has been lifted from my shoulders.

Chapter Twenty-One

LYING ON THE COUCH IN THE LIVING ROOM, WATCHING THE trashiest British reality show I can find, I hear Killian stomping down the stairs, and I glance up and feel my jaw drop as I take in his appearance.

Normally he's in boots, and they clunk loudly against the wood floors, and it sounds like we're being attacked by a giant. But this sound is different. It's lighter and softer.

I pick myself up from the couch to peer back at him as he enters the room.

He's in his green and white kilt with the same slate gray jacket he wore at our wedding. There is no way to fully prepare myself for the effect that kilt has on me.

I completely skip over confused and directly into aroused.

Then it dawns on me. I bolt further upright. "We're going to the party?" I chime excitedly.

"Get dressed before I change my mind," he mutters lowly.

I'm not even focused on the sexual favor I have to perform in order to get him to do this, but I'll worry about that later. Right now, I'm busy barreling up the stairs, thinking about which dress in my closet will work for tonight's event.

I settle on a gold velvet gown that hugs my curves. The plunging neckline is covered by a piece of netting covered in gems. My hair doesn't take long to pull into a half-up style with a clip at the back of my head. I spray my curls with something to clean up the frizz. Then I quickly apply some makeup and scurry downstairs before Killian has a chance to back out.

I'm not sure why I'm so anxious for this party. Maybe it's the promise of ten thousand dollars for getting him to go. Maybe it's the sex. Or maybe it's for the look on his family's face when he shows up and blows them all away.

When I come down the stairs, Killian is waiting.

"That was…" His eyes lift from his phone as he settles his gaze on me. "Fast."

I stop near the bottom step, struggling for something to say. "Ready?"

He swallows. "You look nice, wife."

"Not too bad yourself, brute."

I grin to myself as I sit down on the bench to put on my shoes. Moments like this always strike me as ironic, the way we can banter like a married couple and how *real* it feels, even though it's not.

As I slip on my heels, I glance up at Killian's hair. It's past his shoulders now. It looks silky smooth and well kept, but honestly… too long.

Standing up, I tug on the ends. "Can we please trim this up?"

"Now?" he asks in disbelief.

"It'll only take a minute." I grab his hand and drag him back up the stairs. "Come on."

Begrudgingly, he lets me pull him into my en suite bathroom. I pull the chair from the vanity and gesture for him to sit. A small giggle escapes when I see how massive he looks on the tiny thing. But it puts him at the right height for me.

Snatching a towel off the rack, I drape it around his shoulders and fasten it into place with a hair clip. Then I pull open the top drawer and retrieve the scissors I use to cut off my split ends.

I feel Killian's eyes on me as I move around the bathroom. When I spray his hair with water, he winces and curses under his breath. And I'm not gentle when I comb through the long strands.

"Who has been cutting your hair?" I ask as I try to line up the ends.

He shrugs. "Random women. Sometimes the housekeepers. Sometimes me."

"Tsk, tsk, tsk," I reply.

Leaning back, I take a look at him. "How much can I take off?"

"It's hair. I don't care how much you cut. It grows back."

I screw up my lips as I think this through, trying to imagine what he'd look like without the messy mop of wild brown hair on his head.

"Okay…" I reply. Then I lean in and start chopping. He barely reacts as long chunks of hair fall off the white towel and onto the floor. It's a little nerve-racking to watch the way his signature look slowly morphs into something cleaner and simpler.

"Are you a hairdresser?" he asks as he watches me work.

"No," I reply as I style the length I left on the top. "But I've always loved styling hair."

"So, why don't you do it?"

"As a job, you mean?" I reply.

"Yeah."

I stop and look at the finished product. It's not too short but still looks fresh on him. And I think back to when I was growing up. There was never a moment when I considered this as a career path.

"I'm a writer," I reply without enthusiasm.

"I haven't seen you write a thing," he replies.

"I need to trim your beard now," I say, quickly changing the subject.

Leaning over, I get dangerously close to Killian's face as I comb through the length of it, trimming the excess as I go. His eyes stay glued on mine, but I don't dare look at him. It's too close. Too intimate.

"Who decided you were a writer? You?" he asks softly.

I force myself to swallow. But I don't answer.

"Do you light up when you write the way you're lighting up right now?"

I freeze. In my mind, the answer is immediate—no.

"It doesn't matter," I reply as I set the scissors on the counter and unclip the towel from around his shoulders.

"It doesn't?" he asks.

"No. It doesn't matter whether I'm supposed to be a writer or a hairdresser or a grumpy Scot's wife. Because no matter what I do, it will never be enough."

"Enough for who?"

"Drop it, Killian," I harp in return. Then I gesture to the mirror. "Just look at yourself. Tell me if you like it."

With a disgruntled sigh, he stands from the tiny chair and turns toward the large mirror. Pausing for a moment, he stares at his reflection with hesitation.

"You don't like it," I say, suddenly nervous about his reaction.

He angles his head back and forth to see the new look. Immediately, I notice that he appears older with a more sophisticated style. But older in a good way. There are patches of gray starting to peek out around the edges of his hairline.

"I love it," he says in a low whisper.

"Don't lie."

"I'm not lying," he says as he turns toward me. "You did a bloody good job."

I swallow again, twisting my mouth in uncertainty as I force my eyes away.

"Good. I'm glad you like it."

When I turn to walk out of the bathroom, he snatches my arm and pulls me back toward him.

With two fingers under my chin, he angles my face upward. "It does matter."

I clench my jaw and fidget impatiently, waiting for him to let me go so I no longer have to stare into his eyes. "Okay," I mutter unconvincingly. "We're gonna be late."

Relenting, he lets me go, and I march out of the room. Blinking the emotion out of my eyes, I paint a smile on my face and try to look forward to the way his siblings are going to react when they see him.

When we climb into the car, I start to feel Killian tense beside me. His leg is bouncing, and I can hear the clicking of his jaw as he clenches it. Peter tries to make small talk to cover up the fact that Killian is a mess of nerves.

It's glaringly obvious to me that Killian's choice not to leave his house in six years wasn't much of a choice at all. He's struggling right now. I wish there was a way to help him, but I don't know how.

Reaching my hand across the seat, I rest it on his bare knee. It doesn't do much to calm the jittery movements. He stares out the window with a scowl, so I reach over his lap and take one of his large hands in mine.

While Peter continues to chat with us about the weather and the holidays, I squeeze Killian's hand and watch as the jumping in his knees quiets.

That is, until we pull up to a large house outside the city. It's nowhere near as big as Barclay Manor, but it's still large nonetheless. There are other cars parked in the large circular drive, so Peter pulls all the way up to the door to let us out.

Killian doesn't even move until Peter opens his door.

"Have a lovely evening," he says before we both climb out.

"Thank you," I reply softly.

There is a bagpiper near the door, playing as guests arrive, although we seem to be the last to get here. It takes me off guard to see him there. I sort of assumed this would be an intimate family gathering, but judging by the size of the house and the noise coming from inside, this is a full-blown New Year's bash.

Standing at the front entrance, I wait for Killian to take the first step. But he's hesitating. So I wait beside him. After a moment of loaded silence, I turn toward him.

His face is tense, and his chest moves with slow, shallow breaths. Reaching out I take his hand again. "We don't have to go in if you don't want to."

He shakes his head. "We're going in. Just give me a second."

"Take all the time you need," I reply, giving his hand a squeeze.

His gaze cascades down to our linked hands and then up to my face. After a moment, he seems to reach a conclusion, and he turns toward the front door with purpose.

"Let's get this over with," he mutters before pulling on the handle.

We enter through a foyer first, much like something from a normal-sized home. Nothing like the mansion we live in. He takes my hand again and walks through the hallway of the family home until we reach a large living room.

The moment we step inside, the conversation immediately dies.

I glance around at the crowd, recognizing Anna first. Then I find Killian's brother, Lachy, talking to his other brother, Declan, both decked in matching kilts like Killian is in. They are all staring at us with their mouths hanging open, frozen in shock.

It's Killian's sister who approaches first. Anna hurries over to us with her arms stretched wide for a hug. I notice tears in her eyes as she throws her arms around her brother. When she finally releases him, she smiles at his new haircut.

Then, Anna hugs me, whispering a grateful "Thank you" as she does.

A sense of pride floods through me at that sentiment. I really didn't do much, and she probably doesn't want to know what I really had to offer in order to make him come, but she doesn't need to know. At least he's here.

Next, Lachy wraps me up in a hug. "It's been too long, little sister," he says with a playful tone.

"Och, leave them alone, Lach. You know what they've been up to in that big house all this time."

"Declan!" Anna snaps, scolding him with a slap on his chest. The men laugh, and I instantly glance up to see Killian's reaction. The tension in his face is gone, and he's even cracking a smile now.

The rest of Killian's family comes over and greets us. We're offered drinks and food, and we stay at each other's side the whole time. An hour easily goes by before his aunt finally comes over to greet him.

I met her briefly at the wedding, but it was clear to me then, as it is now, that she is not the biggest fan of Killian. My shoulders immediately tighten as she approaches him.

"It's about damn time, nephew," she says.

She's an elderly woman, probably in her late seventies. Like Killian, she has dark hair and pale skin. Unlike Killian, she is gaunt and thin.

"Hello, Auntie Lorna," he replies in a low, muttering voice.

"You look good," she says with a drink in her hand, letting her gaze scan his clothing. "And you brought your American wife."

My jaw tightens as I glare at her. If this is the woman pulling the strings on this whole scheme with Killian, I have a very bad feeling about it all of a sudden.

"Of course I did," Killian replies, pulling me closer. I rest a hand on his chest and stand close to him.

"What would your father say about your long absence?" she asks over the rim of her crystal glass.

"I'm sure he'd be very happy to see Killian doing so well," I reply, tapping my husband on the chest.

His aunt laughs into her wine. "You didn't know him."

"I'm sure if he was here," Killian says, breaking in, "he'd love Sylvie too."

My heart has the stupid idea of beating faster hearing him say that. But I quickly have to remind myself it's just a trick. He doesn't love me. But he's doing a great job at pretending.

"Well, he's not," Lorna replies.

I notice the way she glares at him as she says that, and it makes my nostrils flare with anger. She slowly walks away from us, and I fight the urge to throw my punch in her face.

"Oh look!" one of the younger women, who I assume is Killian's cousin, calls as she points above our heads. "Mistletoe!"

"You know what that means," Declan adds with a haughty smirk.

I glance up and see the green ball hanging over our heads. I glance at Killian and give him a playful expression. Then, he does exactly what I hoped he would do.

He scoops me up by the lower back and tips me dramatically as he plants a deep, passionate kiss on my lips. His family cheers around us, and when he finally pulls me upright, I find it harder to wipe the smile from my face.

He's starting to relax. I can tell.

When we first entered the party, Killian wasn't himself. He was too tense to be the sarcastic, snarky asshole I know.

When Killian and I move to the corner of the room with fresh drinks in our hands, I turn toward him and whisper, "Your aunt is a real cunt."

He chuckles to himself. "You're not wrong."

I glance around the room. "So, this is her house?"

"Yep."

"Does she have anything cool we can steal?" I mumble into my glass.

"Nothing I want," he replies.

"Come on," I mutter, grabbing his hand. "I'm sure we can find some trouble to get into."

No one notices as we slip out of the room. I pull him past the kitchen and up a flight of stairs. We come across an office, two bedrooms, a large bathroom, and the primary bedroom. We end up in what I assume is her bedroom, and I immediately start to snoop.

"Why does she hate you so much?" I ask as I peer at all of the jewelry on her dresser.

He shrugs as he leans against the doorframe. "She blames me for my parents' death."

My head snaps in his direction. "What? Wasn't it a car accident?"

"Yeah," he mumbles as he nods his head.

"That's terrible."

"I don't want to talk about it," he replies, looking down.

Picking up a pearl necklace, I hold it up over my dress. "What do you think?"

"She'll kill you if she catches you going through her things."

I scoff. "I'd like to see her try. After the way she spoke to you tonight, she's lucky I'm not doing worse."

"Aww," he says as he steps toward me, smiling. "You sound a little protective of me, mo ghràidh."

I give him a twisted expression. "No. I just think she's a bitch, and clearly, being a bitch to you is *my* job."

He saunters up behind me, grabbing me by the hips and grinding himself against my backside. The intimacy still takes me by surprise, but it doesn't stop the blossoming heat building in my belly.

I stand up straight as he brushes my hair away from my neck and kisses me delicately above my shoulder. Letting out a small hum, I let my eyes close as I savor the warmth of his touch.

Then I open my eyes and stare into the large mirror in front of us. My eyes devour the sight of us together. Something about it is satisfying, as if we fit so well together that I can't possibly deny it. But the longer I look at us, the more shame I feel.

So I spin toward him and push him against the wall. Before he can say a word, I grab him by the neck and drag his mouth toward mine. I kiss him with fervor, devouring his lips and tongue. He matches my passion and kisses me back with just as much.

I feel his cock beginning to stiffen against my stomach, so I reach down and stroke it through the thick fabric of his kilt.

"Wait, wait, wait," he mutters, pulling away from the kiss.

"What?" I ask breathlessly.

"I can't do it in here."

"Sure, you can," I reply, pushing him back with a smile. Then I look down at where his cock is pitching a tent. "Because you certainly can't go back down there with that."

Digging a hand in my hair, he tilts my head back as he smiles down at me. "Then, maybe you can take care of that for me, darling."

I quickly shove away, torn between wanting to cuss at him for teasing me with that pet name and desperately wanting to *take care of that for him.*

Naturally, I side with the latter.

My hand drifts downward, sliding his kilt up until I brush the fabric of his boxer briefs.

"Well, that's disappointing. I thought you weren't supposed to wear anything under these."

He chuckles as he kisses my neck again. "It's a wee bit cold out for that. Don't you think?"

When I reach the waistband of his boxers, I gently tug it down, releasing his cock. The moment I have it in my hand, the heavy weight against my palm, I let out a mewling cry. He sucks eagerly on my neck as I stroke him, my fingers barely reaching all the way around.

"Wrap your lips around my cock, darling. I need to feel that mouth of yours."

My core lights up with desire, and I don't hesitate as he uses the hold on my hair to guide me to my knees. My head slips under his kilt as I pull down his boxers further to see his entire cock for myself. My eyes widen when I take in the size.

Long, thick, and bulging at the tip, I admire it for a moment too long. Wrapping my fingers around the base, I drag the head across the surface of my tongue. He lets out a growling moan as I do.

Closing my lips around the tip, I taste the precum leaking as I suck eagerly, licking my way around the rim. He groans again.

"Do that again, darling."

I tease the head of his cock again, flicking my tongue just under the tip. His hand finds my hair again as he guides his dick farther into my mouth. Having his impressive length on my tongue is satisfying, and I challenge myself to go deeper and deeper with each stroke. I wrap my hands around the base and fill the space my lips can't reach as I suck, feeling the way he tenses on every upstroke.

I can't get enough of his moans, so I chase them with each movement of my mouth. Arousal pools between my thighs. With my free hand, I gently cup his balls and massage them as I bob my mouth up and down on his shaft.

"Fuck me, mo ghràidh. That mouth of yours feels so good."

When I feel him nearing his climax, I ease up. I'm not ready for this to be over. I've never enjoyed a blow job in my life, but hearing Killian's praise becomes my motivation. I need more of it.

"Sylvie," he mutters in a raspy tone. "Look at me."

I pause my stroking and gaze up at him. Holding his kilt up, he stares down at me, his face frozen in pleasure. "Keep going."

Using my hands and mouth, I draw him closer to his climax again, this time gazing up at him as I do. I feel addicted to his pleasure and the intensity of his gaze, needing it more than my own. I'm moaning wildly around his dick, squeezing tight and sucking hard, knowing full well he's about to unload in my mouth at any moment.

And I want it.

"I'm almost there, darling. Don't stop."

When he finally seizes up in my hand, I wait eagerly for the salty release on my tongue. When I finally get it, I'm not disappointed. I feel it hit the back of my throat, so I quickly swallow before I risk gagging.

Killian lets out a string of curses at the sight. I wait for his climax to end before I pull my mouth away, quickly wiping the mess from my lips. And when I venture to gaze in his direction, I notice he's staring at me as if he's seen a ghost.

"What?" I say as I stand up.

He shakes his head. "Nothing."

But I notice that his hands don't leave my body for a second. He holds on to my arms, dragging me closer to him. Then, instead of kissing me, he cradles me against his chest. I don't expect it, but I also don't push him away.

I let the pounding of his heart echo against my ear, and I try to push away any nagging reminder that this isn't what people who hate each other do.

Chapter Twenty-Two

WHEN KILLIAN AND I MAKE OUR WAY BACK DOWNSTAIRS TO THE party, I instantly feel the scrutinizing gaze of his aunt, but I do my best to ignore it. Instead, I grab another drink, and we walk hand in hand over to his siblings, who are standing near the large Christmas tree.

I can't explain the good mood I'm in. I'm not one for holidays. I don't generally like family gatherings. And I know in nine months, I will be gone from this country forever.

But with the music playing and the scent of something sweet and spicy in the air giving this party a cozy, warm vibe, it's impossible not to feel good.

"Our brother's not being too difficult for you, is he?" Declan asks with a stern expression. Judging by his sudden comfort in talking to me and the slight slur in his words, I'd be willing to bet that's not his first glass of whisky.

I bump Killian with my shoulder and shoot him a smile. "I can handle him."

When I turn back to the group, I notice the way they're all looking at us. It's easy to forget that these three know the truth while no one else at the party does. They wouldn't actually suspect that Killian and I are casually hooking up in the privacy of our home.

Why would they?

Well, these three and his vicious Aunt Lorna are the only ones who know.

Feeling her eyes on me again, I look over my shoulder and find her staring menacingly. It's like those eyes are the cruel reminder of what I've agreed to. These people have made me an accomplice in something vindictive and cruel.

Which I totally agreed to and knew the entire time.

When I turn back to the group again, I feel a bit more uneasy.

"Killian never was one for manners," Lachy jokes, smiling at his brother.

"My manners are just fine, thank you," Killian replies. "Besides, no one here is nearly as harsh and cutting as this one."

He looks down at me, and I fake a smile. I'm supposed to joke back, but I'm starting to feel sick.

Lies, lies, lies.

The room starts to grow uncomfortable, and I peel my arm away from Killian's.

"I have to use the restroom. I'll be right back," I mumble softly before squeezing through the party toward the hallway. I reach the bathroom without incident, but as I close myself in and stare at myself in the mirror, I feel the same scratching anxiety crawling up my spine.

Relax, Sylvie. You're not doing anything wrong.

I take three long, deep breaths and try to remind myself that this is for the best. This isn't my family. They're just trying to help him.

Those three things just keep echoing through my head, over and over. For the most part, it works. I manage to talk myself down from the panic attack threatening to set in.

But when I open the bathroom door, I'm met with those menacing eyes again, and it takes me by surprise. Lorna is waiting for me in the hall.

"Excuse me," I mumble softly before trying to squeeze past her.

"You and my nephew are getting along well," she says, stopping me in my tracks. We're alone in the hall, far enough away from the party to not be overheard.

I swallow my discomfort and turn toward her. "It's all for show. I promise you."

"It doesn't look like it's for show."

Her expression is cold and flat. It reminds me of my mother, and I tighten my hands into fists to fight the anger coursing through my veins.

I hide it by giving her a simple shrug. "Does it matter? We'll still get through the first year, and everything will go as planned."

Her eyes crease as she leans against the wall. "Will it?"

"Of course."

As she takes a step toward me, I bite back everything I want to spew at her.

"Good," she seethes. "Because if anything goes wrong, then you won't see a dime of that money."

"You don't think I'm aware of that?" I snap back.

"If I were you, I'd be more careful not to let Killian mistake your feelings for him. You are nothing more than a clause in a contract."

"What do you think I'm doing?" I reply in a heated but hushed tone. "I'm doing everything I was told to do."

She steps closer, so we are basically in each other's faces. "I see the way you look at him. I don't even want to know what filthy things you did to him upstairs. And I'm telling you now, harboring feelings for my nephew won't change a thing. You can't stop us from getting that house, and if you even think about getting in our way, you'll be going back to America worse off than when you came here."

I want to shove her. My hands itch to reach out and throw her against the wall, and I don't care how elderly she is. But one deep breath stops me.

Instead, I get in her face. With a snarl, I point a finger at her and it takes her by surprise. Her eyes are wide with fear as she gazes up at me.

"Don't you dare threaten me. I'm only here for my money, and then I'm gone, but don't forget that you need me. So you should think twice before you get in my face again."

I hear footsteps behind me, but I'm too lost in my rage to stop. There's a nagging reminder in the back of my mind that I don't want Killian to hear any of this. He can't know the truth.

"Sylvie," he mutters from the end of the hall.

Without turning my gaze away from Lorna, I continue. "You are nothing but an old hag, and you don't care about Killian at all. So if you know what's good for you, you'll leave him alone. Don't look at him. Don't talk to him. And if you even *think* about coming to Barclay Manor, just know *you'll* leave worse than when you came."

"Sylvie." Killian's voice is a harsh bark. Then I feel his warm hand around my arm, and I stand upright to find that my hands are shaking. I gaze up into Killian's eyes, and instead of a scowl of anger, he gives me a hint of a smile.

He runs his thumb along my jaw. "Come on, darling. Let's go home."

In the distance, I hear cheers and the crowd singing "Auld Lang Syne."

Shakily, I nod. I bury myself under his arm, and he pulls me out of the hallway toward the front door. We leave without even saying goodbye to his brothers and sister.

"Happy New Year!" someone shouts toward us, but we are moving too quickly toward the exit.

The next thing I know, he's covering me with his jacket and pulling me out the front door. Peter is there waiting for us, and Killian guides me into the back seat. There are fireworks lighting up the sky in red and gold, but I'm too focused on him. Once we're settled in the car, Killian tilts my face toward him again.

Gazing up into his eyes, I feel something I never felt with him before. It's a feeling without words, or if it has words, I don't have the capacity to conjure them at this moment. It feels like *mine* and *home. Safety. Comfort.*

I look at him, and it feels like I'm looking at myself.

He inches his face closer to mine, and I close the distance, finding his lips with mine. I kiss him differently this time. Not like I need something physical, but like I need something emotional. When our lips touch, it's like I'm pulling him inside me. Inside my mind and my heart.

When he pulls away, our eyes meet. A spark of something cosmic glistens between us.

A wave of panic starts to build inside me. This can't be happening. I can't feel this way for anyone, least of all him. I don't *want* to fall for Killian.

I *hate* him.

He smiles crookedly down at me, and it shakes me from my panic.

"Forget the blow job; seeing you give that old biddy a piece of your mind was the hottest thing you've done all night."

I force out a chuckle even though inside, I'm being swept away by fear. But for some reason, I find myself clinging closer to him. As if *he* could possibly protect me from falling for him.

Beneath all of that uncertainty is more anger from the altercation. I just keep replaying her words, hearing her talk about him. I've never felt so enraged in my life. More than the night I ripped up my parents' painting. More than any moment with them.

She was cruel to someone I'm supposed to despise. So why am I so mad?

Killian puts his mouth next to my ear, and when he whispers, it feels like words written in breaths. So low even Peter can't hear in the front seat.

"I need to be inside you, Sylvie. I need to make you my wife."

Goose bumps cascade across my skin as a wave of heat pummels me from the inside. Squirming in my seat, I turn toward him and find his mouth with my lips.

The kiss is all the answer he needs. *Yes. Yes. Yes.*

Chapter Twenty-Three

WE PRACTICALLY SPILL OUT OF THE CAR AS IT PULLS UP TO THE house. Killian lifts me into his arms, carrying me through the front door. When he finally sets me down, I tear his coat off my shoulders as his lips devour my face and neck.

This need for him is acute and burning. And I know he feels it too. We are tearing each other's clothes off, fumbling with buttons and zippers. We're still standing in the foyer when he yanks my dress over my head, and I pop a couple of buttons off his shirt as I claw it open.

It's a miracle we even make it up the stairs, but by the time we reach his room, our clothes are gone. He lifts me off the floor, and my legs wrap around him as he carries me inside and tosses me on the bed.

His cock is jutting straight out from his body, and the sight of it again sends a thrill of excitement and trepidation through mine. Standing over me, he grabs my legs and drags me to the edge of the bed. He reaches down and grabs a handful of my hair at the scalp.

"Let me see that pretty mouth wrapped around my cock again, darling."

Without a second thought, I sit up and take his swollen shaft in my hands. Eagerly, I put my lips around him and cover his length with saliva, sucking hard on the tip like I know he likes. His hips cant forward as he lets out a moan.

"What a wee good wife you are," he mutters, holding my head and slowly fucking my throat.

I know the *wife* bit is a role-playing thing, but also…being treated like his wife makes my body grow hot with arousal. I love the thought of being his.

Which is very unlike me. I don't want to feel like someone's property. A thing he could use to fuck and get off.

But right now…I do. I *really, really* do.

When I feel his cock swell, he yanks me off with a growl, and I watch him fight the urge to come all over my face.

I've never felt so hot in my life. There's a fire blazing under my skin.

When a drip of cum leaks from the tip of Killian's dick, I reach my tongue out and lick it off with a hum.

"Bloody hell, woman," he mutters.

I smile up at him as my hands slide up and down his legs, eager for more.

When his eyes cascade up to the headboard and back, I see a glint of mischief in his expression.

"I'm gonna tie you to my bed and have my way with you now," he says, and somehow I grow even warmer with need.

"I'm all yours," I whisper, watching the corner of his mouth lift in a lopsided smirk.

Then he picks me up under my arms and tosses me back on the bed like I weigh nothing. I let out a shriek of laughter as he crawls ominously toward me.

I squirm with anticipation as he hovers above me. "Arms up," he says in a sexy, growling command.

Immediately I obey, and he notices. "Oh…look who listens to me now."

Biting my bottom lip, I fight a smile. "Don't get too used to it."

He sinks down and presses his lips to mine in a sweet, slow kiss. When we pull apart, he stays there for a moment, frozen in place while we breathe the same air. It's a tender, intimate moment.

Slowly rising back up, he takes my right hand in his. Craning my neck, I watch as he pulls a leather strap already attached to the bedpost and winds it around my wrist. It matches the one from the bedpost of my own bed, which I found when I first moved in.

I can still remember how much I bristled at the idea of being tied up then. Now, I yearn for it.

His fingers move with expertise as he finishes the knot, keeping the loop around my wrist gentle and not too tight. When I test the hold, it doesn't budge. Then he does the other, and immediately, I'm overcome with a feeling of aroused anticipation.

Moving down my body, he peppers me with kisses, stopping at my breasts to massage and suck tenderly on each one. I let out a hum of pleasure as more moisture pools between my legs.

"Killian," I cry out in a breathy plea. "I need you."

"I'm here, mo ghràidh." His deep voice vibrates through my torso as he mutters those words against my rib cage.

It's like my lungs won't hold air as I gasp with each inch his mouth devours, lower and lower. My thighs are rubbing together in search of that delicious friction. When his beard scratches the insides of my legs, I tremble with excitement.

"Open for me, beautiful," he murmurs.

My legs part, and he doesn't waste a second before lunging his mouth toward my core, licking and nibbling fervently.

"God, I love the taste of your cunt," he says with a carnal rasp in his voice.

Hanging my head back, I let out a groan as the pleasure assaults me. When he plunges a finger inside me, growling against my clit, I nearly come undone.

"So tight." He sounds overcome with lust, and he keeps up his thrusting, dragging me to the precipice of my climax.

"Killian, please!" I shriek, my arms jerking against the holds.

"Tell me what you want, darling."

I look up from the mattress and stare down my body at where he's stationed. His lips are wet with my arousal, and it makes me feral for him.

"I want you to fuck me. Please."

He chuckles, giving me that disarming smile. "Such a filthy mouth on you."

"I'm literally begging you," I reply.

For a moment he seems to consider my request, but eventually ignores the plea and dives back in between my legs. Curling his finger inside me, he adds a second and thrusts harder. I'm strung tight, ready to detonate at any moment.

"My wife comes first," he growls between my legs. Then he wraps his lips around my clit and sucks, using his tongue to flick the sensitive bud.

And that's it. I'm done.

My orgasm nearly shatters me into tiny pieces. It's too intense. Too good. So pleasurable it hurts.

My legs are thrashing, my arms are tied down, and the sounds that are coming out of me are downright pornographic.

When I finally relax back into the mattress after what feels like a never-ending climax, the space between my legs is soaked and sensitive.

Killian doesn't waste any time. Climbing to his knees, he positions himself between my legs and presses my thighs upward to make room for his wide hips.

I hold my breath in anticipation when I feel the warm head of his cock press against my tender opening. When the head breaches the entrance, I start to panic. The skin is pulled so tight it burns.

"Go slow," I whisper. "You're bigger than I'm used to."

With a grunt, he slides in a little deeper. My skin breaks out in goose bumps as the adrenaline and arousal mingle into a heady desire. Killian is staring down at the spot where his massive cock is disappearing inside me. He's moving slowly with delicate care not to hurt me. I don't think he's even all the way in when I feel as if I can't take another inch.

I tug against the arm restraints again. His attention snaps up to my face. "I won't hurt you, darling. You can trust me."

As our eyes meet, I feel that tug of emotion again. When did this happen? When did the man who uttered such hateful words to me become the one who holds my fear and pain in his hand, offering me safety and comfort instead?

I have no reason to trust him, but I do.

He looks back down as he eases out and thrusts back in again, a little deeper this time. "I don't know what you were so worried about," he says in a strained tone. "You're taking every inch, mo ghràidh. And you're taking me so well."

God, those words might as well be a stimulant. They buzz through my body, making everything feel so good. I wish he'd whisper them to me as he fucked me, like some secret code that unlocks the nerve endings in my body.

"Go faster," I whisper, and immediately his hips start to piston. With every thrust, he goes deeper, and I wait anxiously for the pain that never comes. Finally, he pounds fully inside me until I can feel his hips against mine, and it's a perfect fit, as if he's made to be inside me.

Pleasure blossoms down my spine from the sensation, and as he moves, filling me again and again and again, I become overwhelmed by it. It's all too much.

My eyes won't leave him, watching the look of ecstasy on his face as he fucks me, moving harder and faster as he uses my body to chase his own pleasure. He can't tear his gaze away from where our bodies are joined, and it's endearing how much he likes to watch it.

I wish I could see inside his mind. I want to know if he's feeling this all-encompassing thing that I feel. Is this still just casual sex to him? Or is he being swarmed by this feeling of something *more* the same way I am?

When he lifts his gaze to my face, our eyes meet, and that connection is back. I let out one pleading cry, and he answers the call, collapsing his body over mine and kissing my lips as he keeps up the relentless driving of his hips. His arms frame my head as his tongue tangles with mine.

My legs wrap around him, and I'm amazed at how well we fit together, even with our different sizes. Our bodies are so close it's as if we are one.

Keeping our lips together, he fucks me harder as he whispers, "I'm going to fill you up. My wife. I'm making you mine."

I wish I could wrap my arms around him. More than anything, I need my body to say what my mouth sometimes struggles to express. But with my wrists still tied, I have no other choice.

Hesitantly, I stutter. "F-fill me up, Killian. Make...me yours."

"You are mine."

With a deafening groan and a shuddering in his hips, I feel his climax tremble through us both. His cock pulses inside me, and I'm overcome with warmth. With his body still draped over mine, I swim in his nearness. I absorb his scent, his touch, his breath. Every part of him becomes a part of me.

This is so much more than sex. He has to see that.

When he finally lifts from my body, our lips touch again in a more hesitant kiss. Then, he climbs away from me and watches intently as he pulls his cock from inside me. His eyes don't leave that spot, and when I feel the cum dripping from my pussy, he quickly wipes it with his thumb.

I let out a gasp when I feel him gently pushing it back inside.

Our eyes meet again, and he shoots me a soft smile. "Well, it's official, darling," he says softly. "You're really my wife now."

Chapter Twenty-Four

"What are you reading?" Killian asks from the doorway of the parlor. I glance up from the book in my lap with a sheepish smirk.

I'm not ashamed of my curiosity. I found this book in the library months ago. But it wasn't until the night Killian tied me to his bed and claimed me as his, that I realized this might be something I'm slightly intrigued about.

Slowly I lift the book to let him read the title.

The Act of Submission

His eyebrows lift in astonishment. "Forgot I had that," he says. "Are you reading it because you're curious, or are you reading it because you want to try it?"

I let out a sigh. "I don't know. Is this what you like?" I ask.

His gaze bores into mine, the tension growing charged with every passing second.

"Sometimes," he mutters. Slowly, he walks deeper into the room, closing the distance between us, and I have to force myself to swallow. Killian carries himself with a presence that sometimes steals my breath, and I think I've spent so long pushing him away that I haven't given myself a chance to appreciate that.

"I love the trust that it requires," he adds, looking into my eyes. "I love feeling so connected to someone that they give me full control over their body."

When he reaches the chair I'm sitting in, he places his hands on either side, caging me in. I feel his presence like the heat emanating from a fire.

"Is that something you want with me?" I add.

His eyes close briefly as he replies, "Oh, absolutely, mo ghràidh."

"Well then," I smirk. "Maybe someday."

That word, *someday*, stings, but I quickly brush it off. Killian and I don't have a future full of somedays, and it's not something I like to focus on too much.

He grins back at me. "Yeah, someday."

When I turn my attention back down to my book, he stands up and goes to the bar for a drink. I'm finding it harder to focus on the words on the page since we started talking about it. After only a few months, I've noticed how much Killian has changed. He seems less drawn to recklessness and outbursts, and for a man who was introduced to me as such a partier and playboy, I'm just not seeing that anymore.

It piques my curiosity, remembering something Anna mentioned back when I first came around.

"Did something happen that made your aunt so angry?" I ask.

He chuckles. "What didn't I do to make her angry?"

"No, I mean…with the house."

"Och," he replies, turning toward me with a drink in his hand. Leaning against the bar, he takes a deep breath and stares off as if he's reminiscing about a tough memory. Then he nods toward the book in my hands. "Has a lot to do with that, actually."

"This?" I ask, lifting it from my lap.

"Aye. You know that party we had a couple months back?"

I nod. "Yeah."

"Well, I used to have a lot more of them. Sometimes with

that crowd. Sometimes with others. And after a while, I got a bit of a reputation. Nearly every weekend, people would come. They'd invite their friends, and I knew it was getting out of hand.

"My house was filled with strangers, but I loved it. They weren't...regular parties, you understand?"

"I think I do," I mumble, gazing up into his eyes.

"They were out of control, but I felt free. And soon my house wasn't such a prison anymore. It was like...an escape. A place where normal people would come to let go. To express themselves. To try new things."

"What happened?" I ask, although I have some idea.

"Word got out to my family. They found out that our family home had turned into a sex club on the weekends, and they weren't happy about it."

I bite my lip as a feeling of regret washes over me. I understand now why his aunt was so angry, but at the same time, I feel so much empathy for what that must have been like for him. To feel something important to him ripped away.

"So you had to stop the parties," I add remorsefully.

He nods his head, looking melancholy.

"I'm sorry."

He gives me a shrug. "It's not your fault."

He's right. That part is not my fault, but him eventually losing this place that brings him comfort, is my fault.

"You know...someday you could open a real place like that, and it wouldn't have to be your home. I think it sounds wonderful."

I'm trying to give him hope or solace or something, but his expression isn't giving me the assurance I want.

Then, finally, he leans down and presses his lips to my forehead as he mutters, "No, I couldn't."

I glance up at him with confusion.

With a smirk, he adds, "But maybe...*we* could."

"Killian…" I start to protest his relentless argument that any of this is real, but the words die on my lips.

Setting his drink on the bar, he comes toward me again, and I feel myself burning from the inside out with that heated look in his eyes. Then he cages me in again, leaning so close, I forget how to breathe.

"I thought we settled this already," he mutters lowly. "I *am* your husband, Sylvie. You are my wife."

When he says my name like that—not *cow*, or *darling*, or mo ghràidh—it feels too real.

"I'm not—" I argue, but he quickly cuts me off with a scorching kiss. His tongue invades my mouth, and I forget what I was about to say. I can't believe I'm letting him disorient me like this. I have to get him out of my head before he costs me everything.

With a hand against his chest, I forcefully shove him away. We're both left gasping, and he's wearing a smug grin on his face as he wipes the moisture from his lips with his thumb.

"You can believe whatever you want, Killian Barclay, but just because I let you touch me doesn't make me yours. I'm nobody's wife."

As I suspected, this only makes him laugh. "You can believe whatever you want, Mrs. Barclay," he replies, accentuating the title to drive home his point. Then he picks up the book in my lap as he adds smugly, "But you are my wife, and it's only a matter of time before you truly submit."

I sit up, straightening my spine as I bring my face to his. With a look of steely determination, I snatch the book back and toss it to the floor.

"Never," I mutter, staring into his eyes.

With a grin, he kisses me again. And when he drops to his knees and begins to tear my clothes off, I let him.

He can have my body for now, but I refuse to let my husband have my heart.

PART FOUR

Killian

Chapter Twenty-Five

THERE WAS A TIME WHEN I LOVED BEING ALONE IN MY HOUSE. I liked the quiet peace of solitude. No one to harass me or hound me with questions. No one to worry about me or tell me what's best.

Now, I find myself gravitating toward *her*.

I hear my wife's gentle footsteps everywhere I go. I hear her humming to herself down the hallways of my home. She lives here like a ghost, haunting each room with her scent and her delicate presence. The rose and lilac of her hair. The lotion she puts on her face every night. Everything about her has seeped into the crevices of this house, deep into the stones. She's even stained the upholstery and curtains.

When she came six months ago, I hated it. Now, I love it.

Sylvie is willful and stubborn. For every smile she gives me, she scowls ten times as much. I've never met someone so hardheaded and desperate to show her disdain.

I wish I could return that disdain, but somewhere in the last six months, she's grown on me. And it was long before she started climbing into my bed every night around Christmas.

It was her fire. Her passion. The way I recognized that level of heat was because I could feel it too. It was as if she spoke a language I understood.

I never intended to fall in love with my wife.

But Sylvie came to my home with a sense of loneliness that I related to. And even if she wants to deny it, somehow, we met in the middle.

I don't feel the need to fill the space in my life with parties and strangers anymore. I don't miss any of that, although if I'm being honest, I hope Sylvie and I can get to a place in our relationship where I can introduce her to that lifestyle.

She might be a stubborn hothead, but I bet she would submit to me beautifully. I'd love to make her mine, have her on her knees for me, completely at my control.

Coming in from the fields, I stand in the doorway of my home, and I listen for her. In the deep, endless quiet, I hear the faint clicking of something upstairs. So, I move toward the sound, walking quietly so I have a chance of taking her by surprise before she can put on her armor of contempt.

When I turn the corner toward the library, I pause in the doorway and watch Sylvie at the desk near the window. She's typing frantically on the old typewriter she once broke into this house to see.

Her wild honey-colored curls are piled on top of her head in a messy bun. She's wearing a long-sleeved flannel I recognize as my own, and her gray-sweatpant-covered legs are folded in front of her as she leans over the typewriter.

Honestly, I don't know how I'm supposed to resist her when she looks like this.

I clear my throat to grab her attention. The clicking stops, and she turns toward me with a gasp.

"You jerk!" she snaps. "You scared the shit out of me!"

I chuckle to myself as I enter the room. "What are you working on, mo ghràidh?"

She's stopped reacting with venom toward my terms of endearment, ones I used to use with sarcasm, but no longer do.

"I was feeling inspired so I started working on a new story," she replies, turning back to the typewriter.

"On that old thing? Don't you have a laptop?"

She shrugs. "It's oddly motivating. I think it's the clicking noise. Was it bothering you?"

I shake my head. "Not at all."

"Pity," she says flatly, and I chuckle again.

"Can I read it?" I walk up next to where she's sitting and lean against the table, crossing my boots in front of me.

"Absolutely not," she replies.

"Why not? Is it about me?" I tease.

"Maybe."

"So, it's about a dashing Scotsman with a massive cock?" I respond with a lopsided grin.

She rolls her eyes. "More like an ugly brutish drunk who can't hold his whisky."

I feign a gasp. "I'm offended. Does he at least know how to please his woman?"

She can't fight the smile this time. "He's average."

Standing from the table, I cage her in, placing my hands on either side of the desk and press my lips toward the back of her neck. "Well, I bet the heroine has never complained before." Then, I kiss her tenderly below her ear, and I revel in the way her skin breaks out in goose bumps.

I'd be lying if I said I didn't love fighting with my wife. I enjoy how easily I can push her buttons, and doing so has quickly turned into my favorite thing to do.

Right after making her moan and purr in my bed every night.

I've witnessed the pleasure of countless women in my time, but Sylvie is by far my favorite. Because she fights it. Even her own orgasms are hard-fought. It's like she prefers to suffer, as if it's programmed in her psyche. So if I have to devote every moment of my life to teaching her to indulge in her own pleasure, I'll do it.

"So, does your book require any *research*?" I ask as I deepen my kisses down her neck. I tug back the collar of the shirt she's wearing to pepper more kisses along her shoulder.

She lets out a pleased hum. "Not that kind of research."

Her words sound bothered, but her tone gives me hope. The thing I love about Sylvie is that she's always in the mood. I still laugh to myself every time I remember that morning she woke up to tell me we *wouldn't* be partaking in a physical relationship, but she has never pushed me away since.

She is quite literally addicted to my touch.

"Killian…" she whines. "I was trying…to focus."

"Then, let me clear your mind." My hand drifts around to the front of her shirt, popping open buttons as my lips continue their journey down her shoulder.

"You're not clearing it," she groans. "You're fogging it up."

I get her shirt open enough to find her bare breast inside. My hand engulfs the small mound, massaging and pinching it to hear her voice grow higher and more erratic.

"Then tell me what your book is about, and I'll leave you alone."

Her laughter vibrates through her back as I continue to kiss her. "That's blackmail, you asshole."

"Mmmm…" I hum against her skin. "Call me more names while I undress you."

"We are not—"

Her words are cut off as my hand slides down inside her joggers, quickly slipping under her knickers to find her soaked and ready for me.

"What were you going to say, darling?" I reply as my middle finger sinks between her folds, curling to find the spot that drives her wild.

She clings to my arm as she turns her face up toward mine.

"You're such a dick," she murmurs just before our lips crash together. My finger plunges inside her at a steady pace, and I find it so exquisite how she tenses up around me the faster I move.

My cock is leaking at the tip inside my trousers, and I'm growing more and more restless to free it.

While my finger is still buried deep inside her, I happen to glance up at the typewriter and catch only one small line.

He's the last person on earth I want to love, but I can't help it. I do.

A smile tugs on my lips as I turn my attention back to her. With my finger still hooked in her warm cunt, I wrap the other arm around her waist and hoist her out of the chair. Dropping her onto her feet facing the desk, I retrieve my hand from her joggers and quickly work to undo my own trousers.

It only takes a second before my cock is free, and I move fast to tear down her bottoms, aligning myself with her waiting heat.

"Grip the desk, mo ghràidh. Hold on tight."

Shoving her shoulders down to bend her over more, I watch as she white-knuckles the edge of the table just before I shove my fat cock inside her. She moves to her tiptoes and lets out a relieved squeal of pleasure.

It still takes her body a few strokes to open for me before I can work myself all the way in. Once her pussy is stretched and she can accommodate my size, I pound harder against her.

"Go ahead, darling. Call me a name now. While you're mewling like a goddamn cat in heat."

"Fuck you," she mutters, shoving her hips back against me to increase the intensity of my thrusts.

"You can do better than that," I reply with a grunt.

"I hate you, you brute."

"I know you do," I reply with a smile. "Keep going."

She responds with a high-pitched moan. "You...asshole."

"You said that one already," I tease her.

"Just shut up and fuck me," she pleads.

Looking down, I enjoy the sight of my cock disappearing

inside her, but I want her to see it too. So, in a rush, I pull out and lift her up onto the table. Her bare ass rests on scattered papers, crumpling and tearing them as I rip her joggers completely off. Then, I hold up her right leg and ease myself back in.

"Look how well you take me, mo ghràidh. Like you were made for me."

Her gaze moves downward and she watches with me as I move inside her. When she turns her attention upward to my eyes, I find a hint of something warm and affectionate on her face. Her fists grip my shirt and she drags my lips to hers.

She holds tight to my body as I fuck her, and I know in this moment I could never possibly tire of this. Her body would never feel anything but perfect to me.

Her teeth bite on my lower lip as I feel her body tighten and tremble with pleasure. I groan against the pain as I start to come, pounding three more times inside her. Filling her up gives me more satisfaction than I ever expected it to. It's like I'm giving her something she can't give back. Something she can't refuse or fight. She takes every drop because deep down, she wants it too.

We pant against each other for a moment before I slowly ease out. When I see a drop of my seed dripping free, I quickly push it back in with my thumb. She never argues with that either.

Without a word, I pull her underwear and sweats back up. She presses her lips together as I set her back in the chair the way I found her. But now her hair is falling out of its bun, her shirt is crumpled, and her cheeks are flushed. And she's wearing that postorgasm dazed expression.

"Write *that* in your book," I say as I press my lips to the top of her head.

I watch as she bites her bottom lip and fights a smile.

After tucking my cock back into my trousers and zipping them up, I leave the room and head toward the door to get back to work outside. I do so with a smile, knowing her scent is still on my skin and her ring is still on my finger.

Chapter Twenty-Six

"Supper is ready, Mr. Barclay," Martha says from the kitchen as I close the door behind me. I somehow lost track of time and didn't realize how long I had been out at the farm on the edge of the property. The groundskeeper lets me lend a hand during the planting season, and I can often get lost in time out there. With nothing but the earth under my fingers and the calming silence of the glen, I find it therapeutic.

"Thank you, Martha. Let me just get cleaned up then," I say as I tear off my coat. "Have you seen Sylvie?"

"Still upstairs in the library," she calls after me as I jog up the stairs. I don't bother tiptoeing now. Although I probably should have because when I find her in the library, she's no longer at the desk typing away. She's in a restful sleep on the lounge while the fire crackles in the fireplace. The room is warm when I walk in, but as I rest a hand on her fingers, clenched at her chest, I find them cold.

Grabbing the blanket off the back of the sofa, I delicately drape it over her, tucking her in with care. She stirs slightly from my touch but drifts back off immediately.

As I stand up, I notice the typewriter still sitting on the desk.

But instead of just a few pages strewn about the surface, there's a thick stack now. Frowning, I cross the room and pick them up, reading the title at the top of the page.

Idle Hands.

Before I read any further, I turn back toward where Sylvie is sleeping. She hasn't moved an inch since I laid the blanket over her.

It would be an invasion of privacy for me to read this, but also…this is a story directly from her mind. How could I possibly resist?

Gently sitting on the chair, I tell myself I'll only read a few pages. But those first few pages fly by, and soon I'm five chapters in. It's messy and poetic, much like she is. The story doesn't resemble ours, and to my initial disappointment, the main character is not a mean Scottish drunk who lives alone in an old house.

But by chapter ten, I realize that's a very good thing because the man in this story is god-awful. He is a famous musician who is loved by many, but behind closed doors, it's revealed that the woman secretly writes his music for him. Regardless of that, he constantly dismisses her, never gives her credit, and makes her believe that she's worthless.

With every page I turn, I grow more and more frustrated, at some points worrying that *I'm* the arsehole male character who treats her like she doesn't matter. Is this how Sylvie sees me?

Do I dismiss her? Make her feel unwanted and worthless?

There's a scene when another man flirts with her right in front of the boyfriend who does *nothing*. Even when Sylvie meant nothing to me, I couldn't bear the sight of her with my friend.

Another hour goes by while I read, and my anxiety is never settled because the story is only half finished. And the heroine still hasn't left that arsehole of a musician.

Setting the unfinished book on the table, I turn toward Sylvie, who is still sleeping peacefully. How could anyone let someone so perfect and brilliant feel worthless? Was it her idiot ex-boyfriend? Or her parents, who she has such a volatile relationship with?

Why won't she just give me the chance to make up for everything they lack?

Staring at her now, I notice that her cheeks are redder than they were before although the fire has died and the room has grown cooler.

Standing up from my chair, I walk quickly toward her and rest my hand against her cheek. I'm instantly filled with dread as I realize how hot she is. It takes only a split second for me to feel incredibly useless and panicked.

I rush to the door, yelling over the banister, "Martha! Quick to the library!"

There's a frantic pounding of feet against the floor as our housekeeper and cook run up the stairs to see why I'm so desperate.

"What is it?" she asks when she reaches the second floor, panting and breathless.

"Sylvie is burning up," I reply in a frenzy.

Martha brushes past me into the library and goes straight to where Sylvie is out cold. She rests her hand against Sylvie's cheek and forehead, making her wince in her sleep.

"It's just a fever," the woman replies. "Nothing to be worried about, sir."

"What should I do?" I reply worriedly.

She lets out a clipped chuckle. "Let's get her to her bed—"

"My bed," I bark. "I mean…*our* bed." I'm a stammering mess and trying to make sense without sounding out of my mind. The housekeepers know that Sylvie keeps her own room even though she's my wife, but barely sleeps in it.

"Of course," she replies, thinking nothing of it. "Help me carry her then."

"I've got her," I say as I easily scoop Sylvie off the couch.

She immediately wakes up and stares at me with a glossy-eyed expression of confusion. "What…are you doing?" she says in a sleepy, slurred tone.

"Take her to bed, and I'll get something to bring that fever down," Martha says, leaving the room—not nearly fast enough.

"You're sick, mo ghràidh." I kiss her forehead, hating how hot her skin is against my lips.

"I'm fine," she stutters, trying in vain to climb out of my arms. She barely has the energy to lift her head.

"No, you're not," I say in a bellowing command. "You have a fever, and you need to be in bed."

When I reach my room, I realize how cold it is, feeling bad that I just took her from a warmer space. After resting her under the covers of our bed, I tuck her in again. She curls onto her side and falls back to sleep in a moment.

Then I get to work building a fire in the fireplace. I don't often have one going in here, but this will warm the room faster than the furnace.

By the time Martha returns with a tray, I have a warm blaze going. She sets the tray on the bedside table. There's a pot of tea, water, some medicine, and a thermometer.

Then, she stands up and stares at me as if she's waiting for further instructions.

"What now?" I ask in confusion.

"Take her temperature," she replies, hiding her annoyance at my stupidity. "Anything over thirty-nine-point-four degrees, and you should call an ambulance."

My eyes widen. An *ambulance*?

"But don't worry, she doesn't feel that hot. Just keep her fever down with some aspirin. Make sure she gets lots of water and lots of rest."

"Wait, wait, wait. *I'm* supposed to take care of her?" I ask in a panic.

The look Martha gives me can only be described as astonished judgment. "Well, you *are* her husband, Mr. Barclay. Who better than you?"

"But I don't know what I'm doing," I nearly shout in return.

Her face cracks with a smile. Then she pats me on the arm. "It's a cold, sir. Just give her what she needs, and she'll be fine."

"Okay," I reply with a nervous gulp. She makes it sound so simple. *Give her what she needs.* But how the hell am I supposed to know what she needs?

"We'll be right downstairs until the end of our shift. You should really eat, sir."

"I'm fine," I reply stubbornly. I can't possibly eat like this. My stomach is in knots, and Sylvie is still burning up in my bed.

The next thing I know Martha is gone and I'm alone with my sick wife. On the bright side, the room is warm now.

I hope it's not *too* warm.

I shrug off my long-sleeve shirt and sit on the bed next to where Sylvie is sleeping. "Sylvie, I need you to wake up, darling."

"Hmm."

"I need to take your temperature."

Her mouth opens as if she's waiting. Quickly, I pick up the thermometer, press the button, and place it gently in her mouth. She closes her lips and we wait. When I hear the beep, I pull it out and read it.

Thirty-eight.

No need for the ambulance, then.

"I've got some medicine for you, mo ghràidh."

With a look of discomfort, she moves herself into a half-sitting position. I quickly shake out two pills from the bottle and place them in her mouth and hand her the water. She gulps it down before falling back down to the pillow.

When she lets out a cough, I pause and stare at her with concern. But it was just a cough, and within seconds, she's back to sleep.

Affectionately, I brush back her hair. Staring at her like this makes me feel as if my heart is suddenly outside my own body. How could she possibly understand the hold she has on me?

Sylvie is not perfect. She has flaws, but she wears them on her skin like scars. And it makes her so much more beautiful.

I have scars too, but I keep mine hidden behind humor and whisky. I stay locked away in my parents' house and I lie to myself every single day, saying I could leave if I wanted to.

For her, I could be better. I could leave this house more. I could be a real man. There's nothing I wouldn't do for her. If that's what she needs.

Give her what she needs, and she'll be fine.

I refuse to be like that man in the book.

Standing up, I tear off the rest of my clothes until I'm down to my boxers. Then, I climb under the covers next to my wife. She gravitates toward me, resting her face on my chest. It pains me to feel how hot her skin is.

But after a little while, I notice that the temperature slowly drops. By the time I drift off, she feels almost normal, so I feel as if I can rest. I know it's just the medicine and the fever will likely be back in the morning, but for now we can at least sleep.

So, I do.

Chapter Twenty-Seven

"WHERE THE FUCK DO YOU THINK YOU'RE GOING?"

When I emerge from the shower with a towel wrapped around my waist to find my wife, with her red nose and glassy eyes, putting on a pair of boots, I gape in horror.

"I need to get out of this house, Killian. I'm going out of my mind," she argues.

"You're still sick," I bark as I cross the room and steal her boot from her.

"I've been lying in this bed for three days. My fever is gone. I just have some congestion left. It's nothing."

My jaw clenches in frustration. The morning after she got her fever, she woke up with nothing but endless sneezing and coughing. I was a mess for days, trying to give her what she needed. Medicine, rest, water, food.

Normally when I get sick, I just sleep for days, but Sylvie is stubborn as hell. Over the last three days, she fought me on every decision. She hated having me dote on her and worry about her. I assume it's because she's just not used to it.

"You're not leaving, Sylvie." I keep my voice low and my tone flat.

She stands up in a huff. "Are you keeping me prisoner now?" The force she uses to yell at me sends her into a fit of coughs. She collapses back onto the bed to catch her breath.

There's a swell of pity in my stomach from seeing her struggle so much. Sylvie isn't like me. She hates feeling cooped up in the house, and I know she longs for fresh air.

"Come on," I say.

She lifts her arm from around her eyes and stares at me skeptically. "What?"

I kneel in front of her and unlace her boot enough to get it onto her foot. "You're not a prisoner here, Sylvie. You need some fresh air, but I can't let you leave alone while you're so sick. So let me help you."

She sits up and gives me a narrow-eyed expression. "Where are we going?"

After sliding her foot into the boot, I tie the laces. "Just on a walk of the grounds. We're sitting on sixty acres, you know."

Letting out a rattling exhale, she fights the urge to cough again. Then, she says in a raspy voice, "Fine."

"It's not raining for once, and I'll stay by your side the entire time."

She cocks her head to the side. "I'm not a child, Killian."

"No," I reply, tightening her laces. "But you are my wife, and it's my job to take care of you."

"It's really not," she replies weakly.

"Shut up, cow," I say, making her laugh. "Too harsh?"

She shakes her head with a soft smile. "Not at all."

Then, she puts out her hands for me, and I hoist her off the bed. I feel her forehead again for good measure, but as she said, her fever is gone, even without the medicine to keep it down.

On the entire walk along the gravel drive out to the farm, I keep Sylvie's hand in mine. It's warm enough now that we don't need gloves, although the leather ones she bought me are still tucked away in my pocket.

"We're not walking all sixty acres, are we?" she asks wearily.

"Of course not," I reply with a chuckle. "Are you feeling okay? We can head back."

She shakes her head. "No, I'm fine." Then she wraps herself around my arm, resting her head on my shoulder as we slowly walk down the path toward the farm.

"What do you do out here all day?" she asks.

With a laugh, I say, "Not much, really. The grounds crew keeps most of it up. I do like to help out where I can."

Then, she squeezes my arm. "You must do a lot. Enough to keep up this physique."

We stop, and I turn toward her. "Are you...complimenting me?"

She rolls her eyes. "Don't get used to it."

"I won't. I think I prefer the name-calling."

"Okay, good," she teases as we start walking again. "You have large muscles, but you're still stupid and ugly."

"Well, that's just a lie," I reply with a grin. "I'm incredibly handsome."

The next time I look down at her, I notice she's chewing on her lip and trying to hide the blush on her cheeks.

When we reach the farm, Ben, the groundskeeper, is standing outside his quaint brick house in front of the barn. I introduce him to Sylvie, and she greets him warmly, which is nice to see. She reserves her bitchiness just for me.

As Ben and I get into a conversation about the garden we've been working on, Sylvie walks away to explore the farm. When she finds the gray mare, I excuse myself from the conversation with Ben and run over toward her.

"Is it nice?" she asks before getting too close.

"She's very gentle." I grab an apple we keep in a basket near her stall and place it in Sylvie's hand. Then I hold her against my body as I ease her hand out to the animal.

"What's her name?" Sylvie asks.

"Moire," I reply, which makes Sylvie giggle.

"What's so funny?" I ask.

She shrugs, wiping her slobber-covered hand on my jacket. "Just like hearing you say that."

"Moire," I reply, drawing it out for her and giving the *R* a bit more of a roll. Then, I tug Sylvie closer and lean in to press my lips to her ear. She giggles from the tickle of my beard.

But when I try to move my mouth to hers, she shoves me away. "Don't kiss me! I'm sick."

"I don't care," I reply as I pull her back toward me. I just want her body in my hands at all times. I crave her against my body and my lips on her every second of my day.

"You're disgusting," she squeals as I hold her face and kiss her hard right on the mouth. I don't care that she's sick or that I've seen her go through an entire box of tissues in a day. If that's disgusting, so be it. She's my woman, and I'll take the bad with the good.

"In sickness and in health, remember?" I say with my lips just inches from hers.

Our eyes meet, and I see the slight panic in her gaze. She gets that way anytime I bring up our marriage, as if she's afraid of it *now*. We've been married for six months. And we have six months to go. I've not made any indication that I expect her to stay after the year, at least not *yet*.

I desperately hope she does.

Sensing her discomfort from that phrase, I quickly let her go. She averts her eyes, and I busy myself with giving Moire another snack.

As I'm petting the horse's mane, Sylvie points toward the barn. "What are those?"

Looking up, I see the boxy white structures on the other side, and my mouth twitches with a smile. "Let me show you," I say as I take her hand and lead her toward the hives. Stopping near the barn, I quickly roll up my sleeves and rinse my hands clean with the spout.

Then, I watch her expression as I pull open the box from the top and lift the frame from out of the shelter. The sound of the swarm is immediate, and Sylvie lets out a squeal as she starts to run from my side. Snatching her by the arm, I give her a stern look.

"Calm down, darling. They won't hurt you."

At that moment, a few dozen bees leave the frame and start to buzz around us both, so I quickly grasp my wife to my side, whispering into her hair. "Just relax. I've got you."

She lets out a muffled sound, and I look down to see she's buried her face in my shirt, her eyes clenched shut.

"Sylvie, look," I say as I prop the frame up on the side of the box. With one arm around her to keep her safe, I press the other to the bee-covered hive to show her how gentle they are.

She whines as she clutches tighter to me.

"There's nothing to be afraid of," I reply. "That honey you put in your tea comes from here."

"Yeah, well, I could also get it from the store."

"Where's the fun in that?" I dig my finger into some of the honeycomb at the edge of the frame, and I show her how easily it drips. My fingers are covered as I bring one to my mouth and lick it clean.

When I look down, her eyes are zeroed in on my hand, so I bring it to her lips. She inspects it for a moment before running her warm tongue along the length of my middle finger. I can't keep in the low growl that emits at the sight and sensation of her tongue against my digit.

"Bloody hell, woman," I growl, making her smile.

Just then, a bee buzzes past her head, and she panics, swatting at it with a squeal. As she starts to run, I lose grip of her, and she gets out of my hands.

"Sylvie, relax!"

But she doesn't. She flails and stumbles until she trips and falls, landing in the grass with a hard *thunk*. That forces another coughing fit, and I rush over, grabbing the worker bee that had gotten himself stuck in her wild curls. The moment my fingers close around him, he stings me, and I toss him to the ground.

When I hiss, Sylvie looks up at me with concern. Between her coughs, she manages to squeak out, "I told you they were dangerous!"

Using my teeth, I pull out the stinger and spit it into the grass. Then, I lower myself to my knees in front of my wife.

"No, mo ghràidh. They're not dangerous. You just have to know how to handle them."

She continues coughing, so I pull her up and pat her back through the spell. By the time she's done, I can hear the rasp in her breathing. The doctor said the virus will work itself out, but the cough could take longer. I wish it'd hurry. I can't stand the sound of her like this.

When she's done heaving, she takes my hand in hers, staring down at my finger. There's a red, swollen lump there already.

"Does it hurt?" she whispers.

"Nah," I say. "Not too bad."

Then she brings it to her mouth and presses her lips to the end of my index finger. "I'm sorry."

"Come on then," I reply after kissing the top of her head. "Let's get back home and get you to bed. Enough fresh air for you today."

"Okay," she agrees.

I pull her to her feet and leave her a good distance away from the hives while I go back to replace the frame I had removed. When I'm done, I return to Sylvie and tuck her under my arm so we can walk back to the house together.

Chapter Twenty-Eight

"Is tomorrow your birthday?" Sylvie finds me kneeling in the dirt by the farm. Squinting through the sun, I stare up at her with a bad feeling in my gut.

"Yeah...why?"

"When were you gonna tell me?" she replies. "Your sister just mentioned it in a text."

I shrug. "Why would I tell you? It doesn't matter."

"Of course it does," she replies. "Anna said you always have your friends over for your birthday."

My only response is a disgruntled sigh.

It's true; I always do have my friends over for my birthday, but that's not always a good thing. The party is nothing more than a binge of sex, alcohol, and debauchery. It just doesn't interest me anymore.

If I could have anything for my birthday, it would just be a typical day at home with my wife. Or perhaps her admitting to me that she actually gives a fuck about me. I'd like that too.

"So, let's throw a party," she says with excitement.

Now that she's finally able to argue with me without setting off a fit of coughs, she takes advantage of it and argues with me ten times as much. I'd be lying if I said I didn't enjoy it.

"No," I grunt as I turn my attention back to pulling the weeds that have sprouted along the fence line.

"Come on, you miserable ogre. I *need* a party. I'm so bored."

"I'll keep you busy," I reply as I glance up at her with a wicked grin.

She rolls her eyes. "We're already screwing two times a day, Killian. My poor lady bits can't take anymore."

Out of the corner of my eye, I see Ben fumble with the tool in his hand before quickly scurrying over to the barn and out of earshot of our conversation. I let out a small chuckle.

Then I turn back toward Sylvie. "Wait… I'm not hurting you, am I?"

"No, my dear husband. You're not hurting me. Besides," she adds with a shrug. "I like a little pain."

My eyebrows nearly shoot to my hairline. *Oh, we're coming back to that.*

"How about for my birthday, we see just how much pain you like?" I ask.

"No," she barks, stomping her foot on the ground. "We can't just sit around this house alone every single day, Killian. We need human interaction. We need to celebrate. We need to have *fun*. You remember what that is, don't you?"

Sitting back on my haunches, I let out a sigh of defeat. I know at this moment that I'm not winning this argument. It's clear. When my wife puts her mind to something, there is *no* talking her out of it.

"Fine," I say with a relenting sigh. "One party. Just a few people. Nothing wild."

"Thank you," she replies with an elated bounce in her feet. Then she holds out her hand. "Give me your phone."

I don't even argue. I just pull it out of my back pocket and hand it over. "Don't go looking at my search history now."

She screws up her face in disgust. Then, without a word, I watch her type out a message.

"Who are you texting?" I ask, feeling a sense of hesitation and paranoia.

"The group chat," she says, showing me my phone screen.

"How the hell did you find that?" I reply in shock.

"It's not that hard, Killian. You don't really text that many people."

My phone starts vibrating with responses immediately. She smiles down at the screen. "They're in."

As she passes back my phone, a sense of dread rises up inside me. I'm always happy to see my friends, but I also know what comes with that. I've always been the single guy at our parties, but now I have someone else to protect. Because if any of those men think they can lay a hand on my wife, this weekend won't end well.

"Barclay!" Liam greets me in his usual bellowing excitement as he jogs up the drive from his car and throws his arms around me for a hug. "How the hell have you been?"

I force a pleasant expression and nod. "I've been good."

"Now that you're married, you never want to party anymore, is that it?" he asks with a laugh, slapping me on the arm.

"I guess you could say that," I reply with a wince.

"Where is that stunning wife of yours?"

My teeth grind as I stare at him, gauging his interest in Sylvie. At that very moment, I hear her light footsteps as she comes down the stairs and meets us at the door.

"There she is!" Liam shouts when he sees her.

I turn around and watch him approach her with enthusiasm, pulling her into a hug. Her eyes find mine, and she widens them briefly as if she's scolding me. She told me multiple times to be on my best behavior this weekend; I know deep down she doesn't mean to not drink too much or to use my manners. She means to avoid acting like some possessive caveman who snaps off anyone's head for the smallest thing.

I can make no promises.

McNeil and I go into the parlor for a drink while Sylvie goes to the kitchen to talk with the staff. I catch a glimpse of her as she walks away. She turns back to me for a split second, and our eyes meet. The subtle warmth in her gaze is fooling me. It's telling me she's happy here and that we make a good couple. Because right now, she *feels* like my wife.

"So," Liam adds as we grab a drink from the bar. "I know I apologized last time, but I just feel the need to do it again."

I shake my head. "Liam, it's fine."

"No, it's not. I pissed you off last time I was here, and it was wrong of me."

"I gave you the green light," I reply, but he puts up a hand to stop me.

"You clearly love your wife very much, Killian."

Forcing myself to swallow and remain stoic, I let out a heavy breath through my nose. Liam's words send a shot of regret to my chest. This marriage isn't even real, but he's right. I do love her.

Instead of arguing with him, I simply say, "You're right. I do."

Then, his face pulls into a grin. "I'm happy for you."

That guilt returns, stinging a little bit more.

An hour later, the rest of the crew starts piling in, and the drinking starts as it normally does.

Greg, Nick, and their ladies congregate on the couches in the parlor, and soon the room is filled with laughter. I stay off to the side, hanging by the bar with a drink in my hand as I watch the rest of them go on and on.

"You've been sipping that drink for a long time," Sylvie whispers after she sidles up next to me.

I glance down at my half-empty glass of whisky. "Taking it easy tonight," I reply.

Her eyebrows shoot upward, and I watch as she bites her lip as if she's fighting the urge to respond with something sarcastic and quippy. Instead, she takes the glass from my hand and shoots back the drink in one quick gulp.

She coughs and sputters after it goes down, making me laugh. "What the hell did you do that for?"

"You might be taking it easy," she replies through a strained voice. "But I'm getting drunk."

I let out a low growl. "Easy, mo ghràidh."

"Oh, relax, you big dumb oaf. What could possibly go wrong? I've got you to protect me."

I watch as she pours herself another shot, but as she moves to shoot it again, I grab her arm to stop her. "Keep your wits about you, wife."

She rolls her eyes before gulping down the next shot. "Relax, Killian."

Then, I pin her against the bar and put my mouth down by her ear. She's so much smaller than me I have to practically bend over to reach her. "I'm not a monster, you know. If you get too drunk, I won't be able to fuck your brains out later, and I plan to. So, I'll say it again…" I take the shot glass from her hand and set it on the bar. "Keep your wits about you."

I watch as she gulps nervously before meeting my eyes. Then, to my surprise, she grabs me by the back of the neck and drags me down for a kiss.

The conversation behind us dies as they notice us practically making out by the bar. Then, of course, there is a round of whoops and whistles.

"The party is starting early!" someone shouts with excitement.

Everyone erupts with laughter as I pull away from Sylvie's kiss. She's beaming up at me as I stand upright and turn toward our friends with a smug grin.

That's when I catch sight of the couple in the doorway, and my smile instantly fades. Standing there by the entryway are Angus and Claire. He's wearing a wide expression of excitement, but she's simply scowling at me and my wife.

That's when Sylvie tightens her grip on my arm as if I'm being claimed. And I'm not going to lie, I sort of love it.

Chapter Twenty-Nine

SYLVIE IS ADORABLE WHEN SHE'S DRUNK. WELL, TECHNICALLY, I think she's just tipsy, but it's enough to have her telling hilarious stories at dinner, mostly about me and the idiotic things I've done. The group adores her. Well, all but the short-haired brunette across the table who is staring daggers at my wife.

I get the sneaking suspicion that something happened between Sylvie and Claire that I haven't been told about. When we all sat around the table, Sylvie aggressively stole the seat beside me from Claire, who already had the chair pulled out and was about to sit.

Everyone at the table noticed. Even Angus, who has been silent ever since.

Guilt pierces my chest again. It's like a blade stuck between my ribs that I can't seem to remove.

Sylvie, in her usual commanding style, completely saved the dinner from debilitating awkwardness and had everyone laughing in seconds. By the time we finished our meal, her hand was resting on my stiffening cock, and I had to fight the urge to drag her up to our room right then and there.

I've barely had anything to drink all night. We've been lingering at the table for a while now, and I can see how toasted everyone is getting. It's about *that* time—when things go from a tame dinner party with friends to something far more wicked and depraved.

My favorite part of the night if we're honest, but not tonight. Tonight, I just want to make them all go away so I can be alone with my wife.

"Wait!" Sylvie shrieks with a slur in her voice.

"Jesus, woman. What are you hollerin' about?" I ask.

"Your cake!"

"My cake?"

She jumps up from the table and scurries off into the kitchen. I can feel Claire staring at me, but I don't look in her direction.

"She's really amazing," Greg's wife, Emma, says with a warm smile.

"Yeah," I mutter to myself. "She is."

Just then the lights go out in the dining room, and a warm glow emits from the kitchen. Before I know it, I hear Sylvie crooning off-tune.

"Haaaaappy…" she starts while waiting for the rest to join in. "Birthday to you," she sings when they do.

Throughout the entire song, she's grinning at me over the candles on the giant chocolate cake, and I can't help but smile in return. By the time she sets it down in front of me, the song is over, and she's gaping at me expectantly.

Closing my eyes, I make a quick wish, and I blow the candles out. Everyone cheers, and I swallow my embarrassment.

While Sylvie cuts the cake and passes out each piece, I find myself watching her with wonder. This is somehow the same woman who threw hot coffee on her ex-boyfriend and broke into a stranger's house. She's the same woman who kissed my beesting and mended my hand when it was bleeding. Every moment I thought I had her figured out, she surprised me with more layers and beauty than I ever expected.

"We should play a game!" Sylvie exclaims, with a glass of wine in her hand.

"Not another drinking game," I mutter.

"No…" She snatches the empty wine bottle off the table and smiles at me. "You've played spin the bottle, right?"

My heated gaze turns in her direction. "Sylvie…"

The party reacts with excitement.

"I knew your wife would know how to get the party started," someone says with a giggle.

Immediately, everyone is on board, practically running from the dining room table and into the parlor. They clear a spot in the middle of the large room. Sitting right in front of the fireplace, they form a circle on the floor, and Sylvie reaches for me, gesturing for me to sit next to her.

Liam grabs another bottle of wine, and I realize how painfully sober I am.

This is a bad idea. I can feel it.

My friends and I have been kinky together in the past. These parties always lead to sex in some way or another, and I've always been open to playing along, although there is only one other person in this room I've actually fucked, and *that* wasn't part of the party.

No, *that* was something very different entirely.

But these couples have no problem with sharing all the time. It's almost as if my house is the safe space where they can fuck each other, and it doesn't mean anything.

But now that I'm married, I realize that it means a hell of a lot to me. For a guy who hangs out with a bunch of swingers, suddenly, I don't feel as if I belong here.

"Okay, so the rules are simple. If the bottle lands on you, you can choose to kiss or drink," Sylvie explains.

"Or more…" Liam adds, making everyone laugh.

When Sylvie moves to spin the bottle, I immediately grab it from the floor and pass it along to Liam, who is sitting on the other side of her. Sylvie gives me a grumpy look as if she's disappointed in me, but I don't care. I sit in frustrated silence while Liam spins.

The bottle lands on Emma. Everyone claps and cheers. Her cheeks redden immediately. Then she crooks a finger at Liam, basically implying that she'd rather have a kiss than a drink. He crawls across the floor toward her, and she grabs his face, planting a long wet kiss on his mouth. Everyone reacts with excitement, even Greg, who's laughing next to her.

When the kiss is done, Liam sits back down, and Nick is next. His bottle lands on Claire, who opts for drinking instead of kissing. After Nick, Theresa goes. The bottle spins until it lands on Angus.

"Get over here," he says to Theresa. I notice the way Claire's mouth sets in a thin angry line.

Theresa laughs as she crawls over to Angus, but instead of kissing him on his mouth, she dives down and latches her lips onto his neck, sucking on his flesh and making his eyes roll into the back of his head.

"Holy shite," he mutters after she releases him. As he touches the now red circle she left behind, he mutters a low "I'm fuckin' hard as hell after that."

We all let out a string of laughter, and I feel Sylvie nestle closer to my side. Theresa looks downright proud of herself now.

Then it's Claire's turn, and I grow tense. I watch with nervous anxiety as it spins, and when it stops pointing dangerously close to me, I panic.

"It's me," Sylvie says, cutting off my thoughts.

"It looks like it landed right between you and Killian," someone argues.

"No, it's on me," she argues. Then she glares at Claire. "So… what's it gonna be?"

"Technically, it's your choice," Claire replies flatly.

"I'm not afraid of a little kiss."

"Sylvie…" I say in warning. But she ignores me. Instead, she leans toward Claire and stares obstinately into her eyes. The tension between these two women is palpable, and I'm legitimately concerned about what my wife is about to do.

Claire leans toward Sylvie, but it's Sylvie who makes the leap. She latches her lips around Claire's, kissing her with passion and fire, and I see Claire's bottom lip pinched between Sylvie's teeth. Claire lets out a whimper but meets Sylvie's fervor with her own, pressing back against her. For ten long seconds, the two of them fight for control of the kiss while the rest of us watch with trepidation.

When they finally pull away, Sylvie's mouth is red, and Claire looks angry and defeated, as if Sylvie somehow won.

"I think it's time for another bottle," Liam says, changing the mood in the room. He immediately jumps up, grabs a bottle of wine, and walks to the wall to dim the lights. I can feel the radiating anger from Sylvie's gaze as she glares at the other woman.

She only relaxes after Claire leaves the room in a huff.

"What was that all about?" I whisper.

Sylvie shrugs. "I don't like her."

"Obviously," I joke.

"Don't act like you don't know why," she replies without looking at me.

My head tilts as I stare at her in confusion. Leaning my mouth next to her ear, I softly whisper, "Is my wee little wife jealous?"

"I don't like cheaters," she mutters, denying that she's jealous of another woman wanting me.

"You're in a room full of cheaters, darling."

"You know what I mean," she huffs.

My hand slides along her jaw, turning her face toward me. "I like to see you jealous."

She jerks away from me. "I'm not."

"Then you won't mind me kissing another person tonight?"

Her eyes turn to fire, glaring at me with rage. "You wouldn't dare."

I chuckle softly. "It's not really cheating. Just a kiss."

Reaching into the middle of the circle, I pick up the wine bottle. "My turn," I announce, stealing the attention of everyone in the circle who are all having their own flirty private conversations.

"Should we wait for Claire to come back?" Liam asks.

"She's fine," Angus replies, waving off his wife instead of looking for her.

Sylvie is still shooting daggers at me with her eyes as I give the bottle a spin. After three turns, it stops in front of Theresa, the same woman responsible for the blossoming hickey on Angus's neck.

The group lets out a collective "Ooooh."

I wink at my wife before leaning in toward Theresa and pressing a chaste kiss on her lips before sitting back in my seat.

The group lets out a collective "Awww."

Sylvie is still fuming. She picks up the bottle and spins it for herself. When it lands on Greg, my jaw clenches. We've stopped doing the drink option, apparently because she crawls defiantly toward him and grabs his face. I watch with buzzing anger as she kisses him deeply, pressing her tongue in his mouth.

"That's enough," I bellow.

Thinking it's just a joke, everyone laughs. But I haul my wife back to her seat next to me just the same. When she lands on the floor, I wipe the saliva from her mouth and give her a warning glance.

"She's been bad, Kill," Theresa murmurs. "How are you going to punish her?"

Sylvie shoots me a tense glare, but I tilt my head back and stare down at her menacingly. "I don't know, but I would like to punish her."

Across the floor, Theresa bites her lip, looking as if she's dying to see it happen. Everyone else is fidgeting, and I know they are craving to see it as much as I'm craving to do it.

I lean down toward Sylvie, teasing her with a smile.

"Go on, then, Killian," Greg says. "Show her what we get up to at our parties."

"What do you think, mo ghràidh?" I whisper. "Can I show them how tough my girl is? How well she takes it?"

"You hurt me, and I'll hurt you right back," she responds with venom.

I smile wickedly. "I'm counting on it."

Then I take her lips, kissing her hard and reclaiming her mouth as my own. After she starts melting into the kiss, I stand from the floor and drag her up with me. The rest of the group stays on the floor, mingling together in a drunken mess until Theresa is in Angus's lap and Emma is in Liam's.

But to be honest, I'm not concerned with them anymore. All I can see in my mind is Sylvie kissing Greg and Claire. Her tongue in their mouths. Their hands on her body. I'm seeing red as I toss her on the couch, kneeling on the cushions as she bends over with her ass in the air. In one swoop, I lift her dress, and she lets out a yelp of surprise.

"This, my sweet wife," I say, grabbing her ass cheeks in my hand, "is mine."

She only whimpers in response. As I knead and massage her pale, tender flesh, I hear the soft moans of those behind me. They must be enjoying the show.

"Tell me I can punish you, Sylvie. I need to hear you say it."

She lets out a tortured groan with her face pressed into the cushions of the sofa.

"Say it, wife. Yes or no?"

Lifting her head, I can see the arousal mingled with resistance in her eyes.

"Don't worry, darling. I'll let you pay me back, but I want to show you how good it feels first—to be claimed by your husband."

Her head falls back, and her spine arches as she lets out another moan. "Yes," she replies breathily.

"That's my girl," I reply with a grin.

Then, I waste no time. Peeling down her thin lace panties, I let my friends behind me take their fill of my beautiful wife's cunt, glistening and pink. When I spread her folds wide for them to see, I hear a muffled "Fuck yeah," coming from the dark side of the room.

"She tastes good too," I mutter lowly before dipping my head down and taking a long salacious lick of her wet pussy. She fidgets and moans as I do.

While I play with her, sliding a finger inside her only to pull it out and tease her arsehole, she squirms and mumbles curses into the cushions.

"All mine," I mutter with a sneer as I take another long lick. "No one else can ever touch you. Is that understood?"

She groans without a verbal response. So I rear back my hand and lick my lips before landing a hard smack on her right ass cheek. The sound that comes out of her is a mixture of surprise and enjoyment—a gasp and a whine.

"You liked that, didn't you, mo ghràidh?"

Biting her bottom lip, she nods.

I let my hand fly again, landing on the opposite cheek but not giving her time to recover before doing it two more times. She howls and mewls, the pleasure fighting for dominance inside her.

"Do you understand, Sylvie? Tell me you're all mine."

"No," she says through gritted teeth, shaking her head. A sinister smile stretches across my face.

"You need more then."

Holding her dress up, I land another harsh smack on her ass. I love the way her flesh reddens with every strike of my palm. Her moans are guttural and needy as I spank her again and again, growing more and more desperate to fuck her with every hit.

"Say it, Sylvie," I mutter darkly. "Tell me you're mine."

She continues to fight it angrily, and I love the way she struggles. She could easily tell me to stop, and I would, but deep down, I know this is what she wants.

"More," she whines, shoving her hips backward.

My hand burns with every resounding slap of her ass. Inside my trousers, my cock is straining against my zipper, leaking at the tip with the thought of sinking inside her. Sylvie's knuckles are white as she grips the back of the sofa through her pain.

Finally, on the last harsh hit, she screams, "Okay!"

I pause, breathing heavily as I wait for her to finally say what I want to hear.

"I'm yours," she cries out in a breathless whimper. "I'm yours, I'm yours, I'm yours."

Without a moment of hesitation, I tear down my zipper and pull out my aching cock. Shimmying my pants down enough, I drop onto the sofa and grab her from beside me.

"Ride my cock and show me, then."

She climbs onto my lap in a rush, straddling my hips as she lowers herself over my shaft. This time, she doesn't give herself time to adjust to my size. She winces in pain as her soaking cunt swallows my length.

I grab her by the back of the neck and hold her face to mine. When I kiss her lips, I taste the tears and sweat on her face as she starts to bounce eagerly on my lap.

"That's my girl," I whisper, kissing her lips.

My heart swells in my chest. There is only her, only us. And I know she could have said those things because of the heat of the moment, but in my heart, I pray they're true.

My woman. My wife. My darling.

Her hands grip tightly to my neck as she grinds her hips on my dick, chasing her own pleasure and crying out loudly with every thrust. Her voice grows louder and higher in pitch the faster she goes, and I know there's no stopping the cosmic onslaught of pleasure as it barrels through her.

Then it's as if she holds me tight to pull me under with her. My cock jerks and shudders as I release my load, growling loudly with my climax.

When she finally collapses on top of me, her head rests on my shoulder, and her heart pounds against my chest.

The moans and cries of pleasure from behind her barely register at all to me. I'm so focused on her, and she's so focused on me.

Her eyes are filled with tears, and she is staring at me with astonishment, as if she's about to say something profound. I wait with bated breath for the words I so desperately want to hear.

"Killian…" she whispers.

Quickly, I brush the sweat-soaked hair out of her face.

"Yes, darling," I whisper in return.

Her lips part, the words lingering on her lips. One moment after another passes by as I wait for something, *anything*.

There is so much torment in her eyes, as if it's so hard for her to express how she really feels, and I know it's there. The hatred she once expressed is gone, but for some reason, she refuses to let me have anything else.

Instead, she closes her lips and rests her head on my shoulder again. Her breath is warm against my neck as she relaxes into my arms.

Chapter Thirty

I HEAR THE FAMILIAR *CLICK-CLICK* AGAIN FROM THE LIBRARY, AND I stop in my tracks as I walk in the back door, shedding my boots from the field before quietly crossing the floor. Sylvie hasn't worked much on her novel in the past few weeks. First, she got sick. Then, we had my birthday party. And ever since then, she's been back to acting strange again.

It's as if Sylvie will only let me in one tiny bit at a time. That night of the party a couple of weeks ago, I think she realized how much we mean to each other now, and she didn't like it. I don't blame her. I didn't like it at first either.

It's such a strange feeling to fall in love with someone you don't intend to. It's like being coerced or tricked. Everything that reminded me of what it was like to despise her is gone. Wiped from my memory forever.

Slowly, I tiptoe up the stairs, mesmerized by the hypnotic sound of her fingers punching those loud keys. As I reach the library, I do the same thing I always do. I stand in the doorframe silently with my arms crossed as I watch her.

"I can see you," she calls, sounding amused while still typing away at her typewriter.

I let out a low chuckle as I step into the room. She doesn't stop what she's doing. In fact, she seems captivated by the story she's typing, and when she reaches the end of the page, she rolls it out of the old machine and loads a new one.

I could remind her again that she owns a perfectly good laptop, but she already knows that. And if this is working, then who am I to stop her?

After the fresh white page is loaded, she rolls her chair backward and stretches her arms over her head, arching her spine and revealing her back and belly. I have to force myself to focus.

It's now early May, and I'm starting to feel a sense of panic building inside me because the days of our marriage are numbered. Sylvie only has four more months here. It will take me four more months to convince her to stay. To be my wife *forever*.

"It's a beautiful day outside," I say carefully.

She looks momentarily surprised as she pops up and glances out the large window. "It actually stopped raining."

"We only have a matter of time before it starts again."

She spins toward me, tugging at the rubber band around the ponytail, letting her wild, warm locks fall around her shoulders. "What did you have in mind?"

"It's a surprise," I reply.

The corner of her mouth tilts upward, fighting a smile. "Fine. I can stand to take a break anyway. Let me get my shoes on."

When I meet Sylvie outside, I watch her expression as she pulls the back door closed and spots Moire standing near the garden wall. Sylvie's jaw drops.

"What is she doing here?" she asks with sweet surprise as she jogs down the gray stone steps toward the large animal.

"I thought you might like to go for a little ride," I say without sounding too enthusiastic about it. I've learned that approaching Sylvie is like approaching a wild animal. Be gentle. Don't be too charismatic. She spooks easy.

"I've never ridden a horse before," she says with fright.

I reach out my hand toward her. "I've got you."

When her gaze lifts to my face, I spot a hint of something affectionate, but she quickly wipes it away. "Promise?"

"Of course," I reply. The desire to call her something special and intimate is strong, but I refrain. *Tread carefully.*

"All right," I say, pulling her toward the saddle. "Left foot first."

She slides her foot into the stirrup and leaps onto the horse's back. As I climb up behind her, she relaxes against my body with a sigh. She's more at ease with me close to her. I wish she could see that.

Sylvie leans back as we take off in a slow trot around the perimeter of the grounds. We don't say much as we go, but my wife and I have reached that point in our relationship where we are comfortable together, even in silence. We don't need to fill it with meaningless chatter. She's not like my sister or my friends' wives. Sylvie lives as if she doesn't owe anyone in the world an explanation or an apology. She doesn't belong to anyone—not even me. At least not in that way.

Sylvie is fearlessly herself. And I love that about her.

Especially when I feel as if I'm constantly battling with everyone to let me be myself—my sister, my aunt, and even my dead parents had a vision for me in their heads of what I was meant to be. I have failed time and time again. I've never truly been what anyone wished for me to be. So it's easier just to be alone. In my house, I can't feel the disappointment.

"Your property goes all the way out here?" she asks when we see the river in the distance.

"Yes."

"I had no idea it was this big," she murmurs to herself.

"This runs right out to the sea," I reply, pointing to the river ahead of us. "It makes me feel more connected to the rest of the world," I add, unsure why I need to be so open with her. My hand grips around her waist. "I sometimes come out here just to stare at the current, watch as it leaves."

She's silent for a while before carefully speaking. "Why don't you leave? You could go too, you know?"

I swallow down the discomfort building in my throat. "Where would I go? I belong here."

"You could go wherever you want, Killian. You could leave your sister and this house behind and live your own life."

My hand tightens around her. "And where will you go?"

I hear her exhale softly. "I don't know, Killian."

"Come with me, and we can go anywhere." It's foolish of me to try, but I have to. I still don't understand, after everything we've been through, why this woman still wants to hold me so far away. As if *nothing* between us is real.

"It's not that easy," she whispers.

"Yes, it is. I'm your husband. I'll take you anywhere you want to go."

"For what? For how long? What happens when this year is up?" Her voice is growing frantic, and I've come to learn the sound of Sylvie getting caught up in her emotions. I'm doing exactly what I'm not supposed to be, spooking her with talk of the future and our feelings, but I can't take it anymore. She *has* to know how I feel about her—how I feel about *us*.

"I'll have our house for good, then," I say in a pleading tone. "My aunt will be off our backs, and we can do whatever we want."

She lets out a defeated sound as she places her face in her hands. "Killian."

My jaw clenches. Is this her way of letting me down? Am I really so wrong about these feelings that she truly doesn't feel them too?

"It's all in my head, then," I reply with a frustrated grunt. "You really do feel nothing for me."

Her head lifts, and I see a tremble in her lips. "I didn't say that."

"Then, what are you saying, mo ghràidh?"

"I don't know. Why are you asking me all of this right now? Why do I have to decide?"

I feel her body shivering against me just as the clouds start to drop a heavy mist on us. Guilt assaults me for being too hard on her, too desperate to know I'm not alone in this.

"It's okay, darling," I whisper with my lips against the side of her head. "Let's just go back home."

As we make our steady walk back to the house, the rain picks up from a light drizzle to a slow fall. When we reach the farm, I quickly put Moire back in the stall and shut the door. Sylvie is standing under the roof of the barn, watching the rain. Judging by the look on her face, she's deep in contemplation and downright worried. It makes me feel like shite for bringing the whole thing up in the first place.

She has only been here for eight months. That's fast for any relationship, especially a marriage. It's ridiculous of me to be pressuring her to be married to me beyond the contract we initially set out.

But as I approach her from behind to apologize, she quickly spins toward me and grabs my face in her hands. It takes me by surprise, so I pull back to stare into her eyes.

"Fuck the house, Killian. Fuck this stupid contract. Let's just blow it all off and go away together."

My eyes widen as I stare at her in shock. "What are you talking about?"

"You said you would take me anywhere I want to go, so let's give the house back to your aunt now and go somewhere!"

My hands cover hers as I gaze into her eyes skeptically. "Sylvie, I meant on a holiday. I'm not giving my house to my aunt."

Her face morphs into an expression of defeat as her lips close, and she stares up at me with sadness.

"Fine," she whispers. "Then…just kiss me."

I stare at her in confusion. "Are you all right?"

But she doesn't answer me. Instead, she tugs my mouth down to hers and bites my bottom lip between her teeth. Latching her arms around my neck, she kisses me as if she's trying to distract me...or herself.

Her body clings to mine, and I feel her legs spreading like she wants me to lift her so she can wrap them around me. But I have the sense I'm being misled, and I'm even more confused than I was before.

What is Sylvie not telling me?

Keeping my mouth against hers, she breathes between us. "I do want to go away with you, Killian," she whispers. "I just—"

The sound of tires on gravel down the driveway stops her words before they leave her mouth. We both turn to watch a car driving slowly toward the house. It's a black sedan, expensive and private, with dark tinted windows.

"Who the hell is that?" I mutter.

"I have no idea..." Sylvie responds wearily.

We each tug our rain jackets over our heads and walk hand in hand toward the house, but I feel the hesitation in my wife's touch. Even if she doesn't know who is at the house, I get the feeling she has a specific fear of who it might be.

By the time we reach the front door of the house, whoever it was has already been welcomed inside. Sylvie glances up at me nervously before I guide her toward the door.

"It'll be okay," I whisper comfortingly.

Then I pull open the front door just as Sylvie peeks around me and tears down the hood of her jacket.

Standing in the large entryway of my house is a couple I don't recognize. The woman is slender with a downturned mouth and long red hair, a few shades darker than Sylvie's. The man has dark curly hair and a receding hairline, leaving the top of his head bald.

Sylvie's hand squeezes mine as if she's suddenly afraid. I glance at her as she gapes in shock at the two people standing before us. I'm just about to scream at someone to tell me what's going on when she finally opens her mouth to speak.

"Mom...Dad...what are you guys doing here?"

Chapter Thirty-One

"SHE DOESN'T LOOK VERY EXCITED TO SEE US, TOR," THE MAN SAYS with a hint of sarcastic humor and a nasally voice. I stare daggers at the two people standing in my home, referring to my wife as if they were the sun, just waiting for her to orbit around them.

"Of course she is," the woman replies, giving Sylvie a smug, teasing expression. "She's just surprised."

"What are you guys doing here?" Sylvie repeats as if to herself.

The woman looks at the man and then back at us. "Well... you said you'd be in Scotland, so here we are." Then, her eyes trail upward to my face. "You must be the man our daughter ran off to marry."

"He exists," the man jokes as they both laugh together. Sylvie and I stay silent.

The woman looks around as if assessing my home. "Truly remarkable design," she says, pointing to the accents and fixtures.

The man quickly jumps in. "And this rug, Torrence. Did you see this rug?"

"It must be hand knotted," Sylvie's mother replies, staring down at the floor.

The two of them go on about the rug as my gaze slides over

to Sylvie. She's staring at them with an expression on her face I've never seen before. Lips parted, eyes moist, nostrils flaring. She's on the verge of tears while being frozen in place.

My heart splinters with rage, but I swallow it down. These are her parents. They might be a bit unconventional, but they are still her family, so I'll use every ounce of strength inside me to watch my tone and bite my tongue.

When I spot Martha reentering the foyer to help greet our guests, I decide it would be best to invite them in and at least try to act civilized.

I raise a hand to guide them toward the parlor. "Please, come in. Martha will make us some tea, and we…" I stammer, unpracticed in my manners. "We can get to know each other."

Sylvie's hand clasps onto my arm, her nails digging into the skin. When she turns toward me, I read the expression of hesitation on her face. *Please, no*, it says.

I pull her against me and press my lips to her forehead. "It'll be fine," I whisper.

Then I rest my hand on her back and lead her toward the parlor. Her parents fuss about the house some more, admiring the art on the walls and the architectural details around the windows. Things I've become so accustomed to over the years of my life that I hardly notice them anymore. Then again, I don't find the value in my home in its history or design. I find the value in its comfort and the fact that it's given me shelter and warmth for just over thirty-eight years.

"Well, we haven't been properly introduced," the man says as he strides toward me with a hand outstretched. There's something odd about him. He won't look me in the eye. He's much shorter than his wife, which must be where Sylvie gets her smaller size from. But although he's a small man, he carries himself much like a lapdog does, not as if he's the largest and most powerful thing in the room, but like he sits on the lap of the person who is.

"Yuri Deveraux," he says politely. I shake his hand, clenching my jaw together.

"Killian Barclay," I reply proudly.

The woman doesn't bother with introductions or handshakes. She pulls her glasses off and holds them in front of her as she studies a painting on the wall.

"Torrence, dear, come sit down," the man says as he takes a seat across from me. Sylvie has hardly uttered a word to her parents, but judging by the look on her face, she's fuming inside. She's sitting next to me like a powder keg with a very short fuse. Reaching over, I clutch her hand in mine, holding it tightly, hoping to calm her if necessary.

"Sylvie and I didn't know you two were in the country," I say calmly.

"Well, we haven't been to London in years, but we had some good friends holding an exhibit there, so we made the trip."

Sylvie's hand flinches in mine, so I squeeze tighter.

I think her father notices because his eyes dart down to our hands and up to his daughter's face. He doesn't keep his eyes on her for long, and I sense a flash of sympathy in his expression. He quickly clears his throat.

"So, how did you two meet?" he asks.

"Umm…" I stammer, glancing at her and searching for an answer.

"There was a typewriter," she mumbles lazily.

"A typewriter?" the man replies, perking up. "Sweetie, have you been writing?"

"Writing?" the woman squeaks from across the room. "What have you been writing?"

While the man sounded curious and interested, her mother's reaction is almost accusatory.

"It's nothing," Sylvie replies, pinching her forehead.

Suddenly, the story of how we met has been swept under the proverbial hand-spun rug because her parents are fully invested in the prospect of their daughter *writing*. I had no clue it was ever so significant.

"What do you mean it's nothing?" her mother replies, suddenly showing far more interest in her than the paintings. She walks over, but instead of sitting with the rest of us, she hovers over her daughter. "Have you been in contact with your professors? Perhaps they could give you a critique. What was the name of that professor at her school, Yuri? The one with the connection at the *New Yorker*?"

"Stop," Sylvie mutters, placing her face in her hands.

"She's just trying to help, sweetie," her father says to her, but it doesn't help.

Just then, Martha comes in with the tea, thankfully defusing the situation. Sylvie's mother finally sits in the seat across from her daughter, her nose poised in the air as Martha pours the tea.

"Thank you, Martha," my wife says with a smile. When the housekeeper leaves us, the conversation picks up right where it left off.

"Like your father said, Sylvie, I'm just trying to help. Getting a publisher's interest early is going to help you cut the competition down the line."

"I'm not publishing it," Sylvie replies obstinately. She stares down at her teacup as she stirs a cube of sugar into it.

"And why not?" Torrence replies with shock.

"Because I don't want to." Sylvie's tone is cutting and clipped.

The table clangs with the force of her mother slamming her own spoon down at hearing Sylvie's response. My shoulders tighten up by my ears as I struggle to maintain my composure.

"Dear," Yuri says, holding a hand toward his wife.

"No," the woman argues. "She's doing this on purpose," she snaps at her daughter.

I clench my fists, and keep my response slow and calm. "I can assure you my wife is not doing anything to hurt you."

"No, but she does it to spite me."

Sylvie glares at her mother, a dead-faced expression covering her features. "How is me living my life and being happy to spite you?"

"Because you won't let me help you. It's as if you don't want to be successful."

"Is that really so important to you?" Sylvie argues.

"It's important to everyone, Sylvie."

My jaw clenches again. I glance sideways at my wife, watching the spark grow closer and closer to the end of the fuse.

I wonder if it's for me that she holds it back. Is it for my sake that she refuses to really let these people know how she feels about them? The Sylvie I know doesn't hold back. She lets her fire burn without care for who is in the path of her flame. But now...she's keeping it all in. And I don't like it.

When the room grows silent, it's Yuri who attempts to carry on a casual conversation. "What have you been writing, sweetie?"

Sylvie smacks down her cup. "Can we just drop it? Forget I said anything about the writing."

The man barely reacts to her outburst. But I notice the way her mother watches her. I can see the criticism perched on her lips, ready to take flight, and I stare at that woman, willing her to keep her ugly mouth shut and to think twice about saying anything critical of my wife.

Naturally, she doesn't heed my warning.

"You always were so volatile," she mutters. "Here we are, at your home to meet your new husband that you haven't told us anything about or introduced us to before today, and you really can't manage to have a decent conversation with us, can you, Sylvie? We didn't raise you like this."

"You didn't raise me at all," Sylvie snaps.

"Don't be ridiculous. You'll never truly know how much your father and I sacrificed for you."

"Did you sacrifice birthdays? Christmases? Did your mother ask *you* to pose naked for strangers when you were sixteen?" she shrieks in frustration.

My head snaps up to level an angry gaze at the two of them.

"That was for an art class, Sylvie. Please, be reasonable," the mouse of a man whines.

Sylvie ignores him. "And you didn't come here to visit me and my husband. You were *in the area* and stopped by. The reason you don't know anything about him is because you don't call me. You don't ask. You don't...care. You show up and talk about the fucking *rug* when you haven't spoken to your daughter in almost a year."

Her voice trails, and I hear the quaver in it that shatters my chest into splinters on the ground. I'm seconds away from throwing these two pieces of worthless flesh out of my house.

I stare at Sylvie's father, mentally begging him to do something. To stand up for his fucking daughter, but he doesn't. He stays silent.

For one second too long.

Sylvie sniffles through the silence as her mother stares contemplatively at her. Then, the woman shakes her head as she softly mutters, "Ever since the day you tore your own portrait to shreds, I knew you'd never be happy unless you were the center of our universe. Poor little Sylvie, always so desperate for everyone's attention. What an entitled little bitch you've turned out to be."

The small round wooden table between us suddenly flies across the room, taking the tea tray, pot, and cups with it. There's a scream of fear and a few curse words to be heard as I launch out of my chair and point an angry finger at the two sitting across from me.

"Get the *fuck* out of my house!" I bellow so loudly the art on the walls trembles from the noise.

"What on earth is wrong with you?" the woman shrieks.

"You," I shout, reaching forward to take her by the collar and yank her out of her chair. "You...are *not* welcome in our home anymore." With that, I drag her toward the door.

Somewhere behind me I hear the man nervously stutter, "Get your ha—hands off my wife."

As we reach the front door, I nearly throw the woman toward the exit. She stares at me with horror before glancing at her daughter.

"This is the kind of man you've married? Someone who resorts to violence and outbursts?"

"Why should we leave our daughter with you?" the man argues as he takes his place at his wife's side.

"Because *I* love her, you fucking twats. And I would *never* talk to her the way the pair of you do. And for your information," I add, pulling open the front door to find a deluge coming down outside. I put my finger in Sylvie's mother's face this time as I lean in. "Your child is *supposed* to be the center of your universe, you ungrateful, selfish bitch."

I toss them both into the rain. They're both so appalled by my reactions that it grates on my nerves. Has no one ever defended Sylvie around these two in her entire life? What sort of damage could a pair of incompetent, emotionally neglectful parents like these do to a person?

They're both gaping in shock on the front step of my house. Before shutting the door, I turn and see the red and gold pattern on the floor. In a fit of anger, I pick up the square rug and roll it quickly in my hands before hauling it toward the frail, frightened people standing just a few feet away.

"Here! Take the fucking rug." It lands with a thud on the ground in front of them, getting soaked by the rain. Then I slam the front door closed and force myself to steady my heavy breathing.

I hear the closing of a car door outside before I dare to leave that spot. When I make out the sound of gravel under their tires, I finally leave the front door in search of Sylvie.

To my surprise, she's no longer in the parlor or in the entryway. I nearly panic when I hear her footsteps upstairs in the library.

"Sylvie!" I shout, desperate for her reaction. I need to hear that she's okay.

A moment later, she's stomping angrily down the stairs, tears streaming down her face while wearing an expression of stubborn rage. In her arms, she's hoisting the typewriter down toward the front door.

"What are you doing?" I stammer before she clumsily tears open the door and storms through it. I watch with confusion as she sends the typewriter soaring into the rain. "Sylvie, stop!"

I grab at her arm, but she shakes it free. Running out into the rain, she stomps her boot into the typewriter over and over, sending shards of broken wood and keys flying. At one point, I just stop trying to save it. If this is what she needs, then I'll let her have it.

Finally, I walk over and take hold of her arm again. "Mo ghràidh," I whisper.

To my surprise, my wife turns toward me in anger. "Leave me alone, Killian! You lied! You don't love me! You're not my husband. None of this is real!"

I grab her by the arms to stop her. "What are you talking about? Of course, I love you."

She struggles to shake free of my grip. "You do *now*, but the novelty will wear off. You'll get sick of me, or I'll ask too much, and then you'll get angry at me. Didn't you see the way they looked at me, Killian? How could you love someone who isn't loved by her own parents?"

My mind is reeling as I stare at her in this state. This isn't the Sylvie I know. Her eyes are wild and frantic and *scared*. I just want my wife back.

When she finally slips out of my grip from the rain on our skin, I watch in horror as she takes off in a sprint toward the trees lining the property and quickly disappears.

Chapter Thirty-Two

THE RAIN PELTS MY SKIN AS I TAKE OFF IN A SPRINT DOWN THE grassy field toward the trees. The sound of the rain muffles her footsteps, but I still see movement up ahead. With the sun setting now, the sky is growing dark, and I'm losing sight of my wife. But I won't panic. She can't go far before she'll hit the road or the river.

"Sylvie, please," I beg only a few feet behind her. "You're soaked, darling."

"Leave me alone, Killian," she shouts back as she continues marching away from our home.

"Where are you going?" I call.

"It doesn't matter."

"Yes, it does. Sylvie, please. Fuck them!"

When she doesn't respond, I pick up my speed. Only a few feet away from her, I'm finally able to get ahold of her. With a rough hand around her arm, I stop her from running any further away. Instead, I pin her against a tree, and I put my face in hers.

"Stop running from me, damn it!"

"Leave me alone, Killian!" she fights back.

"No!" I bellow close to her. "I'm your husband. I won't let you go. I will *always* be by your side. I will *always* care about you, you understand?"

Tears fall against her cheeks, blending with the drops of rain that continue to pour down on us. "You're not really—"

I quickly cut her off. "Don't you say that to me again, Sylvie Barclay. I don't care about some stupid fucking contract. I love you. With my whole fucking chest, I love you. So don't give me any of that shite about not being your real husband, because I'm right here. And I'll never fucking leave you, not like they did."

She collapses against the tree, hanging her head back as she sobs. "It hurts so much, Killian. I feel it all. I wish I could reach into my chest and tear out my heart. Sometimes, it feels like I might die of this pain, this…loneliness. I've been surrounded by people my whole life, but I always feel alone."

"You're not alone, Sylvie. Not anymore."

She sobs again. "I'm so angry all the time, Killian. And no matter what I do, no one cares."

"I care."

"I just want to scream," she cries.

"Then, scream, Sylvie. You can scream all you want at me, and I still won't leave you."

When nothing comes out, I shake her again. "So, no one else loves you. Big deal. But I'm here, mo ghràidh. And I am telling you that I will love you enough to make up for all of them. I will keep you, and you can trust me that no matter what you do, I won't let you go. Because you're *mine*, understand me?"

When her eyes finally meet mine, tear-soaked and red-rimmed, she surrenders. Throwing her arms around me, she latches herself onto my body, and I yank her off the ground, holding her against me as she cries.

For a while, she just rests in my arms, not caring that we're getting soaked by the rain. I just let her cry.

Eventually, she mumbles into my neck. "Killian…"

"Yes, darling."

"Let's go home."

With that, I lift her into my arms, cradled against my chest, and I carry her home.

Sylvie is shivering in my arms as we reach the house. Martha has the door open, waiting for us with a large towel. Sylvie doesn't have so much as a rain jacket on. Every inch of her is soaked to the bone, as am I, but I don't feel the chill. I just feel her trembling.

"I'll run a bath," Martha says as we enter the house.

"Thank you, Martha."

"Poor thing," she mumbles, brushing my wife's wet curls from her face. I'm not sure if she's referring to her wet and cold state or what she witnessed today in how her parents treated her.

Muddy boots and all, I rush upstairs with Sylvie in my arms. I don't care about a single rug or piece of furniture we're ruining as I carry her to our room and take her straight to the bathroom.

Martha is quick with the bath, setting out the towels and putting granules of something into the water that smells soothing. Then she scurries out, leaving me alone with my shivering wife.

I set Sylvie on the counter. Her lips are blue, and her eyes are rimmed red. Every muscle in her body is quivering, so I make quick work of removing her layers. Sweater, T-shirt, bra, trousers, underwear. The cold touch of her skin chills me to the bone, so I carry her to the bath in a rush, setting her in carefully.

Even when she's folded up and sitting in the hot water, she's still trembling. "Come in with me," she says through chattering teeth.

There's not an ounce of hesitation in my body as I tear off my clothes before stepping into the bathtub and facing my wife.

She climbs onto my lap, straddling my hips as she forms her body to me, her face in my neck.

"I've got you," I whisper into her hair.

Warm tears hit my shoulder, and I know she's crying again. "It's okay, Sylvie. Just cry, darling. I've got you."

It feels as if an hour goes by like that, with her tears streaming down my chest and shoulders. When all of her tears have dried up, we relax together in the bath. She's lying flat on top of me as I recline in the water. I finally feel warmed up, and her fingers are no longer like icicles, so she must be warmed up too.

When I can tell she is more stable, I feel comfortable to talk to her.

"What did she mean?" I whisper. "When your mother said you ripped up your portrait."

Sylvie lets out a heavy breath. "On my eighteenth birthday, they made a portrait of me. It was supposed to be a gift for me, and it won all of these awards, so they had this big party at one of the galleries to present it. The painting was even called *Our Greatest Achievement*."

"You didn't like it?" I ask.

Sylvie doesn't lift her face from my chest as she replies, "It was beautiful, but that fucking painting got a party, and I didn't. The day that was meant to celebrate me still somehow became about them, and I realized as I was sitting in the back of that room that I was just another creation of theirs. An imperfect creation. A mistake. I didn't win awards or get put on pedestals or celebrated. I was no one's masterpiece.

"So, that night, after everyone had left, I snuck back into my parents' studio, and I tore that painting to shreds. And they cried about it for days. My mother didn't speak to me for nearly a year. The thing that I had ruined was nothing more than some paint and some fabric and a rainbow of colors, but it would never be *me*. I think deep down, I just had to show them that. But they didn't get it."

I stroke her back, remembering that angry and lonely woman I found almost a year ago. I had no clue the pain she was hiding inside, just as she had no idea of mine. Our own torment blinds us from seeing the torment of others.

But now that I truly see my wife, I think I love her even more.

"You are a masterpiece, Sylvie," I whisper against her hair.

"I'm a mess."

"We're all a mess, but the trick is to find someone who thinks your mess is a masterpiece. Your parents might be blind fucking eejits, but I'm not. I know a masterpiece when I see it."

For the first time since before those monsters showed up today, I see my wife smile.

After a moment, she softly whispers, "I love you."

My heart starts to pound, and I have to force myself to breathe, but I try not to let it show. Instead, I stroke her back and let those three words wash over me.

"I love you too, Sylvie."

She squeezes her tiny body tighter against me, burrowing her face in the crook of my neck. I feel the warmth of her breath against my skin. I'll wait for the day when she can say those words to me while looking in my eyes. I can wait. For today, this is enough.

"I tried really hard not to," she murmurs, making me laugh. When she finally lifts up and looks at me, it feels like fire burning through my chest. "But you made it so hard."

"I'm sorry," I lie. Then she grabs my face and presses her lips to mine. Her soft tongue presses into my mouth, and I slide mine along the surface, feeling as if we are melting into one.

With each stroke of her tongue, my chest grows tighter, and my hands roam more around her body. My cock twitches between us as she starts grinding herself against me.

Suddenly, all I can think about are those three words being spoken between us and everything they represent.

"Killian," she murmurs against my mouth.

"Yes, mo ghràidh."

Pulling away, she holds my face as she stares into my eyes. "I'm ready."

Those two words escape her lips in a soft, breathy whisper, but the power they carry is far stronger than the way she uttered them.

"Ready for what?" I reply, although part of me already knows. "Make me yours."

My cock aches at the realization of what she's asking. "Tell me exactly what you want," I add for clarity.

Her eyes moisten with intensity as she clings tighter to me. "Make it hurt. I trust you. I just need you to distract me from this pain. Help me let all of it out, Killian."

There's an ache in my chest to see her say those words to me. I don't want to hurt my wife, but God, I know it will be beautiful to see the way she takes that pain. My fierce, strong, incredible wife.

"Come with me," I say.

Clumsily, we climb out together, barely breaking contact and not bothering with the towels. As I hoist her naked body in my arms, she wraps her legs around my waist, and I carry her to our room.

Draping her on the bed, I take more care with her than I usually do. I want to be a good husband for her and show her how gentle I can be while giving her exactly what she wants. That I will always keep her safe and protected.

"Do you trust me, mo ghràidh?"

Emphatically, she nods.

"Use your words, wife."

"Yes," she answers without hesitation.

Kneeling down, I trail my lips along the inside of her legs, kissing from her ankles to her knees and all the way to the apex of her thighs. She squirms restlessly, but I don't let myself get carried away.

Sitting upright, I let my fingers graze the skin of her knee. "Your safe word will be *red*, understand? If you want me to stop at any point, just say *red*, and I'll stop."

Breathing heavily, she nods. "I understand."

"That's my girl." Her expressions softens at the praise. "Now, get on your knees."

I can tell a part of Sylvie struggles with taking a command. It's not what she's used to. She's gone too long fighting alone in her life that she's never built up enough trust to allow anyone control over her, but this relief is what she needs.

To let someone else make her decisions. To let someone else carry her pain.

And I will be that for her. I will never let my wife feel alone ever again.

Obediently, she climbs from a lying position and kneels in front of me. Although I'm kneeling as well, I still tower over her, so when she gazes up at me, I pet her hair back from her face and plant a kiss on her forehead.

"Hands on the bedpost."

I watch her throat work as she swallows. Then she turns toward the head of the bed and places her hands on the wood. Climbing from the bed, I go to the bottom drawer of my dresser. There, I find the smooth paddle with a soft leather handle.

I catch her watching me as I pull it from the drawer.

"We're going to go easy tonight, Sylvie. You've been through a lot today, but you asked me to make it hurt, and I will."

I watch as goose bumps erupt along her back. She shivers in anticipation as I climb onto the bed behind her, stroking a hand softly along her bare back.

"I'm not going to strap you to the bed. But you won't let go of that headboard, understand me?"

"Yes," she murmurs.

"Grip it nice and tight, my love."

She shivers again.

Before I rear back the paddle and let it fly, I slide my hand over her ass. "Let me hear you say it one more time, Sylvie. Tell me you trust me."

Turning her attention back to me, she looks into my eyes as she says, "I trust you."

"Good. Now let me hear you scream."

The paddle lands with a deafening smack against her tender

white flesh. She lets out a gasp, flying forward from the force of the hit. I watch as the blood rushes to the spot where the paddle landed, turning her right ass cheek a lovely shade of pink.

"One," I say before rubbing the spot.

Rearing back my hand, I let it fly again. This time, she lets out a yelp. Her knuckles have turned white where they're gripping the headboard.

"Two."

On the third hit, Sylvie cries out louder, and squeezes her face in anguish.

She's so strong. She won't even let me see her pain. Eventually she will.

Her expression doesn't change much through the fourth or fifth hit, but by the sixth, her sounds grow louder.

"Come on, baby. Let it out."

It feels as if I'm coaxing a wild animal from their nest. If she trusts me like she says she does, then she wouldn't be so afraid to let me hear her cry. But it's not really about me. It's about Sylvie protecting herself from others. Always keeping the most vulnerable parts of herself guarded.

The pride I feel when she lets out a wailing cry on the sixth smack of the paddle is visceral.

"That's my girl. Let it go, darling."

Her scream on the seventh brings tears to my eyes. It's not just that Sylvie is finally letting it all go; it's that she's letting *me* see it. Out of everyone in the world, I'm the one she lets in.

Her trembles turn into quakes as she pulls at the headboard through her agony.

"Say the word and I'll stop," I offer when she has to gasp through her sobs. Tears streak down her face, and I'm ready to hold her now. I want to bury myself inside her so that I become a part of her forever.

"No!" she wails. "Don't stop. I can take it."

On each following wallop, Sylvie sheds far more than I

thought she could. It's as if I'm watching her come undone, letting herself *feel* and *express* far more than just pain. She's crying for the fear and loneliness and anger.

I hate that she's hurting, but seeing her work through this pain is the most beautiful thing I have ever seen.

"Two more, mo ghràidh," I say, rubbing at her backside. "You're almost there."

My cock is aching as it leaks from the tip, crying for how badly it needs her like this. Her howls and moans are making me feral, and I don't know how much longer I can wait.

Sylvie's cries turn sexy and carnal through the last two hits, and I wonder if she can feel this energy too. This is what I love about domination, feeling so close to someone that everything is aligned. Our needs. Our desires. It has always been my favorite part, but it was never like this.

Everything is different with her.

After the last smack of the paddle, I toss it on the bed and move behind Sylvie, dropping to my elbows so I can devour her from behind. Her voice turns high-pitched as I kiss and lick every inch of her.

I want her to know I cherish every inch. Every single part of her is mine to love and worship and devour. So I do. She lies on the bed in ecstasy as I kiss and lick every drop of water on her bare skin.

As I move to my knees again, nibbling and kissing my way up, I rest my aching cock on her backside. Then I pull her upright so she's resting against my chest. Gripping her chin, I turn her face toward me so I can stare into her eyes.

"I'm so proud of you," I say, pressing my lips to her jaw. "You did so well."

Her face is still tear-soaked as she smiles, absorbing the praise.

"But I need to fuck you now. I need to be inside you."

"Yes, please," she whines.

I take her mouth in a bruising kiss before I bury my hand in her hair and press her forward so she's gripping the headboard again. Aligning my aching cock with her wet core, I tug on her hips and impale her on my cock.

When she lets out a breathless cry, I moan loudly along with her. Her ass presses backward as I fuck her, finding the spot inside her that makes her scream with every thrust.

"That's it," I grunt. "Show me how good that feels."

"Yes," she replies with a whimper. "Don't stop, Killian."

"Tell me you love me again, mo ghràidh."

"I love you," she says, her stunning soft curls draped across her back as she hangs her head in ecstasy.

"Say it again," I grunt, fucking her with more force, still careful not to hurt her.

"I love you," she screams this time.

Unable to keep it in any longer, I tear Sylvie away from the headboard and roll her onto her back so I can pound her into the mattress with my thrusts. Hooking a leg under my arm, I stay right on that spot she loves, watching her expression for a sign that she's close.

"Come for me, darling," I mutter, fighting the urge to lose it myself. "Come for your husband."

"I'm almost...there," she shrieks, her voice tight and high-pitched.

Reaching between us, I press my thumb to her clit and help her ride out her climax when it hits. Her hips jerk, and her grip tightens, so I keep up my thrusts. She goes breathless, but I don't let her stop.

"One more time, Sylvie. Say it."

"I love you," she breathes, this time gazing into my eyes. It's as if she's yanking me over the edge with her, making me feel the same earth-shattering pressure she was feeling. My cock shudders and shoots inside her, filling her up more than I expected in what feels like a never-ending orgasm.

We rock together, riding out the rest of it in sync. When my body is spent, and my heart has stopped hammering, I slowly rise and look down at her. Brushing her hair out of her face, I kiss her softly again. Our kisses are unhurried now and familiar. As normal as breathing.

"Aren't you going to say it?" she whispers.

"I don't need to say it, mo ghràidh. You should just know."

"Well, I want to hear it anyway," she argues with a twist of her nose.

Caging in her face with my arms around her on the bed, I press my lips to hers as I whisper, "I love you, you stubborn little woman."

She smiles softly up at me as she runs her fingers through my hair.

"How are you feeling now?" I ask in a gentle tone.

"I feel good. And tired."

She looks exhausted, but after the night she's had, I'm not surprised. "I want you to drink some water before you fall asleep, understand?"

Naturally, she rolls her eyes. "Are you going to be bossy now?"

"When it comes to taking care of you, you bet your arse I am."

Tears glisten in her eyes, and neither of us say anything for a moment. "Thank you, Killian."

"I'm your husband. You don't have to thank me."

Very carefully, I rise from between her legs. Resting on my heels, I watch as my seed slowly leaks from its home, so with a smile and a wink in her direction, I very gently push it back in.

PART FIVE

Sylvie

Chapter Thirty-Three

"Killian," I shout down the long hallway. "Are you ready yet?"

"I'm comin', woman. Would you calm down?" he replies huskily as he stomps down the stairs.

"The car's ready," I say, urging him as I give him an impatient expression.

I know I shouldn't rush him. This is a big deal for him, but the thing with Killian is that if he doesn't make it a big deal, then I can't make it a big deal. So, I have to act as if this little trip to the coast is nothing out of the ordinary and a simple road trip.

It's anything but.

I know that. He knows that.

It took me weeks to talk him into this plan, and while I've been slowly easing him out of the house here and there, I know he's ready for a weekend away from the manor. It's the middle of summer now. The weather is beautiful, and I desperately need some coastline sunshine in my life.

I'm trying not to think about how there are only two more months until the end of this contract. And since I can no longer deny that my feelings for my husband are real, I have to face the truth. He's going to lose this house.

Regardless of what happens to us when that happens, I have to protect him. Which means I need to make sure he's ready and able to leave it. I'll figure the *us* part out later.

For now, I need to get this man out of this house. And I'm running out of time to do it.

As he takes my hand in the entryway, I watch the way he swallows and hides his nerves from me.

"Ready?" I ask softly.

His eyes meet mine as he winks. "Ready."

Hand in hand, we walk out to the car parked by the front door. The house staff helps us off, and Killian drives. But I watch his face as we leave the property line, and I watch it again as we leave the county line.

He seems at ease, far more than I expected. His hands are a little tight around the steering wheel, and the muscles of his jaw keep clicking, but overall, he seems fine. There's a lazy smile on his face, his eyes hidden by his sunglasses as we travel down the long busy highways. I look over the passenger seat at my fake husband in those dark jeans and tight white T-shirt and realize just how used to him I've become.

If he truly opened himself up to it, he could get used to a regular life outside that house with me. We could go anywhere we want. Any city. Any country. That dream I had of taking my ten million and running off someplace where I owe nothing to no one could be a dream with Killian. That could be *our* dream.

I just need to make him understand he has so much more life outside of those walls. He reaches across the seat and puts an arm over my shoulder. Leaning toward him, I rest on the center console and place a kiss on his left cheek.

"Next time, I'll take you to a warmer beach. You can't go swimming in these waters. You'll freeze your cute little nipples off," he says as he reaches across and pinches the tip of my breast.

I let out a shriek as I jump backward. "I don't care about that. I'm just excited to get out of the house for a while."

His fingers squeeze tighter around the steering wheel, but I brush it off as nothing.

It's only a short drive to the house we've rented for the next two nights. It's a bed and breakfast that typically rents out at least six rooms, but Killian's reserved them all for a bit of privacy. As we pull up to the old house, I smile at the quaint and stunning sight of it on this desolate coastline.

I jump out of the car and walk immediately toward the endless dark sand glistening in the sun. The wind is strong, blowing my hair wildly in the breeze, but as I stand just on the edge where the dunes meet the drive, I breathe in the fresh air.

It smells like freedom.

"I'll get us checked in. Don't go far," he whispers, kissing me softly on the cheek.

"Okay," I reply, watching him go up the three short steps to the front door of the house.

It's been two months since we first spoke those harrowing words. The ones I tried so hard to deny and ignore. That day with my parents still replays in my mind over and over. It wasn't just that he protected me or defended me. It was the fact that Killian carved out a space for me where there hadn't been one before. Until him, I didn't know what that felt like—to be a priority in someone's life.

That night changed me in ways I don't think he fully understands. It was about so much more than the submission or the paddle. It was the way he let me be me, without expectation or criticism. He took the ugliest parts of me and loved them right along with the beautiful ones. He let me scream and cry and held me afterward like I was the most important person in his life.

I *am* the most important person in his life.

And meanwhile I've been denying how much I cared for him. Why? Because of some stupid contract? Or ten million dollars?

Yes, the past two months have been heavy with anxiety thinking about that looming deadline. And yes, I know I will have to come clean with him eventually about my part in the whole thing. But I have a plan, and that plan involves getting my husband *out of that house.*

If I can do that, I can save everything. Him, us, our future.

He just has to learn to let it go.

"All checked in," he says, landing a strike on my ass and making me jump. Then he slings an arm over my shoulder. Seeing him in such a chipper, relaxed mood settles me too.

So, with a smile, I turn toward him. "Hungry?"

"Fuckin' starvin," he grumbles, rubbing his stomach.

We take a walk together just down the road from the house toward the center of town, where the owners promised us one of the best pubs in Scotland. We sit across from each other at an old table near the window, and each order two ales and two orders of stovies and talk like regular people.

For the first time in our long and twisted relationship, we are just two regular people. A couple of newlyweds on a honeymoon. He even reaches across the table and twirls my wedding band around my finger while he finishes his beer. It's a bit of a nervous habit for him, and I've caught him doing it before with his own ring.

I don't think he's acting *too* much more nervous than regular. He's always a little fidgety.

"What do you want to do now?" I ask.

"Go back to that big ol' house and shag like animals," he suggests while holding his beer to his lips.

"Before that," I reply with a lazy, half-drunk smile.

"Go walk on the beach, I suppose."

"Okay," I say, nodding as I grab his fingers.

The wind has died down a bit as we take a stroll along the water. It's surprisingly blue and clear, but as he promised, it's ice cold. Still, it's beautiful to be out.

"Didn't you ever go on vacation with your family as a kid?" I ask as we walk.

He shrugs. "Of course. We spent summers in Greece and Italy when I was a kid."

"Didn't you like it?" I ask.

"Not as much as being home," he replies, and I chew on the inside of my lip, uneasy with that answer.

I've never pried much into what happened to Killian's parents or why it seemed to have hit him so hard. I don't want to open up old wounds for him, but I can't help but feel as if that wound didn't heal properly. How do you fix what's broken without breaking it further?

Instead, I squeeze his hand and offer him a hint of a smile. His hair has grown out again. Not as long as it was at Christmas, but past his ears again. It's time for another cut, but I also enjoy the many variations of Killian.

In truth, I did fall recklessly in love with him. The hate I once felt never went away—it just changed. The passion is a different color now.

But loving someone is terrifying, and this feeling is nothing like it was with Aaron. If I let Killian get hurt, I'll never forgive myself. As hard as I'm trying to make things right, I feel this looming darkness up ahead reminding me that my bottom line is his best interest, and that's never happened to me before. I've only ever looked out for myself, but now, I have him.

But having him and keeping him safe aren't necessarily the same thing.

"For a woman at the beach with her incredibly handsome husband, you look awfully depressed."

He knocks on my shoulder, and I force a smile.

"I'd be less depressed if you jumped in that water," I tease back.

"With you?" he replies, grinning mischievously.

I yank my hand away. "Oh, absolutely not with me."

"We're married, darling. We do everything together. Come here. Let's go swimming."

I take off in a sprint away from him with a shriek, but I don't make it far before he scoops me up from around my waist. I'm screaming and laughing as he carries me toward the rising tide.

"Killian, stop it!" I shout hysterically.

But I know my husband better than I know anyone, and this man doesn't back down from a challenge. I've brought this one on myself.

The next thing I know, the waves are rushing toward us, soaking us from our knees down in frigid water. But he doesn't stop. He keeps on marching.

I'm caught in a fit of laughter as I cling to his body to climb out of the water. Due to his height, he's getting far wetter than I am.

"You brute!" I scream as another wave crashes into us, soaking us to the bone.

"Just think how fun it will be to get warmed up after this!" he replies with a laugh. His smile is wide and warm and genuine, and it doesn't even matter how cold the water is or how uncomfortable these wet shoes are now. That smile is worth everything.

Chapter Thirty-Four

KILLIAN IS STILL SPRAWLED OUT NAKED ON THE BED WHEN I COME out of the shower.

"Ready for round two?" he remarks with a wink.

Keeping my towel around my waist, I climb onto the high bed and curl up beside him. "You'll be the death of me."

"I don't have to be rough this time," he says, gently petting my hip. Then he starts to crawl down my body, shimmying between my legs. "I can be very, very gentle."

With a smile, I run my fingers through his hair. But instead of going where I thought this would lead, he pauses and rests his chin on my lower belly. "Do you want kids someday?"

My eyes nearly pop out of my head. "Kids?"

He chuckles, making his chin bounce on my groin. "I keep forgetting how much younger you are."

"Young or not, it's a little early to start talking about kids. We're still *fake* married, remember?"

He growls at me for saying that, but at this point, I just say it to piss him off.

"We're *legally* married. And I'm not saying we should have them right *now*," he argues. "I'm just asking if you want them."

"Do you?" I run my nails through his hair again, softly scratching his scalp.

He shrugs. "I picture your belly growing big with my child, and it just does something to me. I never thought like that before."

I can't help the way that makes me feel too. My stomach actually warms as if it can feel it too. My own little piece of Killian growing inside. Creating someone that is truly *ours*. Forming our own family that makes up for all of the shit our own have done to us. We would be so much better than them.

"Is that smile a yes?" he asks, looking so hopeful it crushes me.

How could I take anything away from him, especially something that is so perfect and wonderful?

"Yeah...someday," I reply.

"I can already imagine them scampering around the manor, playing out in the garden, and going with us for rides around the grounds."

And just like that, the good feeling spoils and dies. He still thinks he gets to keep the house after our year.

"Or..." I say, testing the subject. "We could buy our own new house somewhere different. Someplace that's all ours."

His head slants. "The house is ours," he argues. "It will be ours and then our children's. I want it to be their home the same way it was mine. Do you not like it at Barclay?"

I swallow the rising dread. "Of course I do," I reply quickly to cover up the gaping wound this conversation is creating.

"Good, then we'll need to make lots of babies to fill it," he replies, peeling apart my towel to place a kiss just below my belly button. I let out a squeal as I wrap my legs around him.

"I didn't say anything about *lots*," I whine, but he's already trailing kisses down to my clit, quieting my mind and replacing my thoughts of worry with the sensation of pleasure.

―――――――――

I wake in the middle of the night to the sound of groans. On the other side of the bed, Killian sounds as if he's having a nightmare. This is the first time it's happened, so I carefully turn toward him and rest a hand on his shoulder, hoping to ease him out of the dream.

His skin is soaked with sweat and covered in goose bumps, so I cover him with the blanket, hoping that will help.

Within a few minutes, the groaning stops, and he falls back to sleep.

So I wrap my small arms around his waist and try to hold him tight enough to keep it from happening again. It takes me a bit longer to nod back off. Worry follows me into my dreams.

When I wake up again, it's still dark. But the other side of the bed is empty.

I sit up in a panic, looking through the darkness of the unfamiliar room for him. Then I hear thrashing downstairs.

In a rush, I dive out of the bed and snatch a robe off the hook, wrapping it around me as I scurry down the stairs. "Killian?" I call for him.

When I reach the main floor of the house, I hear heavy breathing from the dining room, and I burst through the doors to find the chairs all tipped over and a bottle of whisky resting unopened on the carpet.

It takes my eyes a moment to adjust before I spot Killian sitting on the floor with his back to the wall, much like that first night ten months ago.

Please, don't let there be any blood this time.

I rush to his side, placing my hands on his shoulders to find him clammy and cold. His head is in his hands, and he's breathing like he can't take in enough air.

He's having a panic attack.

My voice shakes with fear as I call his name. "Killian, breathe. It's okay. I'm right here."

"I can't," he gasps. "I can't do this."

"It's okay," I repeat. Again and again, I stroke his back and tell him it's okay, and I don't know if it's enough.

"I can't, Sylv—I can't...do this," he stutters. Struggling with his words, he suddenly snaps, shoving the table hard until it flips on its side. His arms are shaking so bad as he buries his face in his hands again and wheezes through his tears.

"It's okay," I whisper, afraid to upset him again. This fear is paralyzing. What am I going to do if I can't get him to calm down?

"I'm going to call an ambulance," I cry, about to run for my phone.

He nearly screams. "No! No...no, no, no." His head shakes emphatically, and I kneel closer to his side.

"Okay," I say, trying to calm his fears. "I just need you to be okay, Killian, so please breathe."

"I'm trying," he replies, but this time, his voice cracks into a sob, and he starts to really lose it.

In my head, I just know that if Killian loses it, then I'm lost. He holds us together. He's our strength, our force, the thing that keeps us together. Without him, I have nothing.

I hold his face in my hands, tears spilling over my lashes as I press my forehead to his. "We can do this," I cry. "I just need you to breathe."

He tries to suck in air, but his breaths are too shallow and don't pull in anything. It's all just short gasps and choppy inhalations.

"Hold on to me, Killian. Please hold on to me. I've got you, okay? Just breathe."

His grip is weak and trembling as he attempts to hold tight to my arm. And for the next thirty minutes, we struggle for each breath. Each inhale is a chore, and I keep second-guessing myself, afraid that I've royally fucked up by not calling an ambulance, but he refused even to let me leave his side.

The only thing I have to offer is my comfort, and it's not enough. He struggles in pain, and it tears me apart to watch.

By the time I see the sunrise start to bleed into the sky out the window, he is finally through it.

He's practically deadweight, collapsed on top of me as if he doesn't have the energy even to raise a hand to my face.

"Let's get back to bed," I whisper when I feel certain the worst of it is past us.

He nods with exhaustion and lets me pull him off the floor. We stumble together up the stairs, and when we reach the room, I wipe his face clean with a warm rag and kiss his eyes as he finally drifts off to sleep.

But I don't go to sleep. I sit next to him and replay over and over and over what a terrible wife and person I am. I've dragged him out here before he was ready just because I wanted to believe he could do it. I wanted to believe that he was capable of something, and for that, I could have seriously hurt him.

I *did* hurt him.

I can't stop crying as I rest my face on my knees and stare at him, realizing just how much I love him. The thought of putting him through that again guts me to my core. Right now, the only thing I want to do is take him home and curl up with him in *our* bed.

But I know deep down what this means.

First, it means that Killian needs help far beyond a weekend away and a wife who can love the pain out of him.

Second, it means that my dream of creating a life with Killian, safe from that awful contract, no longer exists.

I cannot and will not take that house from him. Not until he's healed and ready to do that himself.

While Killian sleeps, I hatch my plan. And I worry about him, about us, and about me if this somehow doesn't work. Because now that I've come here and flipped my whole life around, I no longer care to know what my life could be like without him. I don't want that.

I want him. I want this life that I borrowed.

After picking up the mess in the dining room, I come back upstairs to find Killian lying in bed with his eyes open. I stop in the doorway and stare at him, waiting to see how he's feeling.

"I want to go home," he mutters lowly without looking at me.

"Of course," I reply, my lip quivering as I try to hide the fact that I'm barely holding it together.

Carefully, I cross the room and climb into the bed to face him. When my head hits the pillow, his eyes meet mine. The restraint I was carrying until this moment is gone.

My face crumples, and my tears fall. "I'm so sorry," I sob.

He reaches for me, dragging me against his body as he tries to quiet my cries. "Stop, Sylvie. You don't need to apologize. I just wasn't ready."

"I knew you weren't ready," I cry. "I knew it, and I tried to push you anyway. I thought you could handle it."

"Shhh…" he whispers with his lips in my hair. "You had no idea, mo ghràidh."

"Have you ever had that before?" I whisper, carefully wiping my tears as I pull away to stare into his eyes.

I see the movement of his Adam's apple as he swallows the heavy weight of emotion in his throat. "After my parents died, yes."

"I'm sorry," I whisper again.

He touches my cheek, but his face doesn't have the same animation it had yesterday. It's dull and tired, and I cry again at the memory of his smile on the beach.

"It's okay."

It's not okay, I think to myself. None of this is okay. Nothing his family is doing or what I've done is okay, but he's toughing it out. He's surviving the only way he knows how.

I just wish I could help him more, but I can't if I don't understand.

So very gently, I brush back the hair in his face. "What happened…to bring them on?"

He looks uncomfortable as he swallows again. "My parents were always really hard on me. My father was a very strict man, and he had so many expectations for me and the kind of man I was supposed to be. I always did as I was told, and I always made him proud."

"That sounds like a lot of pressure," I whisper, touching his hand.

He nods. "On the night of the car wreck, I was leaving the house to pick up Anna from my aunt's house. My parents had been out at a party. It was dark, and the roads were slick. I remember seeing their headlights and briefly wondering if that was them. They swerved toward me so fast there was nothing I could do. We collided, and they both died on impact."

I let out a gasp, gripping his arm tighter as tears pour over my lashes. "Oh my *God*, Killian."

"I found them. I didn't have a phone on me. I had to wait with them, with a concussion, until a car drove down that long empty road and found us."

I squeeze my eyes closed and let the sobs rack through me.

"That wasn't your fault. You have to know that," I reply through my cries. "Please, Killian. Tell me you know that."

His eyes are wet with dark circles around them. He looks so tired and in pain. But he does eventually nod. "I know it's not. It was an accident. My father had a lot of alcohol in his system, and the swerve marks were still on the road, but it didn't stop my family from treating me differently. As if I could have saved them. As if I wouldn't have given my own life just to see that night end any other way."

I squeeze him tighter. "Don't say that. They died, and that was terrible, but it wasn't your fault, Killian. And you didn't deserve to live your entire life with that sort of pain."

Then, his eyes focus on my face for a moment. "I thought for a while I was really getting over it. I thought I could finally move on. Having you has helped, Sylvie."

"We can get you even more help," I reply, nestling closer. "Whatever you need, we can do this together."

With one more brave swallow and nod of his head, he pulls me into his arms.

For a while, I convince myself this could work.

Deep down, I know that nothing else matters. Not really. Not the contract or the money or even the house. Eventually, everything around us will cease to exist, and while I've spent my entire life numbing the pain of being agonizingly unloved, as I hold Killian in my arms now, I realize something more profound.

The world outside this room is cosmic and too massive to comprehend.

But the world that exists between him and me is more so. The love we share is infinite.

Chapter Thirty-Five

I've never been to Anna's home before, but today I'm not going for a tour and a chat. I'm not even coming to bargain. I bang on the front door of her quaint house near town. Her heels click against the floor before she opens it and stares at me in shock on her doorstep.

I'm sure she's surprised to see me because I'm coming uninvited, but also because Killian and I are still supposed to be on our trip by the sea.

"Sylvie," she stammers. "Is Killian all right?"

I push past her, barging into her home and marching right into the sitting room at the back of the house. Much like her first visit to my apartment, I come with some astounding news for her.

"Call it off," I bark as I slam my bag down on the table.

"Call what off?" she asks, scurrying in behind me.

"The contract, Anna. That stupid fucking contract." My blood is already boiling, and I know the further we get into the conversation, the hotter I'll get.

"I don't understand…"

I slam my hand down again. "You are *killing* him!"

She puts up her hands in surrender, and I can tell by the look of fear on her face that if I fly off the handle again, I'll never get my point across. Now is not the time to be angry. Now is the time to be clear.

Taking a deep breath, I close my eyes and refocus. "Anna, you cannot take that house away from Killian. You think you're helping him, but you're not. His issues run deep, and forcing him out of that house could kill him."

"Did something happen?" There's a tremble in her voice and fear in her eyes.

"Yes, something happened. He had a fucking panic attack on the floor of that B and B in the middle of the night. It looked like he tried to drink the anxiety away but didn't make it in time. Anna, he's *not well*. And that fucking aunt of yours…"

I clench my hands into fists and try to ease my temper again. "I know what happened to your parents, Anna, and I think that awful woman is trying to punish Killian for it. And I refuse to let her get that house from him. I *refuse*."

Anna blinks, and a tear slips down her pale cheek. She quickly grabs a tissue off the table and wipes it away. Then she sits on the chair and places her face in her hands. She's struggling to maintain her composure, but at this point, I want to see her lose it. She should be screaming and crying the same way I am.

But I think this poor motherless girl fell into the wrong hands and did everything she did with the best of intentions. "But the contract is already in place, and the trust says…"

"Fuck the trust!"

"We can't, Sylvie," she argues. "The trust states that after one year of marriage, you will inherit the house and hold enough power to transfer the deed to my aunt, which *you* swore to do in that contract. And that contract is airtight," she says.

I drop into the seat across from her. "So, what if I break the contract? I just won't sign the house to her."

"Then, *you'll* owe her the ten million."

"I don't have ten million dollars!" I shriek.

"Then you should be careful what you sign," she replies coldly.

I squeeze my eyes shut and try to breathe.

After a moment, she adds in a sniffly whimper. "I don't want to hurt my brother."

Opening my eyes, I stare at her imploringly. "Then, don't let your aunt take it from him. Beg her. Do whatever you have to. Blackmail her. Threaten her."

"It won't matter," she argues. "What's done is done."

"Ugh!" I stand up in a huff and cross the room, feeling like a rat in a cage. That same rage that burned through me that night when I ripped the painting flows through me now. I want to lash out at her, at her aunt, at *everyone*.

And this isn't even my family. This isn't my home.

When I reach the window, I take a long, deep breath. And I realize what I have to do.

"So, the only way for Killian to keep his house at this point is if the marriage fails."

She sniffs, and I see her in my periphery as she looks up toward me. "Yes, technically."

"And I wouldn't be indebted to her for anything?"

Anna shakes her head. "No, but…"

Her voice trails, and I feel the needles of emotion starting to form in my throat.

"He would need to sign the divorce papers, and you know he wouldn't do that, Sylvie."

"I know he wouldn't," I reply as my eyes fill with moisture.

"So, what are you going to do?"

"What are my choices?" I ask, turning toward her and shutting down the faintest sign of weakness.

Her pale brows wrinkle as she contemplates it for a moment. "Technically, if you leave the country for more than thirty days."

"We don't have time for that," I argue. "I'd have to leave *now*. I can't just disappear on him."

"Then…you'd have to cheat on him."

I drop into the chair and let the realization wash over me. There really is no way out of this that won't end in catastrophe. I can't cheat on Killian. I *won't*. I won't even lie about it. It would devastate him.

"I'll explain it to him," I say, my voice tight with the threat of tears. "I'll tell him everything and explain that we *have* to divorce before the year is up. Then we'll be fine. He can keep his house, and we can stay together."

She nods through her tears, but I can see the uncertainty on her face. It matches mine. I'm sure deep down, she's scared of what this means for her family. To disobey her aunt. To have lied to her brother. To know that nothing can be achieved peacefully. Not really.

"He really had a panic attack?" she whispers.

I nod. "Yes, and he tried to hide it from me. Said he used to have them a lot, which explains why he never leaves."

I watch as she winces in pain, maybe from remembering what those panic attacks look like. I'm sure she's been telling herself whatever lie she needs to get through the guilt of what their parents' death did to her brother. He has put on the facade of someone being *fine* for nearly two decades. But rather than taking care of anything, they let those wounds fester instead of heal, only making it worse by throwing shame, guilt, and isolation on top of it all.

I may never understand this family, but I don't have to. I just need to make this right for him.

"Maybe I should tell him," she says, but I cut her off.

"We can tell him together."

"When?"

I take a deep breath and work through the dates in my head. The sooner, the better. It's nearly August, which means we have only a month left.

"Let's give him a week to recover from the trip. Then we'll talk to him."

She nods. "Okay."

With nothing left to say, I stand up from the chair and cross the room toward to where I dropped my purse. Just as I make my way toward the door, Anna calls, "Sylvie."

I turn toward her.

"You've been really good for him. And I had hoped you'd be enough to get him to leave the house on his own."

"He needs more than me," I reply. "He needs you too."

Her lips tremble as she nods. "You really do love him, don't you?"

Choked with emotion, I nod.

Then, to my surprise, her mouth lifts in a crooked smirk. "Then, you'll figure this out. I know you will. I have a feeling you always get what you want."

Not always, I think to myself. If I had gotten what I wanted, I never would have come here. I never would have needed ten million dollars, and I would have never married a stranger for it.

But I'm here now, and I fully intend to get what I want this time.

———————

"Stop the car," I say as Peter delivers me back home. We're halfway down the drive toward the house when I see Killian walking through the trees in the same direction.

As the car comes to a stop, I call back, "Thank you," before shutting the door and jogging over to where my husband is quietly strolling.

"I'm not disturbing you, am I?"

He greets me with a smile as he puts out his arm and welcomes me into his embrace, holding me tight to his enormous chest.

"I found a Q," he says, and I pull back to stare at him quizzically.

Then, he holds up a tiny round button with the letter Q in the middle. "Is that from the typewriter?" I ask.

He chuckles and then nods. As I gaze up at his face, I can still make out the sunken, tired features of his eyes and the lifelessness of his smile. The panic attack was almost twenty-four hours ago. Is it normal to still look so tired?

People don't just bounce back that quickly, Sylvie.

"What is that doing all the way out here?" I ask, taking the letter and inspecting it.

"The rain washes everything out," he says, glancing toward the river. His gaze grows unfocused as he stares into the distance. I clutch his arm and try to squeeze him tighter.

How on earth could they possibly do this to him? It's not fair. It's *cruel.*

But I'm going to make it right. I just have to keep telling myself that.

"I'm sorry our trip was ruined," he mumbles softly without looking into my eyes.

I grab his face and force his eyes down to me. "I don't care about the trip. I care about *you.*"

"It's not right to keep you locked up in this house with me."

My stomach sinks as my eyebrows pinch inward. "Don't say that," I argue. "I'm not locked up. And I love it here. You know that."

"For how long, Sylvie? How long can you really stay like this? You're a lot younger than me. You have your whole life ahead of you."

"Killian, stop!" I snap, wrapping my hands around his neck and pulling him closer. "Please stop talking like that. We're going to get through this together. We'll get you the help you need, and I will be there every step of the way. So stop talking like that."

As his eyes bore into mine, I search for the same fire I saw in the man I first met. So much life, vigor, and personality. Have I ruined that? Have I put out that light?

I don't know what else to do, so I press my lips to his, hoping it will reignite the spark we had before. Before that stupid fucking trip. Before I royally fucked it all up.

On top of that attack, he's now dealing with the guilt of bringing me down with him. I can't stand it, so I try my best to make him believe that's not true.

He kisses me back, but it's weak and missing something.

"Come on," I whisper, pulling him toward the house. "Let's go inside."

I hold tight to his hand for the rest of the walk, but neither of us speaks. When we reach the house, I pull him all the way to the bedroom. I know I shouldn't, but I can't help myself. I'm desperate for him, for all the parts of him that make up the whole of this person I love. He's shattering into a million tiny pieces, and I don't know how to hold him together anymore. So I figure if we keep doing the same things we once did, he'll be himself again. And we'll be us.

I let him undress me, and then I undress him, and when I lie in our bed, using his body like my security blanket, I imagine this is what he wants too. His grip on my body is so tight, and his grunts are so loud, and I hold him the same way I did last night. I give him every part of myself he might need to make himself better, and I pray it's enough. My pleasure, my voice, my body.

When he finishes, he trembles inside me with his lips latched onto my shoulder, biting me just enough to make it hurt. Then, he kisses it better, trailing his lips to my ear, where he softly whispers, "Mo ghràidh."

And I fool myself into believing this is a step in the right direction. But then he pulls out of me and rolls to his side of the bed. I'm left there lying alone, feeling the drip of his seed between my legs, and he does nothing to stop it.

Chapter Thirty-Six

WHEN I WAKE UP THE NEXT MORNING, HIS SIDE OF THE BED IS empty again. Just like last time, I sit up in a panic.

"Killian!" I shout as I burst out of our bed and bolt toward the door. It's morning, and the sky is bright, but as I run from the room, I barely even notice that something is amiss in our room. In nothing but a pair of panties and one of his shirts, I scramble down the stairs, desperate to hear his voice.

Instead, I hear Anna's. And my heart drops.

My footsteps hurry down the rest of the stairs, but when I hit the landing, I nearly trip over the two large suitcases sitting at the bottom. *My* suitcases.

"What the…?"

Dread swarms like bees in my belly as I walk slowly into the parlor. When my eyes find Anna sitting on the chair, tears streaking her face, I know exactly what's happened.

"Anna, no…" I whisper at the sight of her.

"I'm sorry, Sylvie. The guilt was eating me alive. I had to tell him."

"Everything?" I whisper. And when she nods, it's like a punch to the gut.

Then I hear his familiar stomping. Turning, I spot my husband coming toward me, but his eyes don't meet mine. "Killian," I say, pleading as he brushes past me.

"By now, you've realized I know everything," he mutters darkly. There's a slur to his voice, and my heart shatters at the sound.

"Don't do this," I beg.

"I have to," he replies.

"No, you don't," I argue. "We can work this out together."

"I won't lose my house. You have to leave," he murmurs, reaching for his drink on the bar. I sprint toward him, grabbing the glass from his hand.

"Stop it!" I scream before flinging it across the room.

Anna screams and covers her head from the shards of broken glass. Then, I look into his eyes and point my finger as I shoot my accusations.

"Stop it, Killian. Yes, it's true that my part of the plan was to have your house taken away from you, but I'm not going to let that happen now. And you can't be mad at me for that. We barely knew each other then."

"But what about now?" he bellows.

"I was just at her house yesterday, Killian," I shout, pointing to his sister. "You know I was doing everything in my power to fix this!"

"I know you were doing everything in your power to get your money."

"You nasty brute," I snarl in his face. "You know that's not true. You *know* how much I love you. You think I wanted this?" I cry. He turns away from me, marching from the room in anger. "You think I wanted to fall in love with you?" I continue.

"You think I wanted to fall in love with *you?*" he replies in frustration. "It's better this way, Sylvie. Sign the papers, go back to America, let me keep my house, and I don't have to worry about keeping you locked up in this old place for the rest of your life."

"That's what this is about, then. You think you're sparing me from your sadness. In sickness and in health, remember?"

He ignores me, refusing to look me in the eyes as I watch the pain hit him again.

I wish I could hit him with this rage that's rolling through my veins. I hate what he's saying. I hate it all. He's taking away my choice. Where is the part where I get to decide to stay? To be with him forever? Where can I choose us?

He grabs my bags, and I quickly tear them from his grip. "Killian, stop it! I'm not leaving. We can figure out another way."

Shaking his head, he still refuses to look into my eyes. "This solves everything, Sylvie. If you truly want me to keep my house, then walk away."

"Don't ask me to do that," I cry.

"You were going to go anyway, weren't you? So, just go."

A tear rolls over my cheek. "What happened to being your *real* wife? Is this really so easy for you? To just write it all off like it never happened so that you can have your fucking house?"

Finally, for the first time, he looks into my eyes. And the sadness I see in them makes it hard to breathe. "What do you want me to do, Sylvie? Everyone I love is trying to hurt me. Nothing I do is ever right, and even if I did keep you, I'd only drag you down with me. And I refuse to do that. So, I think it's best you just go."

"You don't mean that," I reply tearfully.

He leans forward, and my palms itch to reach for him. "It's the first time in my life I've ever been truly sure."

With that, he turns away and storms out the front door, leaving me to fall apart alone.

None of this feels real. I pack the rest of my clothes. I gather my things. I wait for him to walk back through that door, but he never does.

How can I seriously consider this? Just leaving like nothing happened?

But I have to. Because if I don't, then he will suffer.

So, with shaking hands, I do it all. Even in the library, I gather everything I've left up here. But when I spot the novel I typed on the old typewriter still sitting on the table, I leave it. I hope he finds it. I meant what I told my parents—I will never publish that story, and I don't want to.

It was for him anyway. The main character was never me; it was him.

I set the story where the typewriter used to be, and I walk out of the room.

Peter said we have to leave for the airport in an hour, but I'm all packed, and I can't stand to keep walking around this quiet house, emptying it of pieces of me. When I reach Killian's room, I crawl into the bed and hug the pillows, sobbing into them and praying he changes his mind.

When I hear his footsteps on the stairs, I perk my head up and watch for him. He enters the doorway, and I see the red spots on his face and the puffy bags under his eyes. Where does he go to cry when he's alone? The thought nearly slices me open.

"Please don't do this," I beg him one more time.

"I've set you up with an account to help take care of you until you can get back on your feet. It's not ten million, but it should help."

I squeeze my eyes closed as more tears leak through my lashes. "I don't want anything from you, Killian. Truly, I don't."

"I know," he mumbles quietly. "But this is the right thing to do, Sylvie."

"I know," I whimper.

"You should publish that novel," he says, stepping closer. "It's good. And don't go near your parents. They're not good for you. Maybe start fresh."

"I can't," I sob. "Killian, I can't."

He crosses the room, not daring to get too close to where I'm curled up in his bed. "Yes, you can. You can do anything, Sylvie. You once broke into this house. You moved across the world to marry a complete stranger. You turned my entire world upside down, mo ghràidh. You can do just about anything."

I'm soaking his pillow with my tears as my body shudders through the sobs until my bones are sore and my muscles ache. "Are you sure you're going to be okay?" I whimper.

He swallows, clenches his jaw, and nods. "I promise."

Part of me wants to ask if I can contact him. If I can come back after the thirty days is up, and the contract is voided. I need to take some sort of promise with me so that I'll have a line back to Barclay Manor, but deep down, I know he won't give that to me. That's the point. We're supposed to do this on our own.

No matter how much it hurts to think about it.

There's a honk in the distance, and I squeeze my eyes shut again. Maybe if I just lie in this bed, they won't make me leave. They'll have to carry me out if they want me to go.

"Come on, Sylvie. We can do this."

When I finally peel myself off the bed and stand in front of him, I drink in my last look. The last moment when I will see him as my husband. The last time I will see him as his wife.

After I've had my fill, I move toward the door. But first, he scoops me into his arms and holds me tight against him. Even as I wrap my hands around him, I feel half gone.

"I'm gonna miss you, my wee little wife," he whispers in my hair.

"Please take care of yourself, you brute," I reply.

But when I finally tear myself away, I don't look back. I can't. If I look into his eyes again, I'll never leave. And right now, he desperately needs me to.

Chapter Thirty-Seven

KILLIAN AND I GOT MARRIED LAST YEAR ON SEPTEMBER 18. THE divorce papers showed up just shy of one year later, on the twelfth. They were hand delivered by a notary who had to watch me sign them while I sobbed into the sleeve of my sweater.

And just like that, it was over.

I found a furnished short-term rental in Manhattan, but I spend every night tossing and turning because I forgot how loud it is here. I miss the quiet of the country, the creaks of that old house, and the sound of his footsteps when he would come in from the fields.

I miss his voice, the deep, rasping texture of it when he'd growl into my ear. I miss the feel of his enormous hands in mine. The safety, the comfort, the familiarity.

Almost immediately after leaving Barclay Manor, the loneliness crept in. I've typed so many messages to him just to delete them later. If this is what missing someone feels like, I wish I had never fallen in love with him at all.

Killian wasn't just my husband for a brief, strange period. He was the first person I ever truly cared about. The first person who loved me for me. The first person it hurt to say goodbye to.

Walking down the streets in New York, I try to imagine that it was all just a dream, but then I swear I hear him call my name in the distance or the buzz of a bee, and I'm transported right back to where it all started.

If I could tell him anything right now, I'd tell him that I'm trying. I moved some of my things out of storage. I've started working on a new novel. I even made a friend in my building who tells me way too much information every time we strike up a conversation, but he makes me laugh, and someday, I imagine I might tell him about the bougie swinger parties I used to go to with my fake husband in Scotland.

But not yet. Maybe someday I will.

For now, I try to get through each sunrise and each sunset. I bring my laptop to the coffee shop and I watch the people walk by while trying to piece together some sort of story that sounds half as fascinating as ours.

I imagine he's over my shoulder reading it like he did that day. In my imagination, the couples always start as enemies, more at war with themselves than each other. But then they eventually realize that the only people willing to fight with them are the ones who care about them.

Or at least that's how this new one is going.

"Sylvie?"

I glance up from my laptop at the sound of a familiar voice. It takes my eyes a moment to recognize the woman glaring at me from a seat near me. Her hair is much shorter, in a pixie cut, and the scowl she often wore when I saw her has relaxed into a soft frown.

"Enid?" I question, trying to remember the last time I spoke to my parents' right-hand woman.

"I thought you lived in Scotland with your mean husband," she says in a bitter tone.

In the past, I might have reacted in anger, but now I only laugh. "No, not anymore."

"Oh," she replies, swallowing her discomfort. "I'm sorry about that."

I shrug. "Thanks."

"Do your parents know you're back?"

My spine stiffens. Rather than have a conversation with this woman from the next table, I decide to join her at hers. For a woman I *still* despise, this feels like a very mature step for me.

"No," I reply. "Please, don't tell them."

She scoffs. "Oh, I don't work for them anymore."

My jaw drops. "What?"

"They fired me back in July."

I knit my brow as I recount the last time I saw them. They never said anything about firing Enid, and she's been with them for years.

"Artists," she says with an eye roll. "So temperamental."

"Did it have to do with me?" I ask, which immediately makes me feel like an idiot. Of course, it doesn't. Nothing in my parents' life ever has to do with me.

"Yes," she says plainly. Staring right into my eyes, she says, "I told them what a self-serving, entitled, talentless brat you are."

We stare at each other before a chuckle bubbles from my lips, spilling out into a full laugh. Tears fill my eyes, and I can't seem to stop myself.

She doesn't laugh with me, but she doesn't look as mean and miserable as she usually does either. Who knows, maybe Enid got laid this year and it made her loosen up a little.

When my laughter finally dies down, I wipe my tears and let out a heavy sigh.

"I thought you'd like to hear that," she says softly.

"I did. It's probably the most they're ever going to stick up for me, but it's nice."

She nods. "You're probably right. Just remember, it's not you. It's them."

"Oh, you're on my side now?" I reply with a laugh.

She shrugs. "They don't sign my paychecks anymore. And I started to feel as if they never really *saw* me anyway."

"I know how that feels," I reply, staring down at the coffee cup in my hands. "Well, thank you for telling me that."

"You're welcome."

I'm about to stand up to return to my table when she asks, "Is it true your husband threw a *rug* at them?"

This time, we both break out into laughter just before I tell her the whole story.

Most nights, I don't sleep much. I've been home now for over a month and a half, and I still blame jet lag for the reason I'm wide awake at 3 a.m. Part of me wonders if it's because I know somewhere he's awake too. When he's active, I can't rest. We are that in tune now.

With time, I'm sure it will wear off, but so far I can't get through a single night without crying myself to sleep.

On this particular night, I wake up at three in the morning with a new text message. I bolt upright as I stare at the screen.

Killian: I like the ending.

The sight of his name makes my chest seize up, and my cheeks grow hot. Just four words, and I feel whole again.

It takes me a moment before I realize he is referring to my story.

I quickly type out my reply.

Me: Thank you.
Killian: You should publish it.
Me: I wrote it for you.
Killian: I love it.
Me: I'm glad.

We're silent for a moment, both of us probably unsure where to go from here. What do we say to each other now? My fingers are aching to type out *I miss you. I love you. Please let me come home.*

But he responds first.

Killian: How are you?
Me: I can't sleep.
Me: How are you?
Killian: I'm trying.

My chest aches, and I choke down a sob. Deep down, I keep asking myself this one burning question. If Killian thinks he's sparing me from a life spent in that house, what is left to motivate him to get out? Won't he just fall back into his own ways? Why can't I help him?

Killian: I need to hear your voice.

I dial his number so fast my fingers hurt. As the call rings, I chew on the inside of my lip, waiting to hear his voice.

"What time is it there?" he asks in a growly whisper.

My skin erupts in goose bumps at the sound. His voice seeps into my pores like warm honey.

"Three thirty," I reply.

"It's half past eight here."

"You're up early."

"Couldn't sleep," he mutters.

"Me neither."

"Do you feel different?" he asks. "Being home."

"What do you mean?"

He clears his throat. "I mean, do you feel like you belong there?"

I shake my head. "No. I don't know where I belong."

I belong with you, I want to say, but I hold myself back. Putting too much pressure on him isn't what I want to do either. I can still see the gaunt look in his eyes that day after the beach. I can't do that to him again. I can't be as bad as the others.

If letting Killian Barclay go is what I have to do for his own good, I'll do it.

"Do you feel different? Now that I'm gone."

He clears his throat. "The house feels smaller. I don't like how quiet it is without your footsteps in the hall."

I swallow the pain climbing up my throat. *Don't push, Sylvie.*

"How did your aunt react?" I ask.

He lets out a breath of laughter. "She lost her mind, but Anna spoke to her. The house is mine, and she can't take it away."

"Good," I reply, and I mean it. Nothing pleases me more than hearing him say that. "It's all over, then," I add. The contract, the marriage, the whole thing.

"Aye," he replies. "It's over."

"What will you do now?" I ask.

He doesn't reply, and I hear the struggle in his heavy breath. I'm waiting, hoping, praying that he'll say something that might possibly involve me.

"I need more time, mo ghràidh. And I can't ask that from you."

I blow out a silent, quivering breath as I stare down at my bed, letting a tear fall directly from my eyes to the pillow. "I'll give you whatever you need, Killian. If you tell me you need my help, I'll help you. If you tell me to wait, I'll wait. That was the vow we took, remember? It might be over, but I still believe in those words we swore. I'll do whatever you need because that's what wives do."

He lets out an exhale that sounds hopeful.

"Oh, darling," he replies. "Sylvie, I don't want you to wait."

My heart shatters. I didn't know heartbreak could hurt so much, but it's true. It's agony.

I physically bow over in my bed from the pain, holding in a silent cry as he devastates me with his words.

"I need to do this on my own, love," he continues. "And I'm afraid it might take forever. So, if you want to make me a vow, then promise me that you won't put your life on hold for me. You're not coming back to Barclay Manor, and we are not married. Tell me you understand."

The phone line is silent as I cry into my pillow.

"Please, Sylvie. I need to hear you say it."

He must hear the wet sounds of my next inhale because he makes a sympathetic sound.

"I'm sorry," he whispers.

After a moment, I work up the courage to give him what he wants. "I understand. I won't wait for you, but I will be here to help you. No matter what, I will always want to help you."

"That's good enough then," he replies softly. "Then, right now, I want you to get some sleep."

"I don't want to hang up," I cry.

"Then, keep the phone on your pillow. I'll be here until you fall asleep."

Wiping my tears, I do as he said. I lie on the bed, resting my phone face up on the pillow. Staring at his name on the screen, I let the sound of his breath on the other line lull me off to sleep.

It's the first restful sleep I've had in weeks, and the entire time, I dream of gentle bees and typewriter keys scattered in the grass.

Chapter Thirty-Eight

Dear Sylvie,

*Today marks two months since you left. And I've been seein'
this therapist now for over a month. She suggested I write a
letter to everyone who I need to express something to. And
although she said I don't need to really send them, I decided
that I wanted to send yours.*

There are some things I need to say to you.

*When you showed up at my house, I was stuck. I spent
nearly two decades of my life lost and grieving, but then you
came along. You were stubborn and rude, but you weren't
afraid to tell me what I needed to hear. Out of everyone, you
were the only person who could pull me out.*

*I'm sorry that you had to spend a year with me when I
was at my worst, but I think we were both a mess. And I
want you to know that I'm not angry about the lies you told
in that arrangement. I think part of me knew the entire time
that the real plan was to take my house from me.*

Maybe deep down that's what I wanted.

But then I fell in love with you and everything I wanted

changed. I wanted you to stay. I wanted to be happy for you. I wanted a normal life.

But we were never a normal couple. Or a real couple.

The love was real though, wasn't it?

I'm sorry this letter is such a bloody mess. Clearly, you're the writer.

What I really want to say is that I'm sorry we didn't have a chance to be real. But that day you left, I knew you were different than the woman who showed up in my house the year before. You changed, Sylvie. I think somewhere in our marriage, you forgave yourself for not being perfect and loved yourself anyway.

Maybe you just needed to watch someone fall in love with you to see it.

I'm glad it was me.

Thank you for the best year of my life. I hope when you get married for real, your real husband won't be afraid to fight with you because you are never more beautiful than when you stick up for yourself. Don't lose that.

Your brute,
Killian

KILLIAN'S LETTER IS FOLDED UP IN MY PURSE. I RECEIVED IT A couple of months ago, and since then, I've heard nothing. I've gotten comfortable with the silence, like learning to live with a nagging pain that won't go away.

He told me not to wait, and I'm not. I even downloaded a dating app recently, although I didn't swipe right on anyone, or even upload my photo. But I figure it's a baby step.

I'm doing exactly what he asked of me. And yet, I still miss him so much it hurts.

I'm not holding on to hope that Killian and I will ever get back together. I'm not.

But I'm also not ready to walk away from that year of my life like it didn't mean anything. Enid says I'm just dating myself now, and I think she's right. I am my own rebound.

So when my phone rings in the coffee shop as I'm typing on my laptop, and I see his name on the screen, I freeze.

It's been so long since I heard his voice. At the prospect of hearing it again, I nearly fumble my cell phone out of my grip as I struggle to hit the Answer button.

"Hello?" I stammer.

"Sylvie," he responds. There's a hint of panic in his tone. I jump from my seat and rush out the front door so I don't have to carry out this conversation in a quiet room with strangers.

"What's wrong?" I ask as fear courses its way down my spine.

"I just need you to talk to me," he says through the phone line.

"I'm here," I answer without hesitation. "Where are you? What's going on?"

"I'm going for a drive."

To anyone else, those words would be simple enough, but for Killian, they have me pausing in my tracks. "Where are you driving?"

"Just into town. Not far. My therapist suggested I do this."

"And you're alone?" I ask.

"Aye."

It dawns on me in this moment that he's doing something difficult, and he needs me. He's asking me for help, and the feeling sends a bolt of excitement through my body.

I know he needs me to stay calm, so I let out a relaxed sigh. "What would you like to talk about?" I ask casually.

"I don't know. Anything. I just need your voice."

He lets out a deep breath through the phone as I pause on the sidewalk, listening for the sound of his car starting.

"I'm here," I say. "It's just a small drive, right? You've got this."

"I'm fine," he tells himself.

"Exactly," I reassure him. "You're perfectly safe."

"I know I'm safe," he argues. "I'm sitting on the bloody drive in front of the house. Are *you* safe?"

A chuckle bubbles out of my chest. "I'm standing in front of a coffee shop in broad daylight. I'm fine."

"Keep telling me that," he grumbles, and I bite my lip with a smile. "It helps me for some reason."

"I'm freezing my ass off, but I'm still fine," I say through the phone line.

I hear the crunch of tires on gravel. "Do you need a better coat?" he asks, his voice tense.

"No," I reply. "It's January in New York. It's fucking cold."

"It's cold here too," he replies.

"How far are you going?" I ask.

"To town and back."

"You can do that," I said. "You did it before, remember? That night you picked me up in the city."

He chuckles. "I was so bloody mad at you."

I laugh in return. "I know you were."

He's quiet for a moment before he responds. "I wish you were in the car with me now."

I let out a sigh. "Me too."

Don't start hoping, Sylvie. Don't get your heart broken again.

I mean, who am I kidding? If he asked me to be there, I'd be on that plane in a heartbeat. But that's not what he needs right now. He needs to do this part on his own. He needs to hear my voice and know that I'm here, but also know that he can do it without me.

"Talk to me," he says in a grumbling tone.

God, I've missed that.

"Um…I'm publishing my book," I say.

"Good," he replies immediately.

"Well, not publishing it, exactly. More like…just printing it. For myself."

"Can I have one too?" he asks, and I bite my bottom lip as a smile stretches across my face.

"Of course."

"Do you have a new boyfriend?" The question catches me off guard. I freeze in my spot as my mouth falls open. Is this really what he wants to talk about while he's trying to calm down?

"God, no," I spit back.

"Why not?" he asks.

"Because the only man who's spoken to me since I got home was a guy at the coffee shop who tried to hit on me by offering me advice on writing my novel."

"You told him to fuck off, I hope."

"I told him I wasn't interested," I reply with a smile.

"I miss the days when you threw your coffees at men like him," he replies.

Still chewing my lip, I pace around the space in front of the coffee shop. The wind is starting to pick up, and my nose is like an icicle, but I'm not going inside. It's easier to focus on him out here. As if being outside brings me closer to him.

"How's the drive going?" I ask.

"Good. Your voice helps. Keep talking."

I let out a sigh. "Why don't you try it without my voice for a while? Just keep me on the line. You know what to do if your attacks come back."

My eyes sting as I wait for him to respond.

Finally, he mumbles, "Just because I can do it without you doesn't mean I want to."

A tight smile stretches across my face as my eyes fill with moisture. "It only matters to me that you're doing it."

"I'm doing it."

For the rest of the drive, he goes in silence. I go back into the coffee shop, and I stare out the window as I listen to his breathing on the other end of the line.

With every drive and every trip and every day that passes, I know he's finding peace inside that he hasn't had in far too long. Even if I never make it back to Scotland or to Barclay Manor or to him, at least I can rest knowing he's found that.

On a warm day in late March, I'm walking back to my apartment when I spot a package on the front steps, and I nearly sprint down the street when I see it lying there. Just a simple brown cardboard package that doesn't look very exciting, but I know exactly what is inside.

Squealing as I pick it up, I do a little hopping dance outside the front door before I unlock the door and run inside with excitement. I quickly pull out my phone, dialing Killian's number, and putting it on speakerphone before setting it on the table.

He picks up immediately.

"Hello?"

"It came!" I shriek, making him laugh.

"For fuck's sake, woman. My eardrums are bleeding. What came?"

"My book! I had it printed and it just showed up."

"Oh, Sylvie," he responds softly. "That's incredible. I'm so bloody proud of you."

Killian and I have hardly spoken since he called me two months ago, asking for me to talk to him while he drove. Since then, I've tried my hardest to not pick up the phone or reach out. But these brief conversations feel like getting to know him for the first time.

Ironically, I think I'm even more in love with him now, and I can't even say it.

"I'm opening it." Grabbing the box cutter off the counter, I quickly slice open the package.

"Careful not to cut too deep. You'll slice the pages."

"I'm careful," I argue.

As the box slides open, I freeze. Ever so slowly, I pull out the paperback book from within. As I lay it in my hands, feeling the weight of all the words inside, tears begin to spring to my eyes.

"It's perfect," I whisper.

"Describe it for me."

"The cover is simple and beautiful. It's green, and the title is in gold. Simple cursive letters."

"And your name is on it?"

With a smile, I trace my name across the bottom: *Sylvie Devereaux.*

"Yes."

"That's your book, mo ghràidh. You wrote that."

A tear slips over my cheek as I flip through the pages, remembering the exact place in the library where I was sitting when I wrote it. It feels as if I'm being transported back in time to my favorite place in the entire world.

Technically, this copy I'm holding is the only one in existence. And, other than the one I promised Killian, it will remain the only one. He begged me to publish it, but I had to make him understand that I never intended to do that. Writing was my passion, but it was never the thing I wanted to squeeze dry. I didn't want to treat my passion the same way my parents treated me. I would just love it and cherish it and celebrate it for exactly what it is.

Holding it to my chest, I do exactly that.

"Feels good, doesn't it?" he mumbles into the phone.

"So good."

"I'm really fucking proud of you, Sylvie."

My eyes squeeze shut as I breathe in those words, letting them fill all the tiny crevices inside me where I need them.

When I hear someone shouting in the background, followed by the honk of a horn in the distance, my eyes open.

"Where are you?" I ask.

"London," he groans.

My blood runs cold. I've missed so much. Why is he in

London? Who is he with? But I don't pry. It's not my business. He told me not to wait, so I'm not.

After a few minutes, he fills the silence anyway.

"Anna and I are just here on a short weekend holiday. It was her idea. After our last talk, I've been doing more drives. More outings. And now, this is my first trip away from home."

Pride swells inside me.

"That's amazing, Killian. I'm proud of you," I reply.

"I was grumpy, but your call made me feel better. Thinking about you holding that book makes me feel better. Sign my copy before you send it."

"I'm not signing anything," I reply haughtily.

"Yes, you are, you stubborn brat. You wrote that book in my home. I want a copy, and I want you to sign it. Then I'm going to put it in my library, and someday, a hundred years from now, a stubborn American girl will break in just to see the great masterpiece of Sylvie Devereaux."

"And get conned into marrying a giant Scottish grump," I add, making him laugh.

"Yeah, that's how the story goes."

I drop into a kitchen chair, fixating on the book on the table. Deep down, I fight the urge to admit to Killian that missing him and being so far from him is harder than I think I can handle. I want to tell him that I still love him, and no matter how many times he tells me not to wait, I will. I can't help it. I'll love him until the day I die.

"Sylvie…" he whispers.

"Yes?" I feel as if he's about to say something big. Tugging my bottom lip between my teeth, I wait, praying it's going to be something I want to hear.

"You're still waiting for me, aren't you?"

I swallow, frozen as I stare straight ahead. I could lie. I could tell him that I've moved on and maybe that would be better for him in the end, but I can't bring myself to do it.

"I will always wait for you."

"I—"

I wince at the sound of Anna's voice in the background, interrupting him. The miles between us feel so vast at moments like these.

"I have to go," he replies. "And Sylvie?"

"Yeah?" I reply softly.

"I'm really proud of you for writing that book."

"Thank you," I mumble just as the phone line goes dead.

Chapter Thirty-Nine

KILLIAN MADE SURE I DON'T NEED TO MAKE ENDS MEET FINAN-cially, but I still have a shit ton of boredom to stave off and time to kill. So, for fun, I sometimes help Enid out with her new gallery. I dragged my feet about it for the longest time because I couldn't stand to even be around art, but she finally wore me down and talked me into helping, to at least get out of the house.

Besides, Enid's place isn't anything like my parents' gallery. It has a younger, fresher vibe. Fewer pretentious ass-sniffers and more expressive realism from modern artists. She actually sells a lot of reprints at prices real people can afford, making it all so much more accessible, and I like that. It's something my parents never bothered to do.

On the weekends, I come in and help answer phones or do other menial stuff she doesn't care for anymore. And as much as Enid drives me nuts with her uptight attitude and crass sarcasm, she's started dating a woman named Nikki from England, who I adore. So most days, it's just me and Nikki sitting up front, making conversation and cracking jokes while Enid does all the work in the back.

By this point, Enid and Nikki know everything about

SARA CATE

Killian—then and now. They find our story both bizarre and romantic, and I can't say I disagree.

"We still talk from time to time," I say as I unpack a box of paper bags and tuck them under the cash register.

"You're not thinking of seeing other people, are you?" Nikki asks.

"Fuck no," I reply. "If anything, I'm just going to board a plane and march right up to his doorstep and say *enough*."

"Why don't you?" she asks. "Go over there and whip your tits out. That'll do the trick."

With a sad smile, I let out a sigh. "Because he needs me to be supportive, and I am. I do support him and everything he's doing. It's incredible, but…" My eyes trail downward, and I clench my jaw.

"You miss him."

Solemnly, I nod.

"You can't wait forever, Sylvie. At some point, you're gonna have to move on."

Despondently, I nod. "I know."

The door chimes as someone comes in, and Nikki greets them casually. "Welcome in."

My eyes lift to the door, expecting it to be another customer, but I'm struck silent when I see the person standing there, staring at me in surprise.

"Mom?" I mutter as I stand up.

"Sylvie?" she says at the same time. "What are you doing here? I didn't know you were back from Scotland."

I close my mouth and square my shoulders. I won't fall silent like I did the last time I saw her. "I've been back since August."

"August?"

Immediately, I recognize how my mother puts me on the defensive, whipping questions around on me. So before answering her, I turn toward Nikki. "Handle this customer, please. I'll be in the back."

"Ummm…" Nikki stammers, but I don't wait for her response.

"Goodbye, Mom. Enjoy the gallery." I spin on my feet and march toward the back of the room.

"Sylvie, wait!" my mother calls.

"I don't have to talk to you," I reply. "In fact, I *choose not to*."

She follows me past the front desk and around the corner to the back of the building. "Sylvie, please. Just wait. Give me a second."

"No," I argue. My blood pressure is rising with every moment. I've been preparing myself for this instance and I just keep repeating the same thing to myself over and over again. *Don't engage. Don't engage. Don't engage.*

"Can't I at least apologize?" she cries.

Out of the corner of my eye, I see Enid standing frozen near the service entrance, but I brush right past her.

"No," I call back to my mother.

Even when I reach the alleyway, I just keep on walking. I have no clue where I'm going, but I can't turn back. I can't get into a conversation with my mother.

"Sylvie, I'm begging you."

I hear the sadness in her voice, but it only makes me angrier. Stopping in my tracks, I spin toward my mother and point a finger in her face. "No! You don't get to be sad now. Not when every conversation we've ever had has made me feel like complete shit."

Tears fill her eyes as she reaches for me, but I quickly wave her off. "No! I'm not engaging. I have to protect *my* peace, which means I can't talk to you."

"Okay, then don't talk!" she shouts. "Just listen."

I let out a frustrated scream because *listening* to her is even worse. It's the last thing I want to do. But now I'm out of places to run. I've hit a fence line, blocking me in.

So I freeze at the end of the alley and let her catch up. I'm waiting for the inevitable, *You don't try hard enough, Sylvie.* Or *I'm just trying to help you, Sylvie.*

What comes out of her mouth is nothing close to what I expect.

"Your father and I were terrible parents!" she shouts. "We are still terrible parents. I wish I knew how to even try to fix it, Sylvie, but I don't. You didn't deserve us, and if I could go back in time and give you to people who would have raised you better, I would."

I shake my head, keeping my back to her as I try to force my brain to block out the hurtful things she's said to me. But even I know that's impossible.

I don't respond as she continues. "There was never anything wrong with you, Sylvie. I'm sorry if I ever made you feel that way, and I'm sure it's too late for apologies now, but I have to try at least. And we might have been terrible fucking parents, but look at you!"

"What about me?" I shout, turning around to find my mother with tears streaming down her face, her hair windblown and sweat-soaked. She's a mess.

"You turned out to be the most resilient, insightful, brilliant person I've ever met."

A wrinkle forms between my eyes as I scrutinize her. What is she getting at? What is the catch? Where is the *but* of that statement?

She just raises her hands and lets them fall at her sides. "That's it. That's all I want to say—just that I'm sorry. And…I'm proud of you."

Still panting from the chase, she lets her shoulders slump with a look of defeat on her face. Then, she turns away from me and walks back toward the gallery.

I let her go without another word. At the moment, I don't quite know what to say. I'm not ready for hugging it out and handing out forgiveness, but I do feel a sense of relief wash over me. It's like I don't feel the same heavy cloud weighing over me anymore. That whole your-parents-hate-you-and-you're-a-disappointment fog has started to clear.

Still standing in the alleyway with an expression of disbelief on my face, I pull out my phone and dial Killian's number. It rings and rings and rings, going to voicemail. And I realize that's to be expected now, especially now that he's probably doing things like going to rugby matches with his friends and spending hours away from the house. And that is *great*, but it's hard not to feel a little disappointed too.

It's like he's moving in the right direction, but that direction is away from me.

When I get back to the gallery, I have to tell Nikki and Enid everything about the bizarre interaction with my mom.

Enid is shocked, and Nikki is a slut for good gossip and drama, so she eats the entire story up, wanting all the juicy details. When Enid realizes Nikki doesn't know the full story about how they came to our house in Scotland and the way Killian escorted them out, she has to tell that part of the story herself.

We're all laughing together when I feel my phone buzz in my back pocket. A sense of relief washes over me as I assume it's Killian. Pulling it out, my face falls when I see that it's not him.

It's his sister.

Quickly, I swipe open the call and step away to give Anna my full attention. Immediately, I hear her panic.

"Sylvie!" she shrieks in tears. "He needs you, Sylvie. You have to come *now*."

My eyes widen with fear as something cold and heavy lands in the pit of my stomach. "Anna, where is he? What happened?"

Already I'm moving. I don't even say a word to the girls as I burst out the front door, walking toward my apartment. I'm just a few blocks from my place.

"He's gone," she wails into the phone.

"What do you mean he's gone?"

"He's *not here*!" Her voice is frantic and screaming. "My aunt called me this morning to tell me that Killian had just dropped off the deed for the house to her, and then he was gone. No explanation. No warning. I'm scared, Sylvie. What if he's gone somewhere to hurt himself? What if we drove him to do it? He was doing so well."

My hands are shaking now with fear, and I know she's being hysterical. I know Killian would never do that. Don't I?

I haven't seen him face-to-face in months. What if he's lied to me? He's made me believe he was fine before.

And he didn't answer my call today.

"I'm coming, Anna," I say because it's the only thing I can manage at the moment. I'm sprinting now, just a few blocks from my street. I'll pack my bag in less than five minutes and be at the airport within an hour. I could be in Scotland by morning, and we will find him. He has to be all right.

"Please, Sylvie. You're the only person I knew to call. He talks about you so much still, so I knew you would help us. He needs you."

"I'm coming," I say again. Nothing could stop me. I've never moved with so much purpose in my entire life. I've never felt something so true and real. There are no doubts or questions. If my husband needs me, I will be there—every single time.

"Anna, I'm almost home. Let me try to call him again. I'll let you know when I get a flight at the airport."

"Please hurry," she sobs.

"I'm hurrying." With that, I hang up the phone.

I have to cross one more intersection before I'm on my street. The light takes forever to turn, and all the while, I'm running through possibilities in my head. Maybe he's on a bender with his friends somewhere, drunk out of his mind. Or he met someone and stayed at her place. Or he decided to leave us all behind and took off like a thief in the night.

Or the very real possibility…he had an attack somewhere, and I wasn't there to help ground him. And he got hurt or worse.

Finally, the light turns, and we cross. I sprint to the next street, making the last turn as his phone's voicemail picks up again.

"Damn it!" I snap as I shove my phone back into my pocket. Then, I look up from the street and stop dead in my tracks.

My chest is heaving for air, and I'm staring down the long street with my building halfway down. There, on *my* stoop, is a large dark-haired man sitting on the steps as if he were waiting for me. I continue walking toward the apartment, not wanting to let my heart get away with my head.

But the closer he comes into focus, the more hope I allow myself to feel.

Then he sees me coming. In one quick movement, he stands, and I gasp as goose bumps cover my skin. My heart might as well fall out of my chest and down to the cement. My hand covers my mouth as I walk toward him.

I'm begging my mind not to play tricks on me. I need to know it's him before I let myself believe it. And when he smiles, that same smile I saw on the beach, I break out in a full sprint. My shoes click against the pavement as my legs carry me the rest of the way, anticipating the moment when I have my arms around him again.

And when I finally get there, I launch myself against him so hard I nearly knock him off his feet.

Chapter Forty

KILLIAN'S BODY IS LARGE AND WARM IN MY ARMS, AND HEARING his breath in my ear feels like home. My arms are clutched tight around his neck as his huge arms engulf me, pinning me in place against him.

He's here. He's in my arms.

Questions are swirling in my mind, but I brush every single one of them aside because he is *here*.

"Hello, darling," he whispers into my neck.

"What are you doing here?" I reply.

After a moment, he finally sets me down, but I refuse to let him go. My hands stay glued to him.

"I came as fast as I could," he replies, brushing a wild curl from my face.

"I don't understand. Your sister said you gave the papers for the house to your aunt. Why?"

"Sylvie, you traveled across the world for me, and I kept you secluded in that house for nine long months. I knew that if I was going to make things right, then it was my turn to come to you.

"And when you told me last month that you were waiting for me, I knew what I had to do."

My face stretches into a smile as I take in the sight of his face again. Warm green eyes, chin-length brown hair, strong brows, and full lips. It's him, and he's standing on the street in front of my apartment in New York City. None of this makes any sense in my brain, but I love it all the same.

"So this is what you were working for," I say as everything suddenly clicks into place. Rather than bringing me back to Scotland, he wanted to come to me. He just had to wait until he was ready.

"Thank you for waiting," he says, lowering his forehead to touch mine.

My eyes close, and my heart swells. Reaching for his hands, I grip them in mine, sliding my small fingers between his thick ones. And I never want to move from this spot.

But then my phone rings in my back pocket again.

"Oh shit, Anna," I say, quickly grabbing it and seeing her name on the screen. When I slide the call to answer, I can hear her panic again.

"Sylvie?" she cries.

"Anna, he's here."

She falls silent. "What?"

"He's standing right in front of me," I say, staring into his soft, content eyes.

"He's *what*?"

I let out a chuckle.

"In New York?" she shrieks.

"Yes, in New York. And he's okay."

"I'm going to kill him," she replies as I bite my lip to stifle my laugh.

"Tell her I was just trying to be spontaneous," he says, but when she hears him say that, she only launches into a fit of curses.

"He said he's sorry," I tell her. "And that he'll call you later."

She's still going on as I hit the End Call button, and the phone goes silent. Killian pulls me back into his arms, and I suddenly feel very desperate to have more of him. I want *all* of him.

But I don't want to be too eager. I still don't quite know what state he's in and how much he's struggling. He's hidden it well from me before, and if I push him too hard again, I'll never forgive myself.

"Want to come inside?" I ask.

I notice the tension in his jaw as he nods and picks up his bag from the sidewalk. A slight crease in his brow has me concerned as I gently pull him up to the front door, unlocking it before welcoming him inside.

He looks ginormous in my apartment, which isn't small by any means. But I'm used to seeing him in a house with thirty-foot ceilings on sixty acres.

He drops his bag by the door and follows me into the kitchen, admiring my apartment and all the personal touches I've added over the months.

"Are you hungry?" I ask as I reach the kitchen counter, placing my back against it and suddenly feeling oddly uncomfortable. We've never had to do this before. Killian and I have always collided like two stars. We never had to do this awkward dance of defining exactly what we are. Are we just friends? Or are we still the same couple we were before?

He doesn't sit at the table like I expect him to. Instead, he stands in the middle of the room, staring at me keenly with his hands stuffed into his back pockets.

"No," he replies flatly.

"Thirsty?" I ask, swallowing as my mouth goes dry.

He shakes his head.

My body is buzzing, and I think if I don't get to touch him soon, I might actually explode. But I *need* to know he's all right first.

"What do you need?" I ask cautiously. "Whatever it is…"

He hesitates for a moment, standing there looking almost nervous as his gaze rakes over my body. My eyes stayed glued on his, wishing I could tell him with just my eyes that he can have everything. He doesn't even need to ask. I am all his, and everything I own is his. In my heart, he is still my husband.

I'm not sure if that's what I conveyed in one single look, but suddenly he's crossing the room toward me, and in two long strides, I'm in his arms again. Pinning my body between the counter and his tall frame, he holds my face in his hands as he stares down at me.

"What I need?" he growls.

Without another word, he crashes his mouth against mine. Our lips tangle and slide in unison, licking and nibbling on each other until we're practically fused. His kiss feels like crawling back into my own bed after months away. It feels like finding the one other soul on this planet that matches mine. It feels like home.

My hands ache to touch him, and I roam his body, remembering every muscle, every ridge, every valley of his hard, sculpted frame.

"I just need *you*, mo ghràidh," he murmurs against my mouth. Wrapping his hands under my thighs, he hoists me onto the counter, and my legs open easily for him. His mouth trails from my lips and down my neck. He pops a button off my blouse, tearing my shirt open to get his lips on my breasts.

I let out a loud whimper when his tongue finds the pink bud of my nipple. "I needed *this*," he growls against my flesh. My hand digs into his hair as I pull him closer. But his fingers don't stop. More buttons go flying as he tears my shirt clean open, shimmying it down my arms and unclasping my bra until I'm topless on my kitchen counter for him. His coarse beard scratches my skin, but I welcome the pain. I need more of it.

When his fingers start fumbling with the button of my pants, a thrill of excitement courses through me. It doesn't take him long until they're undone, and he's working them down my legs, pulling my panties with them. My pants are barely off my ankles when Killian drops to his knees and presses his face between my legs.

"This," he growls against my sex. "I've been dreaming about the taste of your cunt for eight months. *This* is what I needed."

I let out a shriek of pleasure as he licks at me ravenously and sucks on my clit. My back arches, and my head hangs as I'm suddenly reminded of what pleasure feels like.

He touches my pussy like he's missed it, spreading my folds and sinking his long thick fingers inside me. My body winds up quickly, and it only takes a few thrusts for me to lose control. Fireworks explode inside me, radiating pleasure in pulsing waves behind my closed eyelids.

"Fuck me," I cry out, suddenly desperate for him.

Standing in a rush, he kisses me, letting me taste my own arousal on his tongue. His shirt falls to the floor before he starts on his pants. While he works them down, I touch his chest, kissing the spot above his heart and running my fingers through the patches of hair.

When his cock springs free, I forget how to breathe all over again. His size takes me by surprise again, and I reach for him, eager to wrap my fingers around his length. A satisfied groan vibrates from his chest as I do. Lazily, I stroke his shaft, savoring the way it drags reactions from his body. Moans, expressions, trembles.

A drop of cum leaks from the tip of his cock, so I wipe it with my thumb and bring it to my lips, humming when the flavor touches my tongue. At the sight, he turns feral.

With a grunt, he grabs my hips and yanks me to the edge of the counter.

"Watch it with me," he orders with a husky rasp in his voice. As he lines up his cock, I reach one hand for his chest and the other for his jaw, holding him tight as he slowly works his way inside me.

He hooks one arm under my leg for more access as he slowly drives in deeper, stretching me until I have him all. Pleasure, relief, and elation flow through my body, making me dizzy. Our foreheads touch as we stare down at the place we are joined, and it's perfect.

Pulling out ever so slightly, he eases back in. I can feel his restraint crumbling. Pulling him closer for a kiss, I bite his bottom lip, making him howl and thrust his hips harder. He digs a hand in my hair and jerks my head back, smiling wickedly at me as he picks up his speed, fucking me with such force he has to hold me in place.

I smile up at him as our bodies smack together in an echoing cadence of pleasure. It's all so perfect that I don't know if I've ever been happier in my life.

"What a wee dirty wife you are," he grunts, staring down at me with smug pride.

"*Your* dirty wife," I reply with a sly grin.

"You love your husband's cock, don't you?"

My hold on him tightens, and the pleasure starts to crescendo again. "Yes," I cry out. "I love my husband's cock."

He pounds harder, dragging me off the counter entirely. I'm barely hanging on as he fucks me, tossing me around like his rag doll. Another orgasm detonates inside me, and I let out a scream, clutching my legs around him tighter.

He lets out a guttural roar as his own climax rolls over him. His cock shudders inside me as I wrap my arms around his neck, holding tight to him as we ride out these waves of pleasure together.

Finally, once his cock is spent, he rests me back on the counter and peppers kisses all over my chest and neck, and face.

"I love you," he whispers with each one, and I swear I could die of happiness right here.

All this time, I was afraid Killian would move on without me, or that I was the one dragging him down. Instead, I managed to guide him out of the hell he had been living in. And I didn't even know it.

"I love you," I whisper in return.

"I mean it, Sylvie," he says, lifting his eyes to my face. "I'm here, and I'm all yours. For as long or as much as you want me."

A smile stretches across my face as I pull his lips to mine. "I want you forever, Killian."

"Good," he mumbles into the kiss.

When he finally eases out of me, I can already feel the warm cum sliding out of me. With a wicked grin, he leans down and pushes it back in. I bite my bottom lip as I watch him.

"Then you keep this," he mumbles before pressing a kiss to my inner thigh. "Forever."

Chapter Forty-One

KILLIAN IS OUTSTRETCHED ON MY BED, NAKED ON HIS STOMACH, and I can't seem to stop staring at him. He's really here. It feels impossible but incredible at the same time.

"Stop watching me sleep. It's creepy," he mumbles into the pillow.

"Get over it," I reply.

"Were you really that surprised?" he asks, sounding half asleep.

"Yes," I say emphatically. "It's been so long I was starting to assume you were just trying to figure out a nice way to get rid of me."

He groans as he hooks an arm around my waist and tugs me nearer to him. "You're still my wife, Sylvie. I'm not just going to *get rid of you.*"

"Technically…" I start, about to point out the fact that we are neither real nor fake married anymore.

"Don't say it," he groans. "We will be fixing that as soon as I recover from this bloody jet lag."

"What?" I snap, staring at him in shock. "Getting married?"

"Yes," he mumbles.

I let out a gasp as I try to move away. "You're not even going to ask me first?"

"I don't need to ask you," he complains.

"Why not?" I shriek.

"Because I know what you'll say. What the fuck is the point of asking?"

"To be romantic!" I try to climb off the bed, but he doesn't let me get far. Holding me around my waist, he pins me down to the bed, shifting his weight on top of me. I let out a howl of laughter as I struggle to get away, but he's too strong.

"Since when are you and I romantic, wench?" Putting his face in the crook of my neck, he growls, making me yelp as goose bumps erupt all over my skin.

"Fine. I'll marry you again, but you have to stop calling me names like *cow* and *wench*," I say with a moan as his growls turn into kisses.

"No deal," he replies curtly.

My arms wrap around him as I smile. Then I find my mind going back to the house as it so often does. "So…" I start. "Did you really give the house to your aunt?"

"Yes," he says on an exhale.

"And you're okay with that?"

"It's just a house. If it means that much to her, she can have it."

"Where will you live?" I ask, although I already know the answer.

"With my wife, of course," he replies, nuzzling closer to my body.

With his face buried in the pillow and his hair strewn in a mess around him, I stare at him and try to find the differences from the man I knew at the manor. But I don't see anything. It's just him in a different setting.

He does seem at ease now. And not the same sort of *at ease* I thought I saw before when I tried to tell myself he was fine. Now, he seems free.

"How are you feeling?" I ask, brushing his hair out of his face to plant a kiss to his bearded cheek.

"I'm fine," he groans.

"And you won't lie to me?" I ask, biting my lip. "If you're not fine, you'll tell me?"

He lets out a sigh and rolls onto his back. "Yes, mo ghràidh. If I start to feel anything, I'll tell ye. But I promise, I didn't make this trip until I was sure I could do it without worrying you."

A tight smile pulls at my lips as I set my cheek on his chest and wrap my arms around his midsection.

"I'm proud of you," I whisper, feeling him kiss the top of my head.

"Thank you," he replies softly.

I wake up early the next morning, and Killian is already sitting up in the bed next to me.

"How long have you been up?" I ask groggily.

In nothing but his tight boxer briefs, he holds up the green book in his hands, and it takes me a moment to recognize it as my own. "Long enough to read this again. My cell phone doesn't seem to work here."

"I can't believe you're reading that again. I own other books, you know?"

He shrugs. "This is my favorite."

I smile to myself as he continues to read. Then he looks down at me as he adds, "Do you have anything new?"

"It's not done yet."

"Are you going to publish this one?" he asks, stroking my hair. "Nope."

With a smirk, he leans down and kisses my temple. Thinking about writing makes me think of my mom and the weird encounter yesterday. "My mom came and saw me yesterday," I say, making him tense immediately.

"Did she stop by to compliment your furniture?" he asks sarcastically.

I chuckle into my pillow, remembering her obsession with the rug in Killian's house. "No. She came by Enid's gallery. I don't think she was expecting to see me. But she sure had a lot to say."

"Oh yeah?" He's on guard and skeptical as he waits for my response.

"Yeah, she told me what a terrible mother she was and what a good person I turned out to be."

He lets out a laugh and then scrutinizes my reaction. "Wait, you're serious?"

I nod. "It surprised me too."

He sits back and shrugs his shoulders. "It must have been the rug that knocked some sense into her."

"It might have," I laugh.

His eyes rake over me again before he drops the book on the end table and lays his body over my back, grabbing my hands and putting them above my head as he grinds into me from behind.

I let out a sultry moan as he groans into my ear. "This is one way to wake up," I say with a squeak as he kisses his way along the back of my neck.

His cock grows incredibly fast in his boxers as he continues rubbing against my ass. Before I know it, he's pulling my hips up, positioning himself between my legs, and thrusting himself inside me.

"Eventually, I'll learn to take my time with you again," he grunts as he slams into me again. "But right now, I need you too much."

As his hand slides up my throat, a wicked smile stretches across my face. "You won't find me complaining," I moan.

It takes most of the day to get us out of bed. Every time we try, we end up screwing instead. When we do finally get hungry enough, we manage to get showered and out the door.

As we walk together down the street, I keep his hand in mine, squeezing his fingers and clutching to his arm like he might float away on a breeze. I love showing him New York the same way he showed me his property. Especially since it's spring and New York is beautiful in the spring.

We end up taking a longer walk than we intended. To neither of our surprise, we find ourselves at the City Clerk's office.

As we're waiting in line, he turns to me and whispers, "Are you sure you don't want a big wedding?"

I rest my head on his arm. "I'm sure. We already had a wedding."

"It was bloody awful. We hated each other."

The woman in front of us turns and gives us a quizzical look.

"I know," I reply to him quietly. "But that's just part of our story. I don't want to replace it."

He shrugs. "If you insist."

When the clerk informs us that there is a twenty-four hour mandatory waiting period, Killian slips her a disarming smile and begs in his thick Scottish accent.

"You see," he says. "We've already been married, for almost a year. Far more than twenty-four hours, and I came a very long way to make her my wife again. You wouldn't make a desperate, lovesick Scotsman wait, would you?"

To my surprise, the clerk actually falls for it. After a heavy sigh, and a little fudging up the date on our documents, she directs us to head into the office and wait with the others. We take our seat between other couples who can't possibly wait another moment until their union becomes official.

With the filled-in papers in my lap, I rest my head on his shoulder. There are no contracts this time. No ten million dollars or historic mansions. There is just us—two people who, by some slip of fate, ended up in the same place at the same time. It feels like a miracle, and I don't intend to let go this time.

"Devereaux and Barclay," the woman at the front calls.

Killian and I walk to the front together, smiling at the clerk as she reads us the same dull terms of our marriage she reads to everyone. And it might seem like the least romantic wedding in the world, but no one here knows that we've already lived these vows.

Our love has survived the trials and come out the other side stronger for it. Like most relationships, we entered ours as two people who only cared about ourselves, but as marriage tends to do, we learned to put each other first. It's no longer about him or me, but us.

"Ms. Devereaux," the clerk says to me. "Do you promise to uphold the vows of this marriage and keep this man for the rest of your life?"

"Do you, darling?" Killian murmurs with a lopsided smirk. "Do you promise to keep me?"

With a smile on my face and his hands held in mine, I gaze into his eyes as I graciously reply.

"I do."

Epilogue

One year later

"LORNA'S DEAD."

The words pull me out of a dreamless sleep, and I peek one eye open to stare at my husband just to make sure he really said that.

He has his phone in his hand, and he turns toward me with alarm in his features. Quickly I sit up.

"Wait. You're serious?"

"Dead serious."

I snicker. "Killian."

"The old hag is gone. Dec just texted me."

Leaning over, I glance at his phone, and there it is. A single text from his younger brother.

Aunt Lorna passed away in her sleep last night.

"Holy shit," I mutter. "What does this mean? For the house."

Killian shrugs. "I'm guessing she left it to Anna. She sure as hell didn't leave it to me."

"Not that you'd want it…right?" I ask, looking up into his eyes.

Killian and I have made a home here in New York. Sure, we haven't exactly set down roots yet, but we do have a nice life at the moment, enjoying this honeymoon phase we're in.

But I'd be lying if I said I haven't been thinking about what the future holds for us. I'm not even from Scotland, and I'm itching to go back. He says he's fine where we are, but if we had the opportunity to live in Barclay again, would we take it?

"Nah," he replies with a confident shake of his head. "If I go back there, I'm afraid I'd fall right back into the same old routine. Here, I finally feel alive."

Turning toward me, he gives me a charming little smirk. My love for him swells in my chest like a tiny little bomb that goes off every time he smiles at me.

"Besides, I don't need a big house to do this," he says as he drops his phone and tackles me down to the pillows. Burying his face in my neck, his thick beard scratches my skin as he kisses and nibbles the sensitive flesh.

I squeal in delight as my legs wrap around him. And then just as our laughter turns into moans, his phone rings.

"Och," he groans. "Fuck off." He flings his phone off the bed and resumes kissing his way down my neck and across my collarbone.

"I'm willing to bet my left tit it's your sister," I say as he inches his way down.

"Well, at the moment your left tit is mine," he replies with a groan, his teeth gently closing around the sensitive bud. My back arches as I dig my fingers in his hair.

But only moments after the buzzing of the phone stops, it starts back up again.

"She won't stop," I say breathlessly.

"And neither will I."

He continues to kiss his way down, but just as he reaches my belly button, the phone rings for a third time.

KEEP ME

"Fucking cow!" he bellows as he reaches down to the floor to quiet the incessant device. With irritation in his eyes, he lies back between my legs as he hits the Answer Call button. "I've got my mouth just inches away from my wife's pussy, so you better make this good."

Letting out a laugh, I cover my mouth as I listen for Anna's response. I can't make out her words, but I can hear her shrieking at him.

"Aye. I know she's dead. Good riddance."

Anna screams at him so loud it echoes through our bedroom.

Then, she continues on and Killian's demeanor changes from annoyance to intrigue.

"She what?"

Anna continues on and Killian's gaze travels up to my face.

"What is it?" I whisper.

"She left it to me?"

"Left what?" I ask.

Killian listens intently to what Anna is saying, and after a moment, he lets out a heavy sigh. "All right," he says with resignation. "I'll think about it. Thanks for the call."

After he ends the call and sets his phone down, he gazes up at me with concern. "The bitch left me the fucking house."

"Why would she do that?" I ask. "After all the trouble to take it away from you?"

He shrugs. "I don't know, my wee little wife."

Hugging my body closer, he rests his cheek on my stomach, using my body as a source of comfort. I stroke his shoulders and his hair. Feeling the tension in his muscles, the answer is immediate and easy.

Lifting his face, I force him to gaze into my eyes.

"We don't have to do anything. You don't have to go back to the house. We don't have to go anywhere. If the thought brings you any stress, we'll never return. We have everything we need right here."

His brows relax and the lines of his forehead disappear. "You're right. But what about the house? I can't let it out of the family."

"You have brothers, Killian. Let them deal with it. You've gone through enough."

Finally, with a sigh, he nods. "You're right."

"I know I'm right," I reply astutely, making him smile.

"I have everything I need right here."

Lifting up, he stares down at my naked body, pressing his lips to my belly. But instead of moving his way down like I expect him to, he picks up his phone and types out a message.

"What are you doing?" I ask, running my nails along his scalp.

"Sending a text to my brother."

"What did you say?"

The phone blares a *whooshing* sound as the text is sent. Then, Killian shows me the screen. The words in his reply have me feeling suddenly at ease.

Barclay Manor is all yours now.

"I'm proud of you," I say, tugging his mouth to mine for a kiss.

Finally, he pulls away with a wicked smirk. Then he glances down the length of my body as he says, "Now, where the fuck was I?"

I let out a giggle as he works his way down and presses his lips between my legs.

Acknowledgments

Sometimes, a couple comes along, and their story steals my heart. Killian and Sylvie will forever have a special place, and I can honestly say I had a blast writing this book.

If I tried to do this alone, it would be an unorganized, unedited, unpublished mess of a story with a scrambled timeline and constantly changing eye color. Which means I have a lot of people to thank for making it what it is now.

My editor—Rachel Gilmer, and my marketing guru, Alyssa Garcia, and the rest of the team at Sourcebooks Casablanca. Thanks for letting me, no—*encouraging me*—to be me.

My agent—Savannah Greenwell. You're never getting rid of me.

My assistant and spreadsheet mistress—Lori Alexander.

My biggest cheerleader and overall voice of reason—Amanda Anderson.

My beta readers—Jill and Adrian. Your unending support (and emojis) mean the world.

My new Scottish friends—Rebecca and Ashleigh. I loved our chats about kilts and stovies and Hogmanay. Thank you for bringing Scotland to me.

My family—Jeremy, kids, Mom, and Misty. Love you all.

And last, to every single one of my readers who continue to find space on their Kindles and shelves for a spicy Sara Cate title. Who put up with me sometimes making them cry or scream or… you know. Thanks for being here and for keeping me.

Much love,
Sara

About the Author

Sara Cate is a *USA Today* bestselling romance author who weaves complex characters, heart-wrenching stories, and forbidden romance into every page of her spicy novels. Sara's writing is as hot as a desert summer, with twists and turns that will leave you breathless. Best known for the Salacious Players' Club series, Sara strives to take risks and provide her readers with an experience that is as arousing as it is empowering. When she's not penning steamy tales, she can be found soaking up the Arizona sun, jamming to Taylor Swift, and watching Marvel movies with her family.

Website: saracatebooks.com
Facebook: saracatebooks
Instagram: @saracatebooks
TikTok: @saracatebooks